ALL OUR TOMORROWS

For two years Julie had suffered the hurt and shame of knowing her husband Luke was a criminal. Now he was back home again—but where did they go from there? For herself, Julie never wanted to have anything to do with Luke again; but for the sake of their tiny daughter, did she have the right to send him away?

ALL OUR TOMORROWS

BY

JAN MacLEAN

MILLS & BOON LIMITED
15–16 BROOK'S MEWS
LONDON W1A 1DR

First published 1982
Australian copyright 1982
Philippine copyright 1982
This edition 1982

© Jan MacLean 1982

ISBN 0 263 73976 7

Set in Monophoto Baskerville 10 pt.
01 1082   61602

Made and printed in Great Britain by
Richard Clay (The Chaucer Press) Ltd,
Bungay, Suffolk

CHAPTER ONE

LOST in the silence and the stillness, and in feelings she had struggled so desperately to submerge over the past months, Julie Marshall stood on the grassy hillside and stared down into the valley below. She realised now that the pain, honed by the terrible aloneness she had wrestled with since Luke had left, had only been buried, not defeated or erased; now it had surfaced again as she and her brother Frank had ridden to the top of the rise and the sprawling cedar and stone house had come into view.

Her brother, Frank Taggart, stood behind her, knowing from the absolute rigidity of her body that she had forgotten his presence and was immersed in her own memories.

She was young, barely twenty-one, and, he had to admit, a real beauty, a startling beauty, although she had always seemed totally unaware of that fact. She had, he thought grimly, her mother's—their mother's—fine features—cheekbones high and beautifully carved, gloriously dark eyes, so alive and always aware of all that was around her. They held few secrets, but spoke openly, honestly, of what was within—even after all that had happened to her as a result of her ill-fated marriage.

Yes, she'd been quite a conquest for the powerful Luke Marshall, he thought bitterly, a conquest that he, Frank, had regretted from the very beginning. She looked so utterly fragile, but then she had always seemed that way to him—small and slender and vulnerable. Appearances were deceiving, because she was anything but fragile. How she had held on during the past two years with such a ferocious tenacity he would never know.

He watched her closely as her long, dark hair was touched by the gentle wind and her slim hand moved to her forehead to hold it back from her eyes. Yes, clearly she was tougher than appearances led one to believe. Nevertheless, she had changed. Slowly, almost imperceptibly at first; then, when he had at last shown her the papers, it was as if something within her had finally and forever frozen, and would henceforth keep her at a distance from everyone, except himself. He was her one trusted friend; she had told him so over and over again. He was the one in whom she could confide. And in a few days she would be gone. And that would be very right, very right indeed. He smiled and walked closer to her, putting out a tentative hand and touching her lightly on the shoulder.

She felt the sting of tears start in her eyes and wiped angrily at them. 'Why did you bring me here, Frank? Why?' She spoke in a low tone, her voice a choked whisper, and she dared not turn to face him.

'Because Luke asked me to,' he replied cautiously. 'I had no choice, Julie.'

She laughed bitterly. 'Ah, yes, and you always do what the mighty Luke Marshall asks of you, don't you??'

He was surprised and it showed in his voice. 'I don't know what to say to that, Julie. I do what I have to do—you know that.'

'I'm sorry,' she said quietly, 'I shouldn't have said that. You've been so good to me and I should be thanking you, not striking out at you. I know it's difficult for you, having to work for him, considering everything that's happened. I still think you should have quit when you found out.'

'I stayed because of you and the child. What would have happened if I'd abandoned everything and left? You and Beth are the two people I care most about and I won't see you destroyed. It's that simple.'

She turned to look at him, her eyes meeting his steady gaze. He was tall, like Luke, but not quite as broad; tall and thin and wiry. But unlike Luke, Frank was a city man. He preferred life in Calgary to the slow-paced, small-town life of Henderson, Alberta. He maintained his physical condition by running and with workouts in his health club in Calgary, whereas, with Luke, it had always been long hours of physical labour in the sun and the rain, riding and working the land that he loved. Julie shook her head, admonishing herself for allowing such thoughts, such comparisons, to surface. They only made things more difficult. She had realised that a long time ago.

'But why, Frank? Why this? Why now?' She looked back across the valley and then down at the house, hurt evident in her voice.

'I told you, because Luke wanted it. He told me to bring you here. I really had no choice.'

'How long?'

'What?'

'How long has it been finished?' She waved a hand at the house that lay below them, nestled in the valley, the mountains behind it a majestic backdrop.

'A month or so, I guess.'

'You did it for Luke?' she asked, astonished. 'And you never told me about it?'

'I didn't think you'd have to know.'

'I didn't, you know.' She turned to him. 'I would have been gone in a few days. You didn't have to bring me here.'

'But I did.' He looked down at his booted feet, running the toe of one through the grass. 'He said explicitly that you were to see it before you left.'

She shook her head, suddenly hating the sight of the house, hurt immeasurably by its beauty as it stood there in the midst of the valley, a monument to all her broken dreams.

'Well, it was cruel to bring me here, when you know I'm leaving.'

'I didn't mean it to be cruel, Julie.'

'I don't understand why he would ask you to bring me here after . . . when you gave him my letter and the papers to sign.'

'I don't pretend to understand the workings of Luke Marshall's mind, and I never will.' Disgust tinged his words.

'But why, after that?'

'I think it's his way of telling you not to go. I know he doesn't want to let you go.'

Anguish carved itself on her face. 'He doesn't have a choice about that, you know. Not after all that he's done, all that he's destroyed that was precious to me. I'm going and he can't stop me. Beth and I won't be here when he gets back.'

He reached out and pulled her into his arms. 'I know, I know. And you're right in what you're doing. I know just how terrible it's been for you and it's time you began to build a new life for yourself. I'll help you in every way I can, you know that.' He stopped speaking for a moment, but didn't release her. 'I know it's hard for you to understand why I stayed on with him, considering everything, but I have to finish what I started, Julie. I can't quit. People depend on me, people other than Luke Marshall. There's you and there's Maggie. And there's the people of the town—that mill was their concern as well. I couldn't leave them all high and dry after he left.'

Julie nodded. 'I know that—you don't have to explain yourself to me. You do what you must and I respect you for it, Frank. Believe me, I do.'

'Besides, soon it'll be over. Soon you'll be in Calgary in a place of your own, a new job, everything.' He held her away from him and smiled down at her. 'And Richard will be good for you. He's been good for you already. He cares a great deal for you, Julie—I hope you realise that.'

'Yes, he's a good friend. I certainly appreciate the job he's got for me.' She smiled back at him. 'You've both helped to make the past months bearable.'

Frank turned down the corners of his mouth and made a face. 'Bearable? Is that all?'

'Don't tease, you know what I mean.'

She thought of Richard, remembering that he was coming tomorrow to spend the day with her and Beth. Somehow the anticipation was gone; the sight of the house had stolen it all. Besides, she would see him next week, because he'd promised to help her move into her new apartment.

She turned again to face the scene below and, taking a deep breath, sought to dispel the weight of Frank's revelation and at the same time drink in the scent of springtime that had come once again to this land that was so filled with life and promise. It was June, and spring's sweet, smoky perfume lingered in the air. She could almost imagine the brush piled high in the corners of the fields and fired, like giant glowworms, to dot the darkness of night. The smell of fresh, clean earth assaulted and thrilled her senses.

Amidst the swaying grass, experiencing once again the power of this land, its openness and freedom, she gave herself up to the fleeting images of a time that now seemed long past. She had been born and had grown up here. As a young girl, she had ridden like the wind over the rolling plains and lush hills. As a young woman of nineteen, she had become a wife, marrying a man she had loved with a passion and depth that she had not believed possible, entering with him a world that was exciting and beautiful and full of promise. But that time of promise had suddenly disintegrated into the harsh, frightening, and disillusioning present.

Looking up into the blinding light of the sun which shed its champagne gold over the gently swaying grass, she felt the soft touch of the wind from the mountains. The sun slid behind a cloud, casting shadows that moved with deceptive swiftness over the fields and across the valley. Even the clouds were closer to the earth out here, she observed.

'I'll never understand why,' she whispered sadly, more to herself than to Frank. But he heard her and placed a comforting arm on her shoulder.

'Because it's important to him. I guess he sees it as a kind of a symbol of the two of you together. He told me that you'd both planned it, that the house was a dream you both shared, and he wants that dream to live again. He intended to bring you here himself, but with the letter and all, he ordered me to bring you today, before——'

'Before I leave him,' she finished. 'As if a house could change my mind,' she added bitterly. 'Anyway, I didn't mean the house.'

'What, then?'

'I'll never understand why he did it. And why he wouldn't take the stand and speak for himself, at least try to save himself, despite everything.'

He dropped his arms and shook his head, frustration sharpening his movements. 'We've been over this a thousand times, Julie. It does no good to torture yourself with it any longer. He did some terrible things two years ago. By denying Dad the work he loved, he killed him as far as I'm concerned—Dad was dead in three months.' Bitterness and anger filled his voice. 'I'll never forgive Luke for that—never! But as well as that, he embezzled money from the mill, not giving a thought to a town full of people who trusted and believed in him, and not a single thought to his own grandmother or his wife. Oh, yes, it takes a very special kind of man to do all that, believe me.'

She rubbed her forehead with frustrated fingers. 'I thought I knew him as well as I knew myself. But I didn't, not really.'

'Luke Marshall only reveals what he wants to reveal. It's always been that way, but you were too blinded by your feelings for him to see that.' Although Frank's words were harsh, she could see that it hurt him to say them.

'I suppose you're right.'

'I know I am, damn it.' His lips were a thin line. 'What are you going to do about the divorce?'

The word struck her with a force that stole her breath. 'I don't know yet. I haven't thought that far ahead. I'm taking one step at a time and that's all I can seem to manage right now. It'll depend on what he does as well, and whether he agrees or not.'

'You should move quickly and not be put off, by him or anyone. I want you away from here where you'll have a chance to start a new life for youself. I want you happy and I'll do whatever I can to help you.'

They turned and walked slowly up the hill, back to where the horses stood grazing quietly. Julie picked up the reins and held them tightly in her hand. 'You know,' she said, keeping her head bowed, staring sightlessly at the leather straps in her hand, 'I thought what we had, Luke and I, was so special and so rare, something that didn't happen that way between people very often. It seemed almost like a kind of a miracle that we found each other.' Her voice broke and she closed her eyes, as if to blot out the pain. 'But it's dead, Frank. He killed it, and now all I want is to be free. It'll only mean more pain if I stay and I just can't take any more.'

'I understand,' he said softly.

'I've worried about Beth, though, thinking that Luke has a right to his own child and that she has a right to know her father. But it seems that he's forfeited that right, somehow. I won't keep her from him when he wants to see her, but we aren't a family and we never will be.'

Julie quickly mounted, stealing one last furtive glance at the valley that she and Luke had loved so deeply. Then she looked down at Frank, who stood watching her. 'Would you mind awfully if I rode back alone? I just need to be by myself for a while.'

He waved his hand. 'Go ahead. I have to go down and check the house anyway. I'll see you later in town.'

Without another word she turned Jewel's Dancer and galloped away, leaving him standing and staring after her as she disappeared beyond a gentle hill.

She rode furiously, blind to the beauty around her, oblivious to the land that had once held so much promise for her life with Luke. Not once did she look back, wanting only to return to the ranch, get into her car, and drive back into town, away from all the vivid reminders of Luke Marshall.

Her horse, Jewel's Dancer, a spirited Appaloosa mare and a wedding gift from Luke, was winded and lathered when she finally rode into the yard. She dismounted, led her into the barn, and began to remove the saddle. She was startled when a voice spoke suddenly out of the dimness. 'Wow, you were really moving it, little lady!'

Jake Simms' bulky figure appeared from behind one of the stalls. He grinned and walked towards her, putting up a huge hand to pat the horse on the neck. 'Always was impressed with the way you sat a horse, Julie. You're a natural, if I ever saw one. Bet you could win the big one at the rodeo this year with this fancy horse of yours.'

She was in no mood to talk, so she merely nodded and said nothing, even though Jake, Luke's foreman, was a good friend.

The 'big one' was the annual five-mile open country race that was the highlight of the rodeo activities in Henderson. Luke had often come first in the event, riding a much bigger horse than Jewel's Dancer, his stallion,

Whistler, whose temperament and pride had perfectly matched his master's. Julie had never raced Jewel's Dancer and she thought now that probably Jake was right—she could win if she raced her. But she'd be in Calgary by that time.

She pulled the cinch free, lifted off the saddle, and marched over to one of the stalls, bracing herself and then flinging the saddle up on to the boards. 'Well, I'm afraid there was nothing impressive about how I handled her today,' she replied. 'I made her pay for my anger, and that's inexcusable.'

Jake put out a hand and touched her arm. 'I'll tend to your horse, Julie.'

'Thanks, but——' She didn't get a chance to finish as Jake picked up the reins and led the mare into the stall.

She stood for a moment, then decided quickly to accept his kindness and leave. 'Thanks, Jake. I'll see you later.' She turned and walked from the barn and across the yard, past Frank's station wagon to her own car, knowing that she wouldn't see Jake later, that this would be the last time.

She drove, trying to dispel the terrible feelings that continued to well up in her, the sharp pain that resurfaced and melted with her anger. Why, she admonished herself, had she ever agreed to come out here this afternoon with Frank? Why hadn't she thought to ask him the purpose of the trip before she came?

Flicking on the radio, she fumbled with the tuning knob, hating the annoying static between stations. The search itself was bothersome. Impatient, she switched it off. Another five miles and she would come to the main highway that led eastwards into Henderson.

On impulse, she slowed the car, pulled it gradually over to the shoulder of the road, and stopped to look back, perhaps for the last time, on the Marshall land that had been her home and a part of her heart's content for nearly a year, before everything had been irreparably shattered.

She left the car running and got out. After a few moments even the purr of the engine became an intrusion and she reached in and turned it off, then walked to the front of the car, kicking aimlessly at a stone with her boot as she stared out at the valley that stretched before her.

The Little Bow River glistened gold and blue in the afternoon sun, as it hastened to join with the Bow River on the other side of town. She smiled, realising once again how much she loved this valley and always would. That was something, at least, she told herself vehemently, that Luke Marshall would never be able to take from her.

Standing in complete stillness for a few moments, she drank in its incomparable loveliness, regretting bitterly that she was soon to leave it. Then, as quickly as she had stopped, she turned and walked decisively back to the car, got in, started the engine, and pulled slowly away from the soft shoulder of the road. She would allow herself no more such moments. From this time on, she must be strong in her resolve to do what had to be done. She had Beth to think of, as well as herself.

Moments later she saw ahead of her the point where the dirt road linked with the highway. She looked briefly into the rear-view mirror at the funnel of dust that trailed behind her as if to underline, even announce, her departure. Then she turned her steady gaze to the long strip of grey asphalt that lay ahead, seemingly cast out of the sky in a moment of playful abandon, finally coming to lie with a vibrating stillness in a straight line, the abandonment having given way to the control of purpose. The highway lay like a single, shimmering grey ribbon, heading east and leading her away from all that she had held dear.

Ahead, so suddenly that she had forgotten how quickly one came upon it, lay the town of Henderson. Julie drove across the old wooden bridge, the tyres of her car sounding hollow on the loose boards, and down the hill into the town. It was an abrupt little place when you approached it in daylight. At night its cluster of lights warned you of its presence at least twenty miles before you came upon it. Not so in daylight.

At the edge of town she saw the mill and the yards piled high with rows and rows of lumber, and beyond them the Rodeo grounds. Cattle sheds and barns. A huge mound of hay next to one of the corrals. Grandstands of grey, unpainted wood echoed sadly with the presence of ghosts from her childhood. And in the open field behind the grandstands, with the name of the town, HENDERSON, printed across it in large black letters, stood the water tower, in a feeble, failing attempt to touch the sky.

It wasn't large, only a few hundred people. The main street, running directly through the middle of town, was wide, with cars parked facing sidewalks that in places were still wooden. Julie drove past the curling rink, the Town Council building, which also housed the single-roomed library, past the Sheriff's office, the Court House, and the box-shaped store fronts.

At the end of town she drove off the pavement down a short lane and turned up the long driveway that encircled Margaret Marshall's house. Almost, as had happened so often, she expected to see Luke's tall figure come down the front steps to greet her, to reach out and take her in his arms and say in his gentle, loving voice, 'Welcome home, Jul.'

She shook her head, wondering when she would stop looking for him, when she would stop expecting to see him come round every corner, or out of every door. This afternoon she had dangerously permitted herself to slip too deeply back into the past, to be trapped by nostalgia.

Resolutely, she opened the car door, stepped out, and slammed it behind her. Never again, she told herself fiercely, would she allow herself to be trapped by the past. Tomorrow was hers to shape and live as she chose.

Margaret Marshall's house was situated on the edge of town, bordered on one side by another large house, which was not as impressive architecturally, and on the other side by a huge field that sloped gently down to the river. Behind it, in the distance, the mountains carved sharp, clean lines into the blue granite sky.

In Julie's eyes it was the most gracious and beautiful home in the town of Henderson, or anywhere else that she could think of. She had never seen its like before and she often recalled, with no small pleasure, the mysterious fantasies she had woven around it as a young child, whenever her father had brought her to the house on his business visits to James, Luke's grandfather.

She had walked into it, hushed and in awe of the world she had entered, her small hand tucked into her father's larger one. The interior of the house was entirely of light oak, golden floors spreading out before her, disappearing into a staircase that she had been certain belonged to Cinderella. It rose upwards to a second, and then, amazingly, to a third floor. She had never seen a house with three floors; in truth, it was the only one in Henderson.

Often she would wait for her father in the living room, walking across the pale green carpet, so lush and deep that she feared almost to walk on it, looking behind her for the trail of footsteps she thought she must surely leave. The curtains hanging from ceiling to floor, to her an immeasurable distance, were of a heavy silken material that glistened beneath her timid fingers. In the living room and in the library there was two vast fireplaces, each constructed of the same stone that James had brought in for the front steps and the patio, on to which the living room opened. Part of the patio was enclosed in glass, part was open, spreading itself out from the house and finally narrowing into a stone path that wandered down into a garden of magical flowers, a garden that was a myriad brilliant colours and sweet smells.

Its grandeur and extravagance had left her speechless, as had the mistress of the house, the beautiful, tall, dark-haired Margaret, as her father used to call her. To other people, she was Maggie, but to her father she had always been Margaret.

James Marshall had spared no cost, no extravagance for his new bride fifty years ago. And now, four years after his death, the house remained a monument to his love and passion for her. The house, by virtue of its location, was a part of the town, and yet very much separate from it. And that had been the way with the Marshalls themselves. Something had always held them apart from the rest of the town. Not arrogance exactly, but a kind of driving energy that kept James and his grandson, Luke, working hard, long hours so that they had little time for the social life of small-town Henderson.

From the time she had married James Marshall and first come to live in Henderson, the town's social life had been Maggie's territory. She seemed to enjoy it with the same insatiable relish that her husband had for his work. And she had stalwartly refused to alter even the smallest aspect of her life in Henderson because of what had happened, two years ago, to her grandson.

Nevertheless, this unspoken separation still existed, even more so after Luke's trial and imprisonment, for Julie and Beth Marshall, his wife and child. They were a part of the community, living in Margaret Marshall's house, but at the same time removed from the ongoing life of the community.

Julie walked slowly up the stone steps, pushed open the heavy, oak door and stepped into the spacious hallway. She was suddenly very tired. All she wanted to do now was to escape into a benevolent, numbing sleep.

Maggie called to her from the living room. 'That you, Julie dear?'

Julie threw her sweater on to the table and walked across the hall, her boots echoing on the wooden floor, and into the carpeted softness of the living room.

Maggie Marshall inspired respect and awe in all who knew her. She was a tall woman, impressive in the way she walked and stood. She was nearly seventy-five and her hair was a thick and brilliant white, but there seemed to be nothing stooped or aged about her. She moved with an ease and control that Julie had always envied. To Julie, dignity and Maggie Marshall were synonymous.

Nevertheless, Julie had noticed lately that the strain was beginning to show in Maggie, for the light in her startlingly blue eyes had faded slightly, clouded, she thought, by the agonising pain of Luke's absence.

As she entered the dimly lit room, Maggie came to greet her, leaning down and kissing her gently on the cheek. 'I was beginning to worry, my dear,' she said quietly, and something in her voice made Julie look up.

'Is Beth all right?' Julie asked quickly.

'Oh, yes.' She patted Julie on the arm. 'We had a wonderful time this afternoon. We even had a hot fudge sundae down at the drugstore, which you'll no doubt hear about tomorrow. You're later than I expected.'

'I was with Frank. There was no cause to worry.'

'Have you had anything to eat?'

Julie shook her head. 'No, I came straight back. Where's Beth?'

'Sound asleep.' Maggie smiled and took Julie's hand. 'So there's nothing for you to do tonight but have your supper, which I have warming in the oven, and get some rest. Beth'll sleep till morning, I'm sure. She had quite a rigorous afternoon with her Maggie.'

Julie sighed, thinking that it could have been no more rigorous or wearing than her own. 'I might go to bed early tonight, as well,' she yawned. 'I haven't felt so tired in a long time.'

Maggie watched her with obvious concern. 'Come and sit with me for a few moments, Julie, please,' she said gently.

Julie allowed herself to be led over to the chesterfield. Maggie looked at her watch. 'Edna is expecting me by eight-thirty,' she said slowly, looking across at Julie, her eyes asking some question as yet unformed in words. 'But if you'd rather I stayed, I could call her and tell her I'll see her tomorrow. I don't have to spend the night.'

'Oh no, don't do that,' Julie disclaimed. 'I'm fine, really I am. Just tired, that's all.'

'Well, I wanted to talk to you about something else, before I left,' Maggie said, drawing a deep breath, as if to summon the courage to go on. She was beside Julie now, sitting slightly forward, her hands folded in her lap. 'But maybe this isn't the time, maybe tomorrow would be better.'

'Tell me.' Julie smothered another yawn.

The brightness in Maggie's eyes dimmed into seriousness. 'You had a phone call today,' she began, her voice hardening.

'Yes?' Julie stiffened and waited.

'From Richard Buchanan.'

'Oh——' she breathed, relief washing over her.

'Who did you think it was?' Maggie watched her closely, a frown creasing her forehead.

Julie shook her head. 'No one in particular,' she lied. How could she tell Maggie that always, even now, she expected Luke to be on the phone when she answered, to be on the other side of the door when she opened it? How could she tell her that even now, two years later, she still went to the post office hoping against hope to see Luke's writing on an envelope addressed to her, instead of to Maggie?

'I've never approved of that man Buchanan coming here to see you,' Maggie said stiffly. 'I've never believed for an instant that he merely wanted to be your friend. And I still don't.'

'Well, that's all that's between us, Maggie. He's my friend and so there's no problem, really,' Julie replied evenly.

Maggie waved a dismissing hand. 'But it isn't that,' she said quietly. 'He said—he told me that——' Her voice broke and she stopped, seeming to struggle for composure.

Panic filled Julie's throat. What had Richard said?

Maggie stared down at her hands, still folded in her lap. 'He called to tell you that he'd see you tomorrow morning and that . . . that. . . .'

'What?' Julie asked, her voice barely a whisper.

'That he wasn't certain, but he might not be able to help you move into your new apartment on Monday. He wanted to know if you could wait till Thursday?'

'Oh, God!' Julie breathed. 'I'm sorry, I'm so sorry, I never expected him to call. I didn't intend for you to find out this way.'

'Then it *is* true. You *are* planning to leave here on Monday. In barely three days!' Maggie's voice rose sharply.

'Oh, Maggie, please,' Julie pleaded. 'I was going to tell you. I just didn't know how to exactly. I didn't want to hurt you any more than you have been.'

'Hurt? Hurt? How do you think it feels, child, finding out this way?'

'I'm sorry, I really am,' Julie muttered. 'I was going to tell you tomorrow. I know it was unfair not to tell you before now, but it——' She swallowed. Dear God, she didn't need this confrontation with Maggie tonight. Not after this afternoon. 'It was a difficult thing to decide to do, in the first place.' She put her hands to her face, covering her burning eyes with their coolness. 'It's all been so very hard.'

'Three days,' Maggie's voice echoed hollowly.

Julie lowered her hands and looked at the woman who sat beside her. Maggie's eyes were the eyes of an old woman, saddened and wearied from having seen and felt too much.

'Only three days,' Maggie murmured again. 'And you never said a word.'

'Please, Maggie,' Julie urged. 'Try to understand. Please!'

'No,' Maggie said bluntly. 'No, I don't understand and I won't try to. This is insane and you know it. Utterly and totally insane. Why, you're like my own granddaughter. I've loved you like my own.' She gripped Julie's hands tightly. 'Why? Tell me why? He'll be coming home soon and everything will be fine.'

Julie sadly shook her head. 'Oh, Maggie,' she whispered, 'nothing will ever be like it was, not ever again. It's impossible. Too much has happened—too much hurts.'

'He's coming home, Julie, any day now. He is!'

'I know, and I intend to be gone when he gets here.'

'But why? Why?' Maggie cried helplessly.

'Because I need to make my own way. I've learned that much over the past two years. It was a hard thing to discover and a terrible way to learn it, but maybe the lesson itself is enough. I'm more than Luke Marshall's wife, Maggie. I have my own life to live and I'm going to try, on my own, just Beth and me, in Calgary.' Julie didn't tell her that the real reason for her decision was that Luke had taken her father's work from him, had fired him without reason, and had thus succeeded in destroying him. She knew too that Luke had been guilty of the crime for which he had been sent to prison. Her love for him had died, for he had killed it mercilessly, and she could not, would not, live with a man she didn't love.

'And what about Luke? What about him? You can't throw your marriage away, just like that!'

Julie avoided Maggie's accusing eyes. She could never tell Maggie the truth of her feelings for Luke. Never. 'I'm doing what I have to do, Maggie.' She paused and added, 'I won't change my mind. I'm sorry if it hurts you.'

'If it hurts me?' Maggie repeated incredulously. 'And what about Luke? What about him? Do you have any idea what it's been like for him, caged like an animal for two years? Locked away from everything and everyone he loves?' She stood abruptly and walked over to the fire-place, placing a shaking hand on the mantel. 'He loves you, Julie, so very much. And now,' she closed her eyes, squeezing back tears that threatened to overcome her, 'especially now, he's going to need you.'

Julie watched her mutely.

'At least wait for him. Stay and talk to him. Deal with this thing together.'

'No.' Julie's words were like ice. 'I'm leaving, Maggie. I can't wait for him.'

'Why not?'

'Because it would only make something that's inevitable a thousand times more difficult.' And more painful than it already is, she screamed inside.

'You've been hurt by all this,' Maggie went on. 'It hasn't been easy for you and he knows that as well as I do. But you're his wife, Julie. For God's sake stand by him! It's going to be hard for Luke to come back to this town. So many believe that he was guilty, ridiculous as that is, and they won't make life easy for him.' Maggie had never accepted the fact of Luke's guilt. 'Don't turn your back on him now,' she pleaded. 'What you two share is special. Stay and fight for it.' She stopped for a moment, then rushed on. 'And there's Beth. Dear God, he's never seen his own child!'

And he's never asked to, Julie echoed inside. Never once. 'Maggie, listen—please, just listen to me.' She stood shakily, her limbs weak with emotion. 'What I've decided hasn't come easily, believe me. But it's what I'm going to do. All I can ask of you now is that you try to understand.' She walked uncomfortably towards the door, feeling the older woman's eyes riveted on her back. 'Don't worry about Beth and me, we'll be all right,' she added weakly. 'I hope you'll forgive me in time, because I do love you, and I never wanted to hurt you, but there's nothing else I can do but go.'

'You're Luke's wife and you can never walk away from that, no matter how far you go. He didn't marry you lightly, Julie. And you have no idea what these two years have been like for him, what they've cost him, or you wouldn't even consider doing this terrible thing to him.'

'I know exactly how difficult and how horrible they've been, Maggie—I've had to live through them as well.'

Julie turned and walked from the room, across the hall and up the stairs to her rooms on the third floor, fighting every step of the way the icy cold fingers of pain that again gripped her heart.

CHAPTER TWO

'I DON'T know why, but he did it . . . he did it!' Her brother Frank stook in the hallway, his face angry and accusing. 'It's all in there, see for yourself . . . of course they caught him . . . he's guilty . . . guilty!'

His words dissolved in the harsh light that pulsated with a sound that quickly became the ear-deafening scream of a siren. She looked beyond him, out into the strangely-tinted darkness that was now filled with the sound of rushing feet and voices. 'Guilty! Guilty!' they screamed. The blackness, so deep and dark and suffocatingly heavy, was filled with faces, grotesquely angry and distorted. She fought her way through the crowd, through bodies that resisted and tried to prevent her from reaching him.

He was there in front of her, at first sitting at a long table, then standing and facing them all, his face showing no sign that he either saw or cared. He stood absolutely still.

She tried to run to him, felt the straining of her muscles and heard her own voice call his name through the darkness, but she couldn't move. He continued to stand motionless, and nothing she could say or do, she knew, could make him turn to her or come back to her.

Julie began to cry, dry sobs racking her small body. She tried desperately to make him wait, to make him fight them, to stop them from doing this terrible thing to him. 'Speak to them, Luke!' she heard herself scream. 'Tell them what really happened!' The pressure of her words pounded inside her head, but Luke said nothing as the judge pronounced sentence. Only then did he turn to look back at her, his black eyes searching hers, asking silently, desperately, for something. Then he turned from her and was led from the courtroom.

The sound of crying erupted again, sobbing that gradually grew to a shrill scream. 'No! Don't take him! Don't!'

Julie sat up suddenly, her eyes straining into the darkness. A child's frightened wailing echoed in the silence of the large house. She slipped quickly out of bed and ran, her footsteps light and soft on the carpeting, along the upper hallway to her daughter's bedroom. Not turning on the light, she gently lifted the child from her crib, wrapped her in a soft blanket, and sat down in the old wooden rocker by the window.

She rubbed her face against the baby's small head, her silken hair so soft and sweetly scented, and in a shuddering moment was reminded of the child's father. Beth had the same hair, the same silken blackness. Black like the velvet night, like the prairie sky. Julie closed her eyes tightly, fighting the lump that formed in her throat, struggling against the despair that threatened once again to draw her into its hopelessness, its endlessness. She wiped angrily at the tears which streamed down her cheeks. No more, she had promised herself, no more tears. For Beth's sake she had to stop remembering. It was over, finished, and she had to be strong, going on alone and making a life for just the two of them now.

But the dream, always the same dream, plagued her. She pressed a shaking hand to her temple. Would she never find peace? Would the terrifying images that were born from memory never leave her? It was Frank's fault. Tonight's recurrence of the dream was Frank's doing, she told herself. She should never have agreed to go out to the valley with him this afternoon. Until tonight, she hadn't had the dream in nearly two months.

Beth, no longer frightened, stirred in her mother's lap, reaching up a small hand and pulling at Julie's hair, and Julie bent her head and kissed the child on the cheek. 'You little monkey! Did I scare you? It's the middle of the night and now you want to play.' She smoothed Beth's hair back from her warm forehead. The child smiled at her and grabbed for an ear this time. 'No, you don't, Beth Marshall! It's back to bed with you. We'll play to-morrow, in the daytime.'

God, she thought, she's so much like him! The smell of her, the touch of her. So easy and light and clean. Black eyes and hair, as black as coaldust. She sighed, stood up and walked slowly back to the crib, hugging Beth with a quiet desperation. 'If only,' she whispered, 'if only it could have been different.' She lifted Beth back into bed and tucked the blanket around her. 'To sleep with you, wee Beth. Remember, tomorrow we go on a picnic with Uncle Richard—a good picnic.'

'Pic-nic,' Beth mimicked, and laughed. 'Pic-nic.'

Julie smiled at her and gently touched her face. 'Goodnight, my little love.' She turned and tiptoed to the door, leaving it open so she could hear if Beth awakened again.

Returning to her room, she walked over to the window and drew back the white lace curtain. Two years, she thought, two long years, and still it hurts, still the slightest thing has the power to rekindle the pain.

Her bedroom was on the third floor and now she looked down towards the town. A street light glowed in the dark silence, and the stillness and emptiness of the scene which lay below her only accentuated her loneliness. She leaned her warm cheek against the cool window pane as a car came slowly down the road, then turned where the pavement ended, driving back towards town and out of sight. The wind chased dust devils in the driveway. Julie dropped the curtain, her hand falling limply to her side. Loneliness engulfed her and almost she wished that Maggie hadn't gone out tonight—although she wouldn't have gone down to her, for she would share with no one the feelings that seized her at unexpected times like this.

She looked around. Once she had shared this room with Luke. Once this room, this house, were filled to brimming with love and closeness and joy. Now it held a silence and a sadness too deep and too overwhelming to bear.

She slipped back into bed and drew the duvet tightly around her in a futile effort to banish the demons that had not rested in their pursuit in two years.

She thought back to the days of the trial, remembering that in the last nights they had shared together, Luke had made love to her with a desperation and a fierceness that had never been a part of their joyful, passionate loving before. It was as if he had known, even then, that he would be leaving her.

Once again the tears came and she turned her face into the pillow. 'Luke, oh, Luke,' she sobbed brokenly, 'I loved you so.' Finally, exhausted, she allowed the merciful oblivion of sleep claim her.

'Lord, Julie,' Richard exclaimed, 'you look a mess!'

She smiled wanly. 'Thanks loads, that's just what a girl needs to hear.' She knew what he said was true. She had tried to call him earlier and beg off their date, but he had already left and so she had had no choice but to go with him; it would be unfair to let him drive all the way out from Calgary and then tell him she'd changed her mind about the picnic. Besides, maybe it would do her good to get out and be with people. At least be where people were, she corrected herself grimly.

Richard Buchanan was a successful young architect, a major force, if she could believe his description of the situation, and somehow she did, in his father's architectural firm in Calgary. She had met him through Frank, who had known Richard in university; they also belonged to the same health club in Calgary. Although he was twenty-eight, sometimes when she watched him, with his curly, blond hair, glistening almost white in the sun, together with his infectious smile painted the width of his face, she found it almost impossible to believe that he was any more than twenty.

There was much that they didn't have in common, she and Richard, for he was a city man, born and bred.

Picnics were the extent of his excursions into the outdoors, and he would only smile and nod, catering as it were to her descriptions of Jewel's Dancer and her prowess. Why, even today he wore neatly creased trousers and a white shirt. Granted, she smiled, he had left the tie at home.

Despite that, she knew that he was a trusted and good friend, one who had helped her greatly during the past year to feel that her life was not at an end, that she had to make an effort to gather together the shattered pieces and live again. Now, in a few days, she would be going to work for him and his firm. Yes, his friendship, his help and support, were priceless.

'Well, do I get to come in or am I relegated to the other side of this door for the rest of the afternoon?'

'Oh,' she stammered, realising that she had been day-dreaming. 'I'm sorry. Of course come in.' She held the screen door open for him and he entered, carefully removing his hat and placing it on the counter beside him.

He looked at her more seriously, then reached out and gripped her shoulders. 'What are you doing to yourself? You've lost weight since I saw you last, girl.'

'Of course I haven't. I'm fine, really.'

He drew her close and hugged her. 'Things'll look up when you get yourself into Calgary, you'll see.' When she didn't reply, he looked down at her, holding her slightly away from him. 'Nothing's happened, has it? No problems with your plans?'

'No. A bad night, that's all.'

'Have you heard from Luke? Is that it?' he persisted.

Julie looked at him in puzzlement. He rarely ever spoke to her of Luke. 'No, why do you ask?'

'No reason, really. You just look pretty done in to me, that's all. I thought something drastic might have happened, and Luke contacting you was about as drastic a thing as I could think of.'

She pulled herself away from him, not wanting to talk about Luke. She wanted to forget yesterday and last night if she could. 'I don't know why I let you talk me into this today. I've got a hundred things to do before Monday.'

He smiled at her. 'It's because I'm charming, handsome, and persuasive—and,' he added with a hint of intrigue, 'I'm about to be your new boss. I've never accepted no for an answer when the request has been a reasonable one.'

She walked brusquely to the counter. 'I'll only be a few minutes. Everything's ready but for the packing.' She began, in her quick, efficient manner, to fill the picnic basket.

Richard leaned over her shoulder and eyed the fare. 'Umm—ham sandwiches! I love them.'

She jabbed him playfully in the ribs. 'Don't I know it! That, dear Richard, is why we're having them.' She put in a jar of freshly squeezed orange juice and dropped in some bananas and apples.

'Oh, listen,' he said suddenly. 'Did Maggie tell you I called yesterday?'

'Yes.' She reached into the cupboard for some glasses.

'Well, can I call you tomorrow and let you know about Monday? Seems I may have to fly to Toronto that day, and I'm not sure I can get out of it. I was wondering if we could get you moved later in the week.'

'I think it would be better if I went on Monday. I don't have much to move, really. There's just a bit of furniture, and I have movers coming for that.'

'I thought it would be easier, nicer somehow, if you didn't have to do it alone.'

'Thank you, I appreciate that, Richard. But don't worry, I can manage all right. And I'll see you when you get back.'

'You bet your life you will,' he grinned. 'I just thought I'd mention it, in case you wanted to wait.'

'Do you like gingerbread as much as Beth?' she asked him, as she deftly sliced off a huge piece and wrapped it in waxed paper. She was determined to change the subject.

'Indeed I do, if you make it,' he offered seriously.

Julie smiled. Richard was always full of compliments. She could have made the bread of lead and he would tell her that he loved it. Nothing she could do, it seemed, was less than perfect as far as he was concerned. Rather nice, she thought, if unrealistic. 'Wait till you've tasted it,' she warned, 'then decide.'

He leaned against the counter, placing his hands over hers and staying their movement. 'I trust Beth as the connoisseur of gingerbreads, so I'm sure I'll like it.' He turned her round to face him, then leaned forward and kissed her on the forehead, his mouth slowly moving down to claim her lips. 'Julie. Sweet, sweet Julie,' he whispered, as his mouth sought hers again, this time more forcefully.

Her first reaction was to draw away, to wrench his hands from her shoulders. But she found herself coming closer to him, leaning against him and letting the kiss continue. It had been so long since anyone had kissed her, so long since she had felt Luke's hands on her, and she wanted to feel it all again—to be loved and desired. And so she permitted his kiss and tried to respond to him, longing for the feelings that Luke had been able to arouse in her, sometimes with the slightest touch, the merest look.

But it was no good. She felt suddenly trapped and suffocating. She wrenched herself free and turned away. 'Please, Richard, don't. I can't. I can't!' Panic quickened her breath.

He spoke to her without touching her. 'It's all right, Julie. I know it isn't easy. It takes time, after what you've been through. You'll learn to respond to me in time.'

Dear heavens, what was he saying to her? She swung round to see his face, asking herself, for the first time, what he was really expecting of her when she moved into Calgary and went to work for him at the firm. Perhaps Maggie was right, after all. 'I'm not going to get involved with you that way, Richard, if that's what you're expecting.' It was kinder to be blunt and truthful from the beginning. It would prevent a totally impossible situation later, that she knew she could not handle.

But he seemed not to listen to her words. He smiled at her and reached out to touch her face. 'I said it was all right, didn't I? We'll go slow.'

'No, Richard, we won't.' Fear erupted within her. 'We have to get this clear from the very beginning. I'm not looking for another man—I'm still married to Luke.'

'And you're leaving him.'

'Yes, but not for another man. You know perfectly well

why I'm leaving. All these months you've been a good friend and a help to me, but there's nothing more than that between us. I thought you——'

He interrupted her. 'I'm still a friend and I'm still going to be a help to you. And,' he looked at her, seeming to finally comprehend how upset she had become, 'I think we should let it go at that right now. There's no need to get so upset over a friendly little kiss, girl.'

She waited a moment, almost tempted to tell him the picnic was off, certain that she had not been mistaken in what she had read in his advances to her. But no, surely not. Richard was trying to help her, nothing more. She desperately wanted to believe just that.

She closed the lid of the basket. 'There,' she said more easily. 'If you want to put this in the boot, I'll get Beth and a few things for her and be right with you.'

Richard bowed ceremoniously and flashed one of his most brilliant smiles. 'Anything you say. But don't be long, I beg of you. I'm starved!'

'And when are you ever anything but starved, Richard Buchanan?' she laughed, injecting a false lightness into her tone. She was determined to enjoy this day which had begun so badly.

It was a beautiful June afternoon, bright and warm and sunny, the blue sky glowing above them. It was the beginning of Rodeo Week in Henderson and today there would be a town picnic down by the river, and tonight was the first-night dance over at the Rodeo grounds.

Now, driving beside Richard, holding Beth in her lap, inhaling the sweet spring air and allowing the wind to ruffle her hair, Julie was glad that Richard had come. She had attributed her earlier overreaction to her tiredness and let it go at that.

Looking across at him, she realised again how much she liked him. It had been Richard who had helped her to see the choices left to her when she had first come face to face with the fact that she had to leave Henderson and Luke Marshall if she was ever to find any semblance of peace and happiness again. Richard had offered her a public relations job with his firm, when she told him finally of her decision to move to Calgary. Yes, he was a good friend and it was good to be with him now. His easy, laughing manner helped her to relax, and that was exactly what she needed.

'It'll do you good to get out and have some fun, Julie.' He reached over and ruffled Beth's hair, playfully tweaking her nose. 'You too, muffet.' He smiled at her delighted squealing. 'She's a pretty little thing. Just like her mother.'

He parked the car by the river, lifted the picnic basket out of the back seat, and came round to help Julie with Beth. 'Okay, muffet,' he said, 'want a piggyback ride?' Beth responded immediately by lifting her arms up to him and he swung her easily up on to his shoulders. 'We'll bring the food,' he said, grinning up at the small child on his shoulders, as he lifted the basket out of the back. 'You can carry the blanket, Mama.'

They walked slowly along the river, looking for a sunny spot with some privacy, passing some people from the town, people Julie had known for years, ever since she was a child. They greeted her cooly and noticeably averted their eyes. Even after two years, Julie still hadn't grown accustomed to their rejection.

'There's quite a crowd, Richard. And it looks like the weather's going to co-operate this year.' Her voice was strained.

Richard smiled affably at one of the secretaries from the mill office, and whispered under his breath to Julie, 'Smile at them, Julie, and say to hell with them at the same time. I know what you're feeling, but stop it. You have every right to be here. You're worth a thousand of these small-minded, small-town people. So hold up your head and,' he squeezed her hand, 'enjoy my company.'

He stopped by a weeping willow tree. Fresh buds, newly green, were beginning to bloom. 'How about here?' he asked.

'Fine,' she replied absently, quickly spreading out the blanket, glad to have found a spot away from the others.

He lowered Beth to the grass. 'When do you think that mother of yours will let us at the sandwiches, kid?'

Beth held out her hand to Julie.

'Not yet, you two,' Julie laughed. 'Why don't you go and watch some of the games while I unpack things?'

Richard shook his head. 'No way. I have a much better idea. You come with us.'

She shook her head. 'I'd rather not.'

'Come on, Julie. Where's that old grit of yours?'

'Richard, please don't force me. This is difficult enough as it is.'

'You need to show them that they can't affect your life like this.'

'They do affect my life, and that's one of the reasons why I'm leaving here next week,' she replied vehemently. 'I refuse to bring Beth up in a town that treats her like this; when she's old enough to understand their whispers and their slurs, I don't want her to have to bear a burden that was none of her doing.' She tugged at a piece of grass. 'Go with her for a little while and let her watch some of the races and games. I want to stay here.'

Richard didn't argue further but reached down and took Beth's small hand in his, then walked across the grass towards the roped-off section in the middle of the field. Farther on, booths and tents were being set up for the fair that would begin this evening.

Julie watched Richard walking beside her daughter, beside Luke's daughter, and his words to her earlier, back at the house, came back to her. He was serious about her and he was serious about the relationship that he hoped to have when she moved into Calgary. Watching him now told her that. Something in her almost hoped for it as well, when she saw him like this with Beth. Beth needed a father, just as she, Julie, needed a man. She shook her head and closed her eyes. Damn, damn, damn! Beth didn't need a father. She had one. And *she* didn't need a man. She had Luke.

But no more, no more, she told herself. It could never be the way it was. She could never forgive him for what he'd done to her father, to her, and to Beth. No, she wasn't going to stay in this town one minute longer than she had to. And now, she told herself angrily, you will stop torturing yourself unnecessarily with things that have already been decided and need only to be acted upon, and you will unpack this lunch and have it ready for them when they come back.

The lunch ready, she lay down on the blanket and turned her face to the sun and its gentle warmth. Closing her eyes, she forced herself to think of nothing but the sweet smell of June, the warmth of the sun, and the blue sky. Shortly, she heard Beth's excited voice bubbling across the field and opened her eyes to see her running towards her. Julie smiled, thinking that it seemed like only yesterday that Beth had started to walk. Now she was running, a bit shakily perhaps, but running nevertheless. Behind her came Richard and with him was Frank. She sat up quickly, wondering if something had happened, if something was wrong. Maybe he had news of Luke. She waited, searching his face for an answer to her unspoken question.

Beth stumbled and fell and just as quickly was scooped up and placed back on her feet by Frank as he walked briskly onwards. He grinned broadly at Julie. 'Hi, Jul.' She shivered at the familiar nickname. Luke often had called her that. 'Good to see you out on such a fine day.' He looked down at the little girl who was now kicking and chasing a large ball in the grass, stumbling, then picking herself up, only to fall over again. 'Just finding her running legs, I see. Just like her mother,' he teased, 'falling all over herself.' He grinned wickedly at Richard.

It was obvious that Richard didn't welcome the intrusion, even though Frank was a good friend of his. Frank, however, seemed oblivious to the fact. 'I thought I'd stop over here. I went by the house, but you were gone, then I remembered you'd said that Richard was coming today.'

'Want to join us?' she asked. 'We were just going to eat.' She gestured towards the blanket.

'No, thanks.' He shook his head. 'Can't say it isn't tempting, but I've got some work waiting for me back at the office, then I have to go into Calgary.'

'Is there something you wanted to speak to me about?' she asked, once again wondering with a touch of panic if it had to do with Luke.

'Well, yes, there is,' he said reluctantly. 'And I'm sorry

to intrude, but I don't think it should wait till tomorrow.'

She nodded. 'Perhaps we could take a walk along the river for a few minutes.' She turned to Richard. 'Would you watch Beth for me? We won't be long.' She moved across the grass and on to the path that led down to the river, Frank following close behind her, until she reached the sandy river bed, her sneakers sinking into its softness.

'Look, I'm sorry for coming here when you're with Richard. I'm glad as hell that you're seeing him, you know that. It's good for you to get out again. And he's a darn good catch, believe me. One of the most eligible bachelors in Calgary.' He grinned at her, then when she didn't respond but stood waiting and watching him, the smile faded.

'Is it Luke?' she asked quietly, fighting for calm.

He looked startled. 'What?'

'Do you have something to tell me about Luke? Has something happened?' This time the tension in her voice, in her whole bearing, was only too evident.

'How did you know?'

'What's happened?' she asked abruptly, not daring to move, fearing what he would say next.

Frank drew a deep breath and let it out slowly through gritted teeth. 'I found out an hour ago that he was released four days ago.'

'Oh,' she replied weakly. 'I see.'

Frank watched her through narrowed eyes, waited for her to say something else. '*Do* you see?' he asked sharply. 'Do you really see?'

'I don't understand.'

'I just told you that he's been out for four days and all you can say is, "Oh, I see." This is serious, Julie. Where the hell is he, that's what I'd like to know? Why hasn't he come home before now? It's been four days,' he snapped his fingers, 'when he could have been back here in four hours.'

He folded his arms across his chest, all the while pushing the toe of his boot in the sand and moving it round and round. 'What worries me is that I never know what to expect from him next—what his next move will be. When he was in there, it was easier. What he could do was limited. But now——'

Julie frowned, not understanding what he was saying. 'What are you talking about?'

'He'll try to stop you from leaving, you know that. He won't let you go.'

'Don't be ridiculous, Frank! He can't stop me.'

'You can't know him very well, if you think that.'

'When you gave him the papers and my letter, did he ask you to persuade me to stay, to wait for him? He knew I intended to be gone when he got back. He knew that and still he said nothing. Isn't that what you told me?'

'Yes, that's right. Not a word. Just the house.'

'Well, "nothing" to me means just that. He doesn't really give a damn whether I stay or go. Don't forget,' she added bitterly, 'he hasn't written to me, not once. That's message enough, I'd say.'

'Well, don't you think it a little strange that he hasn't come straight here?'

'I don't care what he does. I don't care where he goes. I'm leaving on Monday and that's final.'

'Look, I'm driving into Calgary later,' said Frank. 'Bring Beth and come with me then. A few days earlier might be better.'

'I can't do that,' she sighed. 'I couldn't leave without saying goodbye to Maggie. My leaving will hurt her enough as it is.'

'She knows, then?'

'Yes, she found out——' she stopped, not wanting to get into a long explanation of what had happened. 'I talked to her about it yesterday.'

'Go with Richard, then. I'd feel much better if you weren't here alone, with us not knowing where he is.'

'I've already told you that I can't go. I just can't.' She looked back over her shoulder towards the picnic grounds. 'Look, I have to get back. I've already left them for too long.' She reached out and touched his arm, squeezing it gently. 'Don't worry about me, Frank, I'll be all right. Are you going to be in Calgary for the entire weekend?'

'No, I'll be back tomorrow morning. I'll check with you then.'

'Thanks. And please,' she looked at him gratefully, 'remember how much I appreciate all you've done. Without you, I don't know how I would have managed.'

Frank put his arm around her and they walked back up the path to rejoin Richard and Beth.

As hard as she tried, Julie couldn't enjoy the rest of the picnic. Somehow she managed to endure the time, for Beth's sake and for Richard's, but all she wanted now was to be alone, away from the condemning and speculative eyes of the people of Henderson, many of whom still worked at the mill, and away from Richard's lighthearted bantering. Beth, thank God, was too young to understand any of it. She rolled and laughed and ran on shaky legs, happily oblivious to her mother's bleak mood.

But Richard was not. It was he who spoke first. 'It's too bad that Frank came here this afternoon and managed to spoil our time together.'

'I'm so sorry—it's my fault really. I've ruined your afternoon by being such terrible company.'

'What did he say to you that's had such an effect on you?'

For a moment she thought of telling him nothing. But even Richard, who was always so kind, so willing to believe, could not be expected to accept such an evasion. She stared down at the blanket. 'He told me that Luke was released from prison—four days ago. He doesn't know where he is and he's worried about why he hasn't come back here straight away.'

Richard frowned. 'It does seem strange. It would seem natural that he would want to come back right away.'

'Well, he hasn't, and that's what's worrying Frank.'

'And you as well.'

'Yes,' she admitted. 'A little.' More than a little, if the truth was told, she said to herself. It was so important to be gone from Henderson before he came back. Things would only be more painful, more difficult, if he was here when she left.

Richard gently ran his finger over hers. 'It will be so much healthier for you away from here. Too much has happened to you in this place for you to stay, too many harmful things.'

She nodded, feeling very vulnerable, close to tears.

'Come back to Calgary with me tonight, Julie,' he whispered urgently. 'We can arrange to have things moved from here once you're in Calgary. You don't have to be here and do it all yourself. You need to leave this place and soon.'

Suddenly all she wanted to do was lean against him, against anyone, just to be held and told what to do. She wanted to go with him to Calgary and to let him handle the arrangements, everything. 'Oh, Richard, sometimes I think I don't know what to do. I'm so tired of it all!'

He put his arm round her and pulled her close. 'Come with me then, Julie, and you won't be alone. I'll be there to help you. It'll be all right, I promise.'

'I can't come today. It's impossible, really.'

'Why is it? It's a very simple thing to do. Pack what you need for tonight and I'll send someone for the rest.'

'No. Luke's grandmother will be back tomorrow from Houghton. It would hurt her terribly if I left like that. It's going to be hard enough for her as it is.'

'You have to stop thinking of everyone else. *You* need some attention now, I'd say.'

'You've been so kind to me, Richard, how can I ever thank you?' She leaned her head against his shoulder. For a moment he didn't speak, then he turned his face into her hair and breathed deeply.

'You can listen to me for a minute without getting upset and without interrupting, that's what you can do.' She didn't move, her body tense and waiting. 'I've been thinking a lot about you lately, Julie, and a lot about us.' She moved, suddenly afraid of what he was going to say. 'No, listen to me.' His fingers roamed the soft skin of her arm and he held her tightly against him. 'I would rather you didn't come to work for me at the firm,' he said bluntly.

Julie felt a sickening lurch in her stomach. Where would she go now? What would she do? She had gone ahead with her plans to leave mainly because of the security that Richard's offer of a job had given her. 'I would much prefer,' she heard him continue, 'that you marry me.'

This time she sat up straight, staring at him, wide-eyed and shocked. 'Richard, please don't,' she began.

'I mean it. I've wanted it for a long time, since I first met you. I've never felt this way about anyone before, never. And I want you to know how I feel. I want to be completely honest with you.'

She looked across the field, to where Beth sat fingering a bright yellow dandelion. When she did speak, she chose her words carefully, 'I care deeply for you, Richard, really I do. You are and have been a good friend to me during the most difficult time of my life. But I don't love you, not that way, not in the way you deserve to be loved by the woman who would be your wife. I'm sorry, it would be so much easier for you, for all of us, if I did love you that way. But I don't.'

He cleared his throat. 'You've been through a harsh time and it's left its mark on you, Julie. There are wounds that haven't healed yet, but they will in time. I'm willing to give you that time. I'm willing to give you everything you need to feel healthy and whole again. You're so very young and you have all of life ahead of you, all your tomorrows.'

She shrank at his use of those particular words and tears sprang to her eyes and overflowed. Luke had promised that—all his tomorrows would be hers, he had said when they'd married. He had promised her a bright, shining new world filled with a love such as she had never known existed. And he had stolen it from her, coldly and uncaringly. 'Words are too easy, much too easy,' she said brokenly. 'Please don't say any more.'

'But there's so much to be said, to be shared, Julie.'

'No.' She pulled out of his grip and sat leaning forward on the blanket. 'I'm still married to Luke Marshall. I'm his wife and the mother of his child.'

'And as I've already reminded you, you're going to divorce him.'

'It may not be as easy as all that.'

'Did he say no to your request?' Richard questioned her for the first time about Frank's visit to the prison last week.

'No. He said nothing. There was no response from him.'

'Does he want to talk it out?'

'I don't know.'

'I think the fact that he sent no response speaks for itself.'

'Luke Marshall isn't like other men, Richard. Nothing he does speaks for itself.' Julie touched the rough wool of the blanket with her fingers. 'But that isn't even the point. You've been truthful with me and I've told you where I stand. I don't love you the way you want me to and I don't think I ever will. It's not fair of me to go to Calgary and work for you if that's what you expect of me.'

'It's entirely fair. I expect nothing of you that you're not willing to give, Julie. You need the job and it's yours. I can wait for the rest.'

For long moments neither of them spoke, then Richard stood up. 'I'm going to take a bit of a walk by the river, if you'll excuse me,' he said evenly. 'I won't be long.' He walked across the grass, ducking under the long branches of the tree, then stopped and looked back at her. 'You know, he must be one hell of a guy, this Luke Marshall, for you to go on loving him after everything he's done to destroy your life.' He turned abruptly and disappeared into the trees.

He had left her too quickly for her to deny aloud what she had been denying inwardly for so long now. She no longer loved Luke Marshall. It was over. It was dead.

True to his word, Richard was not gone long. However, neither of them picked up the thread of the conversation that dangled uncomfortably in the air before them. Instead they wandered along the river, then Julie allowed herself to be persuaded to join him for supper at the only restaurant in downtown Henderson. They came back to the grounds to sit on the blanket in the coolness of dusk to watch the fireworks. But despite the brilliant dance of colour in the night-time sky, Julie felt no thrill at the sight. Finally, Beth crawled into Julie's lap, cuddled up against her, and was promptly asleep.

Across the valley the evening train, eastbound, moaned mournfully into the night. Shortly, it came round the bend and rolled along the tracks on the other side of the river. Julie could see the lights in the coaches, the figures sitting and looking out into the darkness. Again it blew its whistle, this time its cry not quite so lonely, perhaps, she thought, because it was closer to people now that it had come out of the mountains and across the empty grass-land. She wondered how the passengers felt looking out at those who watched and waved back at them. Trains and their whistles always filled her with sadness, always made her cry a little. She stared after it, long after it had continued on into town and out of sight.

She turned to Richard. 'We'd better get Beth home, if you don't mind. She's worn out.'

The dance was beginning. It was always held in the open air, if weather permitted, on staging erected especi-ally for the occasion. 'Want to come back for the dance, Julie?' he asked.

'No, thanks, Richard. I think I'm as tired as Beth. I just haven't had the sense to pass out. I've got a lot to do tomorrow, so I'd like to make it an early night, if you don't mind.'

They drove through town, past groups of people dressed for partying and dancing, walking towards the picnic grounds. A group of cowboys and their girl-friends suddenly stepped off the sidewalk and crossed the street in front of them, forcing Richard to brake suddenly. They smiled and laughed, obviously feeling immune to every-thing except the infectious laughter and good times to be had during Rodeo Week in Henderson.

He pulled the car to the kerb in front of the house and turned off the ignition. Julie looked up to see a light shin-ing in her room upstairs. 'Oh, damn, I must have left the light on this afternoon.'

Richard made to move to get out of the car. 'Sure you won't change your mind, Julie?'

'No, really. I don't feel like dancing tonight, Richard.'

'And about coming with me to Calgary? There's room at my apartment for you both until you can move into your own next week.' His voice was hopeful.

She shook her head. 'No, I'm sorry.'

He leaned over and kissed her on the mouth, lingering for a moment, then drawing slowly away. 'Whatever you say.' He got out of the car, walked round and opened the door for her. 'I'll carry Beth for you, if you like, and come back and get the rest.'

'No, I can carry her if you'll get the basket and the blanket.'

He followed her up the walk and opened the back door, which was unlocked. 'Lord, don't you ever lock your doors around here? Anybody could come in and steal you blind.' He walked into the kitchen behind her and put the things on the kitchen table. 'Want me to take her upstairs for you?'

'No, thanks. I like to tuck her in myself.' Julie reached up and kissed him on the cheek. 'Thanks for persuading me to come with you. I needed to get out.'

'Not that it was all that much fun for you, though, thanks to Frank and myself.'

'It was good to get out, no matter what you say. I enjoyed your company and I appreciate you coming all the way from Calgary.'

He kissed her again on the mouth. 'Goodnight, sweet Julie. See you next week in Calgary.'

'Goodnight, Richard.'

He left, closing the door quietly behind him. She waited for the sound of his car driving off, then, holding Beth close to her, walked slowly up the long winding staircase, realising, not for the first time, how large this house really was.

She turned the light on in the hallway, entered Beth's room, and laid her carefully in her crib. She changed her nappy and covered her with a blanket, deciding to wash her sticky hands and face in the morning. The child was so tired that it was best to let her sleep.

Julie tiptoed out of the room, turned off the hall light and walked wearily towards her bedroom. She couldn't remember having left the light on, but she must have. Opening the door to her room, she went in, leaning down to take off her sandals. A movement at the window startled her and she looked up.

A man stood at the window, his back to her. He must have heard her gasp, for he turned slowly and looked at her, his eyes black and burning and familiar.

'Luke,' she whispered, leaning against the doorframe for support.

CHAPTER THREE

THEY stood staring at each other across the illimitable space of two long years, neither of them able to speak. He was thinner, so much thinner, Julie realised at first glance, and there was a tension and a control in him that had not been there when he had left.

Like a wild animal, he seemed wary, ready to spring if attacked, ready to defend even when there was no threat.

She looked into his eyes for something she could not define, for some hint of the Luke Marshall she had known and loved those years ago, but she searched in vain. The eyes that returned her stare were dark and cold. She shivered and dropped her searching gaze, frantically trying to think of something to say to this man who was her husband.

'You look tired,' she offered weakly, her voice a mere whisper. It seemed like such an empty thing to say and immediately she regretted having spoken. She should have waited for him to speak first.

He didn't take his eyes from her, drawing hers back to his, holding her mesmerised and trapped. 'I am,' he grated. 'Two years tired.'

A shiver went up her spine. There was something dangerous in him now, in his look, in his words. 'I . . . I don't know what to say to you,' she stammered. 'It feels very strange.'

'Yes, it does, doesn't it? There are so many things to say and nowhere to begin.'

Slowly he turned back to the window and looked towards the town he had not seen for so long. 'It hasn't changed much really, has it? Not on the surface anyway.' He spoke as if he didn't expect an answer from her and neither did he wait for one. 'I don't imagine people have changed much.' He paused, waiting for something, perhaps for her to speak, but she stood and stared at his back in stunned and frightened silence. She could not bring herself to approach him, to respond. She could only wait.

Luke spoke again, suddenly, with an anger that he did not try to disguise. 'Have they changed, Julie?' He swung round and faced her, his jaw clenched tightly, a pulse beating furiously at the base of his throat. 'Well, answer me! You never used to be at a loss for words—always quite the contrary, if my memory serves me correctly.'

He used to tease her when she would chatter excitedly about things, but he was not teasing now. 'Yes,' she managed to say, her voice almost inaudible.

'What's that? I didn't hear you.' He walked towards her, his steps slow, even, and menacing.

'I said yes,' she repeated unevenly, her voice faltering. 'Yes, they have changed. They aren't like the people I grew up with. Everything's changed.'

'And how's that?' He stared down at her, his eyes narrowed, angry slits.

'There's a barrier. I live in this town as I have all of my life, but I'm not a part of it, not like before. For two years I've lived on the outside. They've had nothing to do with me or,' she hesitated, then added, 'or Beth.'

'And you? What about you, my Jul? Have you changed so much?' Slowly he lifted a hand and passed it over her face, the touch of his fingers burning into her skin.

She closed her eyes, fighting for control. He was too close, too dangerous, and he frightened her as he never had before. She stepped back. 'Please don't, Luke,' she whispered brokenly. 'I can't.'

'You can't what?' he asked, his voice steel-edged.

'What do you want of me?' she burst out, unable to stand it any more, not understanding, but hating the game he was playing.

'Come now, Julie, you were never dull-witted. I'm sure you know the answer to that question.' He spoke with forced casualness.

But she saw in his eyes a hunted, tormented look, that belied the quiet control in his voice, and a deep, raging anger that seemed to know no boundaries. 'What's wrong with you, Luke?' she breathed, terrified.

His eyes widened. 'You can ask that of me?' He threw

his words at her, reaching out and roughly gripping her arms, his fingers biting into the soft flesh.

She struggled against his iron hold. 'Stop it! You're hurting me!' she whimpered.

'And I could kill you,' he grated as he released her, dropping his hands to his sides. 'God help me, I could kill you for what you've done!' He raked his fingers through his hair and fought for control.

'And what have I done?' she asked incredulously, suddenly finding her voice and her own anger—he had no right to come back here and treat her like this.

'You *are* innocent and naïve this evening, my dear.' Sarcasm dripped from each word. 'You understand nothing that's going on around you, if I'm to believe the act you're putting on for me now.'

'It's no act, and I don't understand why you've come back like this, why you're behaving this way. Frank says you've been out for four days. What kept you?'

He moved past her, smiling as she jumped at his sudden movement, and remarked almost nonchalently as he reached for his jacket which lay at the bottom of her bed, 'It's probably very healthy for you to be afraid of me just now, Julie. God knows I've stayed away long enough so that I wouldn't come home and hurt you for what you've done.'

'And what have I done?' she demanded again.

'Am I to believe that you've been living the life of a saintly nun these past two years?' he drawled, a derisive smile painting itself on his mouth.

'You're crazy!'

'No, I've finally come to my senses. After two years of absolute hell, when I feared at times that I couldn't survive another moment, I'm free. Free,' his voice rose, 'to live again. And that's exactly what I intend to do.' He withdrew some papers from one of the pockets of his jacket and came to stand before her, levelling them at her as he would an accusation. 'These are for you.' Hatred burned in his eyes. 'You'll note that they're unsigned, and will remain that way. You see, Julie,' he went on, speaking slowly and emphasising each word so as to lengthen his threat, 'I've decided to keep you.'

Her eyes widened in horror. 'No,' she stammered, her

voice a hoarse whisper, 'you can't!'

'I can and I will.'

She backed away from him, towards the door. 'I'm going. I have a job, an apartment. Beth and I, we——'
She almost had the door open when his hand came down on hers, and pulled her roughly back into the room, placing himself between her and her only means of escape.

You can't run, anyway, Julie,' he said calmly. 'You would have to leave the child with me, and I know that wouldn't suit you at all.'

She struggled to free herself from his bruising hold, but to no avail, for his strength far surpassed hers. He was toying with her, she saw, as a spider would with a helpless moth, and enjoying it too. To fight him would be a wasted effort.

'You listen to me, Julie.' His words were as dark and threatening as his eyes. 'You're my wife and you're going to stay with me. I've given up two years of my life and I'll be damned if I'll give up any more. The Taggarts have had all they're going to get from me. Do you hear me?'

'I hear you.' She spat the words at him, hating him as she'd never hated anyone before. 'But you can't keep me here. I'm not your property, Luke Marshall, and if I want to leave, you can't stop me!'

'Can't I?' He let go of her hand, but did not move away from the door. 'You'll be very surprised to know what I'm capable of, what I can do when I'm pushed to it.'

'Oh, not at all,' she said cuttingly. 'I know exactly what you're capable of, believe me! You're a thief, a man who stole from his friends—people he'd known from the time he was a child, people who dealt with his father and his grandfather before him. That didn't stop you, though. Oh no, Luke, nothing you could do would surprise me.'

'Are you serious?' He is voice was tight, controlled. 'Do you know what you're saying to me?'

'Yes.'

'You believe that I was guilty?'

'Yes,' she replied, more faintly the second time, a nagging feeling at the back of her mind telling her that he shouldn't be so astonished at what she had said; it was inevitable that she learn the truth about it some day. 'I've known for a long time. Frank showed me the papers.'

Luke looked up suddenly. 'The what?' he asked sharply.

'The papers. The accounts that you tampered with to hide what you'd taken from the company.'

He was interested now, following every word she said, leaning forward, almost in wonderment. 'Frank showed you those?' he asked.

She nodded, for a moment hesitant and confused about his reaction, then realising that probably he was trying to turn her away from her real concern. She pushed on. 'That was quite a surprise for me, Luke, but since then I've given up believing in people, and believing in you, especially. I know you for what you are, and nothing you could do now would surprise me in the least. I want a divorce and I intend to have one.'

He flinched as her words found their mark. 'You bitch!' he swore, his control vanishing. 'You wait two years. You wait until a few days before my release, then you send divorce papers to me with Frank. And oh yes, I nearly forgot, a tidy little note to explain why, telling me that you've changed, that people change and that it would be best and easier for everyone if you left.'

The pulse in his throat pounded out a furious rhythm, taut lines carving themselves around his mouth. 'I've lost two years of my life. Nothing on earth could have been harder for me, being caged in that place like an animal, each day as if it were a year. I come home to a child I've never seen, and a woman who believes I was guilty.'

'I know it must have been difficult for you, Luke, I'm not discounting that,' she offered, trying to make him listen to reason.

'Oh yes, it was difficult, very difficult.' He reached down and picked up the papers she'd dropped to the floor, and tore them up. 'There's be no divorce, Julie,' he said harshly. 'I have a wife and a daughter and I intend to keep both.' His eyes blazed. 'Two years of hell should be worth something, surely.'

'And my two years of hell should be worth something

as well! I have a right to be happy. I can't stay with you, not after everything that's happened. It would be a farce if I did.'

'I've told you how things stand. You're not leaving.'

'You can't watch me every second of the day. I'm leaving, and I'm taking Beth with me.'

'You're right,' he said evenly, 'I can't watch you all the time. And yes, you can leave. But know this before you do something rash—as sure as I'm standing here, I'll come after you and I'll bring you back. But by God, I don't do it more than once. If you leave a second time, I'll let you go. It'll be the child I bring back, and I promise that you'll never see her again. Never. And you know me better than to doubt my word on that.'

Julie stared at him, frozen by his threat. 'You wouldn't, you couldn't do that! She's my child,' she whispered brokenly. But she knew that he meant every word he said. She closed her eyes, his threat echoing in her mind.

'She's my child too, Julie, and I damn well would do it. Do we understand each other?'

She nodded, not opening her eyes, but that wasn't enough for Luke. He had to hear it. 'Say it, Julie. I want to hear you tell me that you understand what I've said.'

'I understand.' She looked mutely up at him. 'I believe you.'

He reached out to touch her, but she shrank away from him, her eyes wide with terror. Slowly and deliberately he drew back his hand. 'No need to cringe like a frightened animal, Jul. I won't touch you—at least not tonight.' The tone of his voice mocked her fear of him. 'I'll give you time to adjust to my return before I make love to you.' He stared down at her, at her shirt, the top button open and revealing a hint of her soft breasts. 'Not that I don't want to. I've wandered to the edge of insanity more than once during these last years, just for the lack of you. I have every intention of being your husband again, and soon. You'll share my bed again, Julie,' he said softly, menacingly, moving away from her, turning and opening the door. 'Now I want to see my daughter.'

He stood motionless beside the cot, staring down at the

small child who was so obviously his.

'Please don't waken her. She's had a long day.' Julie tried to control her tears, the fear that welled within her. But all she could think of was that he would take Beth from her. He would take her child if she didn't do as she was told. A terrifying thought swept across her mind. Maybe he would take her anyway, maybe he was hiding his real intention—to punish her for daring to ask for the divorce. It was all too cruel. This child of theirs should have been born of their love, their lives together. Luke should have been with her and the joy of Beth's birth should have belonged to both of them. But he hadn't been, and she would never forgive him for that. 'She doesn't know you, Luke. You'll frighten her.'

But he was oblivious to her words and her presence, aware only that his child lay before him, the child he was seeing for the first time. He moved closer, reaching down and gently laying a hand on Beth's small head, and closed his eyes. He stood this way for what seemed to Julie a very long time. She watched him breathlessly, not daring to move or make a single sound to disturb him.

Finally he turned to her and faced her once again. 'Dear God, Julie, she's my child. My daughter.' The unmasked agony in his eyes and the tortured emotion in his voice was too much for her to bear, and she ran sobbing from the room.

He did not follow her back to the bedroom. She stood perfectly still, holding her breath and leaning back against the closed door, waiting to hear him in the hallway. Moments later his muffled footsteps sounded on the stairway, then in the downstairs hall. The front door opened and closed and he was gone. But where? Her mind was in a turmoil. Why had he gone out now? It wasn't late. Only about ten o'clock, she thought, so where would he have gone? What did he have to do at this hour?

She listened for the sound of his return, to the silence that now pervaded the house, to the stillness that was punctuated only by the hammering of her heart. Maybe he wouldn't come back, maybe he would grant her wish and let her leave. But as quickly as the thought crossed her mind she dismissed it. She knew with certainty that he would stay and he would force her to as well. He no longer loved her, she was certain of that, but as far as he was concerned she was his property and he had no intention of giving her her freedom. Moreover, he wanted his daughter with a passion, and even if he no longer loved his wife, his child was another matter altogether. She had seen that in his face only moments before.

She lay in bed, tense and still in the quiet darkness, waiting for the sound of his return. How could she stand to stay here now? Yet how would she dare to leave? She was virtually a prisoner, held captive by invisible bars, by Luke Marshall. Yes, his power to hold her was greater than hers to escape.

It was nearly dawn when he returned, his footsteps on the stairs alerting her. She lay perfectly still, feigning sleep, praying that he would not come to her. All was silent for a long while and she wondered where he had gone, then she heard him in Beth's room. What if he had come back to take the baby—her baby? The thought panicked her and she almost leapt from the bed, but she forced herself to remain calm and stay where she was. Luke wouldn't take Beth from her, not as long as she stayed with him. He had said so himself and his word was his word. She almost laughed aloud. What good was his word? Wasn't he a thief? Why should he not add lying to his crimes? She rubbed frustrated fingers against her forehead, wishing desperately that sleep would come to end these confused and dreadful thoughts.

Somehow, despite the strain of his presence and the frantic images that plagued her mind, she did manage to sleep. When she opened her eyes the sun was streaming in through the curtains, spreading a golden morning glow throughout the room. Sitting up, she threw back the covers and stretched her body. She felt terrible. Her head was pounding, and it was as if she hadn't slept at all. Then, with a jolting suddenness, she remembered. He was back.

The phone rang downstairs. Once, twice, then it stopped. Tiptoeing across the room, Julie slowly turned the knob. It creaked, no matter how cautious she was.

She walked down the hallway and into Beth's room, her
footsteps cushioned and silenced in the carpet. Suddenly
she uttered a strangled cry of terror. 'Oh God! Dear God,
no!' Beth wasn't in her cot. Running from the room and
down the stairs, she remembered all that Luke had
threatened last night. He had taken Beth, when she had
persuaded herself that he would never do such a thing.
He was not to be trusted. She hesitated at the bottom of
the stairwell, not knowing which way to turn, grasping
the railing for support. It was then that she heard Beth
laugh, a happy, little-girl giggle. Pale and shaken, she
rushed into the kitchen, only to see Luke, a dish-towel
flung carelessly over one shoulder, kneeling beside Beth,
who was sitting on the floor in the midst of her toys,
happily oblivious to everything except her stuffed bear
and Luke's attention. Her small fingers pulled at his gold
wedding band; Julie had noticed last night that he had
not removed it.

The sight of him there beside his daughter was devastating. All the tenderness, caring, and gentleness that he
had once given so generously to her were evident again as
his strong fingers reached down and touched Beth's cap of
silken black hair. The sight of it brought stinging tears to
her eyes, which she brushed fiercely away. Never forget,
she reminded herself harshly, the man is a thief and he
killed your father. He's cruel and ruthless and was never
what you believed him to be. Never. You were a fool to
be so blinded.

Luke must have felt her presence rather than heard her
enter the room, for he seemed engrossed in Beth, but after
a moment he looked up at her and rose slowly to his feet.

'You're still here. You didn't take her,' she said breathlessly, then wanted to swallow her words, wishing them
unsaid as soon as she had spoken them aloud.

His face clouded. 'Is that what you thought?' he asked,
as in disgust he threw the towel on the counter and stood
staring angrily across the room at her. His anger seemed
almost a constant in him now.

He wore faded jeans and a white shirt, its sleeves rolled
up to his elbows. They were clothes that he hadn't worn
for two years and it was even more evident in the daylight

how much weight he had lost, how strained and tired he really looked. But he was still a big man, well over six feet, and the shirt, unbuttoned, revealed a broad and well muscled chest. Julie blushed, realising that he was noting her assessment of him.

'So what do you think, Julie?' he asked coldly.

'I—I don't know what you mean.' She wanted to turn her eyes away from his cold stare but could not.

'Yes, you do, damn it,' he snapped. 'Stop acting as if I speak a language foreign to yours!'

'I don't know what you're talking about,' she insisted, not willing to admit that she did.

'Forget it,' he grated, exhaling a frustrated breath. He stood perfectly still, staring at her from across the room, the power in his look devastating. She felt her legs weaken. 'No, let's not forget about it,' he said harshly. 'Let's get a few things straight right now. Sit down.'

'No, I need to take a shower.' She moved towards the door.

'I said sit down!'

Her eyes darted around the room. Never had she felt so trapped, so utterly helpless. Walking reluctantly to the kitchen table, she pulled out a chair and sat down, self-consciously pushing back her hair from her forehead.

'You thought I'd taken Beth.' It wasn't a question but a statement of fact. It required no response and she gave none. What use, she asked herself, to try and deny it?

'Maybe that's good. Maybe it's a lesson for you, to know how it would feel if you even dare consider trying to leave.'

She looked up at him, her eyes searching his. There was no softness in them, just that deep, burning anger in the depth of their blackness. 'I intend,' he spoke each word succinctly, 'to keep you both, as I've already told you. You've nothing to worry about, unless you're foolish enough to do what I've warned you against.'

Beth continued to play, having shifted her attention from her teddy bear to her blocks, the sound of them striking the floor punctuated by her soft baby noises; her presence provided a strange, almost ironic contrast to what was happening between the two adults.

Luke poured two cups of coffee, came back to the table, placed one mug before Julie and sat down. There was no sign of weariness in him now. It was as if he had willed it away. 'Drink it before it gets cold,' he ordered. 'We have some things to talk about. You owe me some answers and I have some decisions to make about where we go from here.'

Julie shook her head, unable to speak, her heart pounding in her ears. Anywhere but here, she thought frantically, facing this cold and embittered stranger. 'Please, Luke, just let me go.'

He ignored her plea. 'Where's Maggie, and when's she due back?'

'In Houghton, with Edna. She'll be home tonight, after supper sometime.'

He didn't take his eyes from her, but kept her pinned with his glare, as one would a moth to a light. 'And Frank?'

'He's in Calgary on business, something about the mill maybe. He said he'd be back today.'

'Good old Frank, working as hard as can be for everyone but himself.'

The ridicule in his words brought her to life. 'Yes, good old Frank, indeed. He's been a good friend to you. If it hadn't been for him——'

Luke got up, pushing his chair behind him so forcibly that it nearly fell over, and walked over to the counter, throwing the contents of his coffee mug into the sink. 'I went to the mill last night.'

'You did?'

'Yes, I did,' he said roughly. 'And I wasn't very happy with some of the things I found. So your dear brother Frank has some explaining to do when he gets back today.'

Julie didn't bother to react. What would be the use? Luke would reject anything she would have to say anyway. She lifted the mug to her mouth and sipped at the warm liquid, keeping her eyes averted, not wanting to look into the face of his anger any more. She didn't hear him come back to the table, and she was startled when he coolly placed in front of her a picture of herself and Frank and Richard Buchanan. She gazed at it in puzzlement; it must have been taken at a party that they had all been to at Richard's home last year in Calgary, although she had not known that it had been taken and could not guess how Luke had come to possess it.

'Where did you get that?' she asked, not thinking to hide her surprise, not realising how he would probably interpret it.

'Tell me, my dear, what else do I have to thank your brother Frank for?'

'What are you implying?' she demanded hotly, knowing full well what he was saying.

'I'm not implying anything! I can see quite plainly that my good friend Frank Taggart made perfectly sure that you weren't going to be lonely while I was away.'

She couldn't believe her ears. How dared he accuse her—and Frank—of such a thing! 'That's insane,' she said incredulously. 'You can't be serious.'

'I'm very serious. Who is it?'

'His name is Richard Buchanan. He's a friend of Frank's, from Calgary.'

'Is he the one who brought you home last night?'

'No,' she replied, too slowly to be believed.

'You're lying. I thought perhaps Frank had taken you both to the picnic, but he didn't, did he? It was this fellow Richard, wasn't it?'

'Don't be such a fool.' She was the fool, she thought harshly. Why didn't she just tell him the truth and let him interpret it as he wished?

Luke grabbed the picture off the table, crumpling it in his fist. 'Your friend Richard Buchanan called before you got down, to tell you that he was sorry but, as he feared, he has to fly to Toronto on business and won't be back until next Thursday. So he won't be able to help you move into the apartment, but he'll see you when he gets back. He also said to thank you for yesterday.' He threw the picture into the garbage by the stove. 'He thought I was one of the movers, here to help with the packing,' he sneered. 'And what else does he have to thank you for, Julie? What else?' The barely controlled violence in his eyes truly frightened her and she shrank away from him.

'Tell me, how often have you slept with him?'

The question hit her with the same force as if he had physically struck her. She could take no more of this. Now she wanted to hurt him just as he had hurt her, to make him feel some of the pain he was inflicting on her. 'What do you suppose?' she threw back at him. 'He's handsome and rich—and after all, I had my future to think about. Two years is a long time for me as well as for you. You wouldn't let me visit you. There's been nothing, absolutely nothing, between us for two years. What would you expect me to do?'

'I expected, I believed, that there was trust between us and that it would hold us together.' His hands curled into fists, held rigidly at his sides. 'But you're right, I was a fool,' he muttered bleakly.

'Richard loves me and wants to marry me. He was here, you weren't.'

Luke turned away from her, rubbing his neck with his hand, obviously struggling against the emotion that raged inside him. He looked back at her, and for a moment she thought she glimpsed raw pain in his eyes; but whatever she saw was fleeting, gone before she could be sure of it. What bothered him the most, she thought, was the fact that he believed someone had the effrontery to violate what he considered to be his property. Love was not a concern of his.

'What I said last night still stands,' he said finally. 'You're mine and you stay.' The harsh lines of his mouth and the bleak anger that smouldered in his eyes told her that he meant every word. 'A little used perhaps, but mine, nevertheless,' he added cruelly.

He walked over to Beth, bent down and picked her up, holding her close against his chest. 'Take your shower, Julie. I'll watch the baby. Then I'm going back down to the mill.'

There was nothing more for her to say. Her head downbent, she left the room.

CHAPTER FOUR

THE hot water was a balm to her tortured spirit, the warmth of it flooding over her, soothing away the ache and the tension in her body. She stood for a long time in its streaming warmth, then stepped out and towelled herself dry, pinning up her long hair, then putting on a bright yellow sundress. She chose a pair of light sandals from the closet, then turned to look at herself in the mirror. The reflection that stared back at her, remarkably enough, showed none of the strain and hurt of the last twelve hours. No one, to look at her like this, would detect that anything was amiss in her life.

Luke's return to Henderson had been a shock to her, had radically altered all her plans. If she tried to leave now, he would carry out his threats, she was in no doubt about that. So she would have to call Richard when he returned later in the week and tell him she would not be coming to Calgary—although she would not tell him why. Everyone must be made to believe that she chose to stay of her own free will, must come to believe that she was indeed happy and content to have Luke home again. But nothing on earth would make her give up her intention to leave. Not even Luke would want a woman as his wife who hated him as she did. Yes, she stared back at her determined reflection, when the time came Luke would willingly give her her freedom. She would fight him and she would win.

She straightened, her face set with purpose, and walked slowly out of the room and down the hall, stopping at the top of her stairs and listening to the laughing sound of Beth's voice and Luke's deep, resonant one. Beth was glad to see him—but Beth didn't know who he was or what he had done to them both.

She closed her eyes, suddenly afraid of the feelings that were again sweeping through her, fighting them, ordering herself to be strong and to be careful. Remember that, she whispered to herself, and you won't be hurt again.

A knock sounded at the front door and Frank, not waiting for an answer, walked in. He looked up and saw her instantly. 'Well!' he exclaimed, 'you look better today. Your time with Richard was well spent, obviously.' Walking to the bottom of the stairs, he held out his hand to her. She came down, hesitated, then took his hand as he bent and kissed her on the cheek.

'Frank——' she began, about to tell him of Luke's return, but he interrupted her.

'And what's the occasion? Why so dressed up? Did I forget somebody's birthday, or has Richard been able to persuade you to leave today?' He smiled broadly at her, not hearing the footsteps in the hallway behind him.

'Morning, Frank.' Luke's voice, as cold as a mountain spring, froze in the air. Frank swung round, astonishment carved on his face.

'Luke! My God, man, you're home!'

Neither of them moved but stood staring, measuring, Julie thought, the changes wrought in each other over the past two years. The moment of searching lengthened and finally it was Frank who spoke first. 'It's different, seeing you here. You've changed a lot, more that I was able to see when I visited you.'

'Two years make a difference,' Luke replied stonily.

Julie looked at the two men, puzzled by their manner.

'Not if you remember who you are at the core and the why of it,' Frank said evenly.

'Sometimes even that isn't enough.' Luke's voice was heavy and his words fell between them like stones.

A chill ran along Julie's spine, leaving her more afraid than she had been in her entire life. Luke was home and with him had come an ominous sense of foreboding and doom. She fought to dispel it. 'Luke arrived last night,' she said thinly, 'on the evening train from Vancouver.'

Both men ignored her, as Frank reached out his hand. 'Welcome home, Luke. I'm glad to see you back.'

Luke stared at the hand extended before him, but made no move to take it. 'Thanks.' One word, quiet and telling, was all that he said.

Frank dropped his hand to his side and shrugged. 'Suit yourself,' he said coldly.

'Luke——' Julie began, surprise evident in her voice.

'Never mind it,' Frank cautioned.

'No, it's not fair! I don't understand.'

Luke turned on her. 'There's nothing for you to understand. What's between Frank and me is between us and I want you to stay out of it.' He grabbed his jacket from the hall seat and looked evenly at Frank. 'If you're not too busy, maybe you could come with me to the mill. I spent the night there looking things over and I have some questions that need answers right away. I also want to talk to you about the ranch.'

'Sure, no problem.' Frank nodded to his sister. 'See you later, Julie.' He turned and walked to the door. 'I'll wait for you outside,' he said to Luke, as he closed the door behind him.

Julie stood gripping the banister. 'That was unfair and you know it,' she accused hotly.

'Life's unfair,' Luke retorted, his bluntness making her even angrier.

'He's your best friend and look at the way you treat him! He's worked hard for these last two years. What's happened to you?'

'He's been well paid for his efforts, believe me. And I don't have a best friend, Julie. In fact, I'm not sure that I have any friends. I have people who work for me, for money, and a wife who will stay with me because she has no choice. That's quite a bounty of blessings, isn't it? What more could a man want?'

'Dear God, Luke,' she breathed. 'Don't you trust anyone anymore?'

'Should I?' he mocked. 'I think not. That's not how to survive in this world, I've learned that the hard way. Trust people and they'll destroy you if they get the chance.'

'Not Frank, never Frank.'

'Maybe even Frank.' A small flame flickered and grew in his eyes as he came to stand at the base of the steps, reaching up and touching her, his fingers barely brushing her slim throat. 'Just remember this—you're my wife. You carry my name and that makes you mine.' She shivered, unable to take her eyes from his, mesmerized by the passion within them. Then it was gone, as suddenly as it had appeared. He dropped his hand and turned towards the door. 'Be here when I get back,' he warned.

That day was one of the longest of Julie's life. After Luke had left with Frank she wandered about the house, looking for something to fill her time now that she was no longer faced with the rush and confusion of moving. She called and cancelled the movers, and was about to call Richard in Calgary to tell him of her change in plans, but then remembered, the receiver in her hand, that he was on his way to Toronto. She had to do something, but what? Desperation began to build in her again.

How could she possibly stay? How could Luke possibly want her, knowing how she truly felt? But she couldn't chance his wrath, not yet, not now. She had no choice but to wait, to see more fully what he intended; then some day, soon, she would make good her escape. Perhaps with Richard's help she could find a place where Luke would not be able to find her or Beth. She would not let him demolish her plans for a new life, would not let him hurt her again. Beth was playing on the floor in the front hall and Julie looked across at her. She was so utterly and breathtaking beautiful. Fear grasped at her throat once again. No one must take her. No one. Not even her father.

She looked up at the clock. It was nearly six. She didn't expect Maggie for supper, but Luke would be back shortly. Maybe. She had no idea what his patterns would be now; when they had lived together, then she had known, but now he and everything about him was strange to her. She put the steak and onions on to cook and started the salad, furiously shredding the lettuce, then stopped suddenly, closing her eyes. 'Please, God,' she prayed fervently, 'let it be all right.'

'Talking to yourself is a bad sign, Julie.' A voice intruded abruptly and startled her. The knife she was holding clattered to the floor, as she turned quickly to see her brother leaning against the doorway.

'Frank!'

'Right you are,' he replied glibly.

'How'd you get here? I thought you were with Luke.'

'I left him over an hour ago, still poring over books and invoices. The bastard doesn't trust anyone, it seems, not even me.'

He looked down at Beth, who stood beside him and tugged at his leg with her small chubby hands, then bent down and lifted her up, hugging her fiercely and issuing a mighty roar to delight the little girl. 'That baby soon won't be a baby,' he laughed. 'She's grown quite a bit these past months.'

Julie picked up the knife and placed it back on the counter. 'Yes, too quickly almost.' She looked at him. 'I didn't expect you. Do you want to stay for supper?' Almost she hoped that he would, realising how much she hated the thought of being alone with Luke again.

'No, I can't do that. But is there any chance of a coffee?' He pulled a chair out from the table and sat down. She poured the coffee and handed it to him as he leaned back in the chair and looked up at her. 'So he's back,' he said slowly.

'Yes . . . it will at least take the worry and the load off you, his being back,' she offered, not wanting to discuss her own affairs. 'You've had to handle things at the mill as well as the ranch. It's a lot for one man.'

'Oh, yes, indeed it will do that,' he replied sarcastically, fixing a penetrating gaze on her. 'And what are you avoiding telling me, little sister? What are your plans now?'

'He just got back last night, you know. It's too soon to say, really.' She had no intention of telling him of Luke's bitter refusal to give her her freedom.

Frank leaned across the table. 'What the hell are you saying? You're leaving here on Monday, just as you planned, aren't you? You have a job and Richard to think about.'

She raised her hands to him in a helpless gesture, willing him to understand what she was trying to say. 'I have Beth to think about, as well. And Luke. Things have changed.'

'Luke!' His eyes blazed fire. 'You're plain crazy, Julie, if you stay. He hasn't spent much time worrying about you, you can bet on that, and now you welcome him back as if he's been away on vacation. I don't believe this!'

'Stop it, Frank—I can't stand all this pulling on me. Luke and I will have to work it out for ourselves.'

'Then you really are staying?'

'Yes.'

'And what about Richard?'

'He's only a friend.'

'Richard was offering you more than a job with his firm, in case you didn't notice.'

'I noticed. But I don't feel that way about him, and he knows it.'

'I think you're a fool, Julie. An absolute fool. You have a right to your own life now.'

'And Luke has a right to try and make a life for himself.'

'And what about you in all that? Haven't you suffered enough because of the great Luke Marshall?'

'I'm his wife, Frank,' she murmured shakily, hating having to lie to her own brother, but unable to share her desperate secret. She could do or say nothing to risk losing Beth.

'And I suppose you're going to tell me that you still love him, that you still believe that he didn't do it?'

She closed her eyes, crumbling before the impact of his words. 'Please Frank, stop it!'

Frank's eyes narrowed. 'Well, he did do it and you know it. So face it, Julie, now, before it's too late.'

She swung round on him. 'I've faced it all,' she said frantically.

'So come with me now, right now—before he gets back. Pack a bag and bring the baby and I'll take you into Calgary—or to my place. You can stay there until Richard gets back. Do anything, but don't stay here.'

Julie shook her head. 'You know that wouldn't work.' But how could he know? How could he possibly know of Luke's threat to her? 'I can't leave him now, Frank. I just can't,' she whispered brokenly.

'Then you're a bigger fool than I thought you were!' He slammed an angry fist on the table.

She was sobbing openly now and pressed her hands to her face. 'Leave me alone!'

'Yes, I think that's just about enough, Frank.'

Frank swung round to see Luke standing in the doorway, looking past him to where Julie was leaning weakly against the counter, her face pale and drawn.

'Are you all right?' Luke asked quietly.

'Yes. I'm sorry, but everything's been so upset lately. Frank was just——' She didn't finish because she saw that Luke was no longer listening to her, but had turned his attention to Frank; she wondered how much he had heard of their conversation.

The contrast between the two men was startling and more markedly obvious than it had ever been to Julie. Luke towered over Frank and exuded a power and control that was totally absent in her brother.

'What was that all about, Frank?' Luke's voice was cold and precise, his words thrown at Frank like a knife.

'Nothing much,' Frank replied, evidently gambling on the hope that Luke had not heard crucial parts of the conversation. 'Just a disagreement, something that happens often enough between brothers and sisters, I imagine.' He laughed uneasily, clearly uncomfortable.

'She's too upset for that. There's something more,' Luke said flatly.

Frank shrugged. 'Believe what you will.'

'What were you doing here?' Luke asked rudely.

'I came to see Julie and——'

'——persuade her to leave me,' Luke finished with a sneer.

'That, too.' Frank threw caution to the wind. 'She deserves better than she's had these past years. She's got a place in Calgary and a job. Everything's settled.'

'Nothing's settled, Frank, at least not along the lines you're thinking. She's staying, and *we'll* decide where we go from here.'

Frank glared at Luke, waiting for him to speak, for he clearly had more to say.

'As you can see,' Luke continued, 'I did have the nerve to come back to Henderson. And as you'll soon discover, I have the courage to stay.'

Frank's eyes narrowed. 'That's not courage—that's outright foolishness,' he replied scornfully.

Luke smiled. 'Well, congratulations, Frank. You've finally spoken the truth of what's on your mind. You must try to be more honest about such things—it could be habit-forming.' He stopped, then shot back at him, 'Call it what you will, it's what I intend to do.'

'Despite everything?'

Luke smiled again. 'Right.' He raised a hand and pointed directly at Frank. 'After checking things at the mill, it seems I've got plenty to do in the next while—the business is falling apart. It could be accurate to say everything you've managed to do—or undo—since I've been away has given me that incentive I need now to stay.'

'I don't need to stand here and take that from you!' Frank moved towards the back door, but Luke's voice pursued him.

'Oh, yes, you do. You work for me, remember? There's important information and some records missing, Frank, and I want them in the office by nine tomorrow morning.'

Frank turned to face him. 'Are you threatening me?'

'As a matter of fact, yes, if that's what it takes. I don't like what I've found, as you've no doubt guessed.'

'I've done the best I could with a steadily failing business,' Frank retorted. 'And your insinuations about mismanagement are uncalled-for.'

'There was nothing failing about that business when I left.' Luke threw his jacket on the chair in disgust. 'And it doesn't say one hell of a lot for your best, Frank. But then, one might ask, best for whom? I only hope things aren't as bad as they seem at first glance. When was the last time you filled an order from Smith and Hemming? or Sam Kendall? Two of our best customers, and they haven't placed an order in well over a year.'

'Not everyone wants to do business with Luke Marshall's company after what happened. I took care of your business interests and your family for the past two years. It wasn't easy for any of us, but we tried. Now you come back here accusing me of God knows what when all I deserve is a little gratitude, not your arrogance and insults. If you didn't trust me to handle the mill, then why didn't you get someone else to do it? But we know the answer to that question, don't we, Luke?'

Luke drew in a long breath, fighting hard for control. 'Get out of my house, Frank! Any business we have from now on will be conducted at the office—I won't have you here again!'

Julie had been immobilised by the unleashing of so much antagonism between the two men. Now she placed a trembling hand on Luke's arm, feeling the tautness of his muscles beneath her fingers, sensing that a single word, anything, could spark an explosion in him, one that they all might well regret. 'Luke, let's stop this. It's already gone too far.'

'Don't mix in this, Julie,' Luke grated.

'He's my brother and he has a right to visit me. And he's done the best he could for you while you've been away. You can't come back here and treat him this way—it's unfair!'

Luke swore under his breath. 'You're blind sometimes, Julie.'

'Indeed she is,' Frank added bitterly. 'A blind fool for marrying you in the first place and a fool for staying now. Anyone would think she would have accepted long ago the truth about the man she married!'

Without warning Luke lunged at him, grabbing him by the shirt front, one arm drawn back to strike, his face deathly pale. 'Damn you, Frank. Damn you to hell!' Amazingly, he suddenly dropped his hand, turned and walked out of the kitchen, leaving Julie alone with Frank.

It was a few moments before either of them spoke. 'Well, are you coming with me?' Frank demanded. With one part of her mind Julie noticed that he was as pale as Luke had been.

'No.'

He walked to the door and flung it open. 'Leave him, Julie. He's a drowning man, but he's still dangerous. Protect yourself and that child of yours, because as sure as I'm standing here you're going to get hurt if you stay. There's no place for him in this town and there's no place here for those that stand with him—you'll find that out soon enough!' He slammed the door, leaving her alone.

Supper was eaten in strained silence, for neither of them was willing to discuss the afternoon's altercation. When they had finished eating, Luke got up, picked up Beth, and walked out of the dining room and across to the library. Julie washed the dishes and cleaned up the kitchen, then went to fetch Beth for her evening bath. She found the child seated quietly on Luke's knee in the big chair by the fireplace, Luke resting his cheek on the baby's head.

'I came to get her for her bath,' Julie said, somehow hating to intrude.

He looked up at her, nodded, and stood up, still holding Beth close to him. Then he kissed her gently and held her out to Julie. There was a quietness, almost a peacefulness in him that had not been there this afternoon, that she had not seen in him since his return. He did not take his eyes from the child. 'She's very lovely, Julie,' he offered quietly.

'Yes,' she murmured. 'She is, isn't she?'

The moment of intimacy lengthened between them until finally Luke spoke. 'I thought I'd drive over to the Rodeo grounds and see what's happening. Would you like to come?'

For a giveaway second or two she hesitated, horrified to find a part of herself wanting to prolong this closeness and go with him. 'No,' she replied sharply. 'No, thanks.'

'Why not?'

She hadn't expected him to pursue the subject. 'Because Beth is going to have a bath and then it's bedtime. And——'

'And you don't want to be seen with me,' he concluded icily.

'No,' she denied hotly, 'that's not true. It will be very difficult to avoid such an occurrence if you insist on making us stay here with you.'

'Julie,' he interrupted urgently, 'we have to talk. We have to deal with it. There's no avoiding it.'

'Deal with what?'

'With us.'

'I'm not avoiding anything. There is no us—only what

you force on me, and the façade that we'll present to others. You came back and told me exactly how it was to be—you didn't want to discuss anything with me last night or this morning. How do you expect me to react to the fact that you view your wife as property?' She turned away from him, but stopped at the door and added, 'There's nothing for us to discuss, Luke, nothing except a divorce. It's that simple—to me at least. If you have difficulty in understanding it, why don't you check with your lawyer and he'll explain it to you?'

Neither of them had heard the front door open and close, nor had they been aware of footsteps running across the spacious hall-way, and they were both startled when Maggie burst into the room. 'You're home,' she breathed fiercely. 'Oh, Luke, at last you're home!' Tears welled in her eyes and overflowed as Luke and she stood rooted to the spot staring at each other, grandson and grandmother.

'They told me you were back. Edna said her brother saw you down at the mill this afternoon, so I came as soon as I heard. Why didn't you call me?' Her words tumbled over each other. 'Dear God, it's true. It's really true!' Then they were running towards each other and Luke swept Maggie into his arms, holding her frail body and hugging it to himself.

'Oh, Maggie,' he groaned, 'I never thought it would ever come. It's been so long.' He buried his face against her shoulder. 'I wasn't sure . . . I wasn't sure that you'd be pleased to see me, when the time finally came.'

'Idiot!' She was laughing and crying now, her tears mixing with her bright smile. 'What would you think? Not glad to see you? It's been as though I stopped living these two years, everything on hold just waiting for you to come home.' She reached up and touched his face, his hair, pushing back a strand that had strayed over his forehead. 'But we've had each other. Me and Julie and Beth, we made it because we stayed together, the three of us, and waited.' She beamed up at him. 'And now the waiting's over. Now we can live again, the way it was.'

Julie stepped forward, holding a wriggling Beth in her arms. She kissed Maggie on the cheek. 'I'm glad you're home, Maggie,' she whispered. 'I'm going to draw a bath and put Beth to bed, then leave you two alone for a while. I'm sure you have a great deal to say to each other.'

'Thank you, my dear.' Maggie touched Julie's cheek with her trembling hand.

Julie did not look back at Luke, but turned quickly and left the room, closing the door behind her and almost running across the hallway and up the stairs. Tears escaped and ran down her face, blinding her, but granting her no relief. In so many ways, first with Beth and now with Maggie, the man she had loved and married still existed. She hated the reminders that tore at her, that made everything so unbearable. Yes, he loved Maggie; she'd raised him after his parents had died. Yes, he loved Beth; she was his own child, flesh of his flesh, blood of his blood. But he didn't love her, Julie. He had used her and lied to her and for the past two years he had lived without her.

She sat down in the rocker in Beth's room, remembering the one time when she had gone to see him in prison, remembering the look of ice-cold anger in his eyes, and his voice, hard and biting, telling her to leave and never come back. She must wait for him in Henderson with Maggie, he had ordered, but she was never to come to see him again. Those visits from the outside had been left to Frank, for he was the only one Luke would agree to see.

He had told her he would write, but never once had he done so. Julie squeezed her eyes shut and thought of all those letters to Maggie. How horrible it had been to go to the post office, week after week, month after month, waiting, hoping for even a short note from him. But they were always addressed to Maggie, never to her. She had never said anything to Maggie, always silently leaving her mail on the table in the hallway, not showing how terribly it had hurt.

No, Luke loved Maggie and he loved his daughter, but Julie, his wife, was merely a part of the Marshall property, whom he would keep because it satisfied him to do so. But he did not love her, a truth it had taken her a long time to accept. Now she hated him for all the tender lies he had told her—somehow she would escape him, maybe not right away, but soon.

After she had bathed Beth and put on her sleepers, she wrapped the child in a blanket and sat rocking her to sleep in her lap, relishing the clean, sweet scent of her in the quiet darkness of the room. Finally she stood up and gently placed the sleeping child in her cot and left the room.

She looked at the clock in the hallway. It was nearly ten. She listened, but heard no voices. She was tempted to go to her own room and go to bed, but she knew that Maggie would find that strange, so she walked quietly down the stairs and into the library.

Maggie sat before the fire, a wool shawl thrown over her legs, her head resting in the soft cushions behind her. Julie thought she was asleep and was about to leave without disturbing her, when Maggie called out to her. 'I'm not asleep, child. Come in. Come in.' The happiness in her voice was unmistakable.

Julie walked over and sat down in the chair next to hers. 'It's been a long time since he built a fire for me, and I'm going to stay till the last spark flies up the chimney.' Maggie smiled across at Julie. 'An old woman's delight, I guess.'

'Where's Luke?'

Maggie's face clouded slightly. 'He went out. I think,' she hesitated, then continued, 'that it's very difficult for him to be inside now. He hates walls and he just had to go out. He won't be long, I'm sure. Gone down to the Rodeo grounds, I think he said.'

She reached over and patted Julie's hand. 'Your hands are cold, my dear. Lean forward and warm them with my fire.'

They sat for what seemed a long while, not speaking but watching the flames, gold and orange, dancing and leaping. Finally Julie rose, bent down, and kissed Maggie on the cheek. 'I think I'll go to bed,' she said. 'I'm very tired.'

'Of course, you must be. It's been an exciting, wonderful day—enough to make anyone tired.' Maggie's eyes reflected the glow of the fire, tears glistening in them once again. 'Luke tells me that you've changed your mind, that you're staying after all. I'm so glad. I knew everything would be all right as soon as he came home. Thank God he came before you left. He wouldn't have understood otherwise, I don't think. And I want to thank you for the time you gave us tonight—I know you must want him all to your self.'

Julie bent and kissed her again, pressing her hand on Maggie's thin shoulder, not wanting to hear any more. 'Goodnight, Maggie. I'll see you in the morning,' she murmured.

It was late when Luke returned, well after midnight, Julie guessed, and Maggie had long since gone to bed. Julie heard the door of the truck slam, and the front door open and close. She lay still, listening for the sound of his footsteps on the stairs, praying that Luke would find a bed in another room, waiting for a long time for some sound that would tell her where he had gone.

Then she heard Beth cry out. Quickly slipping out of bed, she went down the dimly lit hall to check on her. Beth had thrown off her covers but was still sleeping, so Julie carefully tucked her in again and went silently back to her room, closing the door behind her.

Luke stood by the window where moonlight streamed into the dark room, casting its silver light on his strained features. He stood absolutely still, his breathing barely visible, staring across the room at her. She wanted to move, to draw a breath, to run, anything, but she dared not. His eyes, his body, his very presence riveted her to the spot where she stood.

'Come here.' His voice seemed buried deep in the darkness that separated them. Oh God, why did it have to be this way? she thought desperately, unable to move, sensing his intentions. If it had to be this way, why hadn't *her* Luke returned, the Luke she had loved so completely, so passionately and with such abandon, instead of this frightening stranger?

'Come over here, Julie,' he repeated.

'Luke, please . . .' she began, unsure of what to say, or where to go, the feeling of entrapment smothering her.

'Julie.' He held out a commanding hand.

She walked slowly towards him, her small frame trembling with uncertainty. Finally she stood before him, refusing to meet his gaze.

'Look at me, Julie.'

She forced herself to look into his eyes, into the dark eyes that gazed steadily down at her. She was shivering uncontrollably.

'Are you that frightened?' he asked sadly.

She nodded, unable to speak.

'Why, Jul? I've never hurt you, never.' His voice was a hoarse whisper. 'And I won't hurt you now.' He pulled her gently towards him and held her firmly against his chest. She could feel the beat of his heart against her cheek. 'How I've longed for you, my sweet Julie,' he whispered, dropping kisses on her hair, stroking it with his fingers.

Suddenly her pain found form. 'Yes, you did hurt me,' she blurted out, her eyes glistening with the sting of tears. 'You did so hurt me. And I hate you for it. I'll hate you for ever! Do you hear me?' Her voice rose hysterically. 'You took from my father what he cared for the most, what he lived for—his work, and that killed him—you killed him! And you let them take you away, doing absolutely nothing to try and save yourself. You didn't care what happened to me and to Beth, did you?'

She saw the raw pain in his eyes. 'I can't explain what happened with your father,' he said in a low voice, 'and I didn't know you were going to have a child. You know that, Julie.'

'At first,' she swept on, blocking his protests, 'I thought it was your pride, your stupid foolish pride that kept you from testifying. I didn't understand those sorts of things. I thought that maybe you believed if you got up to speak it might have made you less of a man.'

He expelled a harsh breath. 'You don't understand, Julie. I had no choice.'

Anger spilled into her words. 'That's not true—I didn't understand then, but I understand now. You did it, you were guilty, that's why you didn't get up to deny anything. And that's why you wouldn't talk to me about it.'

'Julie, listen to me!'

'Why?' she demanded. 'Why should I? Are you going to discuss it with me now? Are you going to explain why, after all these years?'

Luke closed his eyes, hesitated, then turned towards the window. 'No, I'm not,' he said flatly. 'I can't.'

'Of course you can't.' She laughed bitterly. 'There's nothing to discuss, is there? I know the truth of what you did and, believe me, you aren't the only one who's paid with two years of his life. Why, you even refused to allow me to come and see you!'

'Did you expect me to welcome you there?' he asked furiously. 'In that place? It was no place for you! I didn't want you anywhere near it. And then when you told me you were expecting a child ... I nearly went crazy! I wanted to see you so much. But not there. It couldn't be there.'

'You never wrote,' she pushed on, ignoring his explanation. 'Not one single letter.'

Luke looked at her as if she had slapped him. 'I did write to you—I did. I always gave——' He stopped abruptly.

'You're a liar,' she cried. 'A liar! I'll never believe anything you say—never again!'

'You really believe that I did it?' It was as if the words were dragged out of him, and she found herself unable to reply. The silence between them lengthened. 'Do you?' he grated.

She could see in his face when he turned from the window that he still dared to hope that she trusted in him. But her pain was too deep and too raw and she wanted him to feel it, too, to realise that she had lived with it for two long years.

'Yes, damn you! Yes, I do believe you're guilty.' Her voice was hard and cutting. 'What else do you expect me to believe? Have you ever tried to tell me otherwise? Your silence has spoken loudly enough about your guilt, and about the truth of your feelings for me. As far as I'm concerned, Luke, you and I share only yesterdays. Because of what you've done, there can be no tomorrows for us— all our tomorrows are dead. We have only to bury them.'

Her voice broke and the tears that had threatened now streamed down her face. 'I hate you,' she cried, her hands tight, angry fists in front of her. 'How much I hate you, Luke Marshall!'

He flinched, and she knew her words had hit their mark. But he made one last effort. 'I want us to try and go on from here, Julie, to forget the past. It's useless and foolish to dwell on something that can't possibly be repaired or explained.' His voice was husky with emotion.

'Can't you see that it's useless and foolish for us to try and live with things as they are? The damage has been too great, Luke. Please let me go.'

His eyes blazed with frustration. 'And do you think you're the only one who's been hurt, who's still hurting?' He grabbed her wrist, his fingers tightening as he pulled her against him. 'I survived in there the best way I could, Julie. I was alone. God help me, I had to do it alone. I'm out now, but I'm not free—you've seen to that. I honestly wonder if I'll ever be free again.'

'It would be better if you let me go.'

His cynical laugh tore through the tension between them. 'Better for whom, my dear? For you and Richard Buchanan?'

'Better for all of us. We can't live together like this, it's impossible.' She tried to pull out of his grip. 'You're hurting me, Luke!'

He dropped her hand but didn't release her from his cold gaze. 'You're my wife, Julie.'

'I haven't been your wife for two years, Luke. And now you're a stranger to me, not the man I married or even thought I married.'

He took a menacing step towards her. 'Then perhaps,' he replied icily, 'we should become reacquainted, you and I.' He pulled her against him, his mouth closing roughly over hers. She struggled against his hold but was powerless against his strength. Powerless, too, to slow the quickening beat of her heart and the warmth that even after everything he was still able to create in her.

'No, Luke,' she pleaded, 'don't do this!'

'I've waited too long for you, Julie, too long,' he rasped. With one hand he began to undo the buttons of his shirt, nodding to her to do the same, but she clasped her arms against her sides in bitter refusal. 'Take it off,' he ordered, 'or I'll tear it from you.'

'I won't!' She threw her refusal back at him.

He was lightning-swift in his movements. His hand flew out and in the next moment the cloth of her shirt ripped in his fingers. He lifted her into his arms, lightly and easily, ignoring her twisting and kicking, laughing cynically. 'Go ahead, fight me, Julie. You never did before. It might add a new twist to our relationship.'

He was crushing her tightly to his chest, the mad rhythm of his heart beating beneath her cold fingers. 'I don't want you! Can't you understand that?'

'But I want you,' he retorted.

She continued to fight him, hopelessly she knew, as he flung her across the bed, pinning her flat with his own weight. Nothing she could do or say would stop him, but that didn't mean that she would surrender herself to him willingly. He would have to take what he wanted, for she would never again give it to him willingly, freely, or with love.

His hands, urgent and hard, roamed her flesh, as his passion and desire for her grew. Frantically she tried to writhe away from him, but he held her fast. With one hand he grasped her face and stared into her eyes, forcing her to meet his gaze. Then slowly, deliberately, he lowered his head and began to kiss her, his lips forcing hers apart, his mouth leaving a burning trail on her skin as it moved from her lips down her throat, then to the soft flesh of her breasts.

In the end it was her body that betrayed her, that melted beneath his touch, that rose in desperate passion to match his own. She clung to him, helplessly hungry for the intimacy that had been denied them both for so long. As his body claimed hers it was as if she were alive again, alive and dancing on the wind, and all time and separation ceased.

Finally, exhausted, they lay quiet and close, the sound of their breathing peaceful in the cool darkness. Julie gently touched the thick mat of dark hairs on his chest, revelling in the feel of him, the strong, steady rhythm of his heartbeat. They lay together thus for a long time, her body cradled against his, for she was lost in the touch and presence of this man who was her husband and her lover, once more.

Finally Luke spoke, his words soft, his breath fanning her face. 'You're mine, Julie, only mine.'

His words froze the blood that moments before had coursed so wildly through her veins. Her body stiffened in his arms. He must have felt her withdrawal, for he hugged her closer to him, as if in an effort to deny their separateness. But his words had rent asunder the tender, vulnerable fabric of their joining. In those single seconds she hated him for what he had done and she hated herself for having willingly followed him. He had not spoken to her of love tonight, only possession. What he felt for her now was pride of ownership, nothing more, and because of that she was resolved to make his victory over her a bitter and empty one.

'I don't belong to you,' she replied coldly. 'I'll never belong to you, no matter what. Our so-called lovemaking was the result of simple animal cravings, nothing more.'

'You bitch!' he growled, pushing her roughly from him and flinging back the sheets. 'And you tell me I've changed!' He grabbed his clothes and pulled on his jeans, coming to stand beside the bed, towering over her. 'We can have it any way you like from this moment on, Julie— willingly or otherwise. But you stay, no matter what. Deny it if you will, the truth is that you do belong to me. And I intend that you'll be the one to satisfy my simple animal craving as you so crudely put it.' He paused, then added threateningly, 'For now, anyway.'

CHAPTER FIVE

LUKE did not remain with her, but left their room and left the house. What time he returned home, if indeed he did at all that night, Julie didn't know. And, she told herself the next morning when she awakened, she didn't really care. She would never forgive him for what he had done. Knowing that she had not wanted him, he had taken her anyway, had forced himself upon her. Fiercely she vowed that he would come to regret the day he returned to Henderson to claim her once again as his wife.

During the next few days the tension between them grew almost unbearable, despite the fact that Luke spent most of his time at the mill, working from sunrise until late into the night, often returning long after Julie, Beth, and Maggie were in bed. But always Julie heard him come in, and always she waited with drawn breath to hear the fateful footsteps outside her bedroom door. But he didn't come to her, not as he had that night, and almost she dared believe that he had changed his mind, that soon he would set her free.

Neither had Julie seen Frank since the afternoon of the argument, although she was certain that he was probably spending a lot of time with Luke at the mill, for once she had walked downtown, leaving Beth with Maggie, and without thinking had gone to the gates of the mill, something she had often done in the early days of her marriage to surprise Luke. She had stopped herself from going in, angry that she would even subconsciously have considered it, but as she turned away from the gate, she had noticed both Luke's truck and Frank's car parked beside the office steps.

She had talked to Richard, telling him about Luke's return and of her change in plans. She had, she thought sadly, resigned a position that she hadn't even had the opportunity to fill. It had been a most uncomfortable and difficult conversation, filled with awkward pauses and unspoken feelings. At first he had been very upset and had wanted to drive out to Henderson immediately and take her back with him. Only when she had told him adamantly that under no circumstances was he to do such a thing had he agreed not to come and not to try and contact her. It was her life, she'd told him, and she would live it as she saw fit. She could not tell him, or anyone, the true circumstances of her so called 'decision' to remain with Luke. Nevertheless, every time the phone rang in the house, particularly when Luke was home, Julie would tense, praying that it was not Richard.

If Maggie noticed anything amiss between Julie and Luke, she had to this point given no indication. She was overjoyed by his return and from the first day had behaved as if he had never been away. She was also planning for the three of them to attend the Kendalls' annual party in Calgary; apparently Mildred Kendall had called as soon as she had heard Luke was back. Julie had tried to dissuade Maggie, telling her that it was too soon to attend such an event, trying diplomatically to convince her to drop her plans. But Maggie seemed totally oblivious to the fact that everyone might not share her joy at her grandson's return. Julie was surprised that Luke had not openly rejected his grandmother's plans, appearing on the contrary to be not at all concerned.

A couple of weeks after Luke's return Julie was sitting at the kitchen table, sipping black coffee and holding Beth on her lap as her daughter munched a piece of toast. She looked up as the back door opened and Maggie walked in. The older woman smiled brightly. 'Well, you're finally up.' Then she frowned in concern. 'You still look quite tired, though.'

Julie didn't explain that it was only with the first faint colours of dawn that she usually fell asleep these days.

'It's a lovely day, my dear, and it's going to be hot, I think.'

Carrying a bouquet of flowers that she'd cut from the garden, Maggie walked over to the cupboard, reached up and took out a vase and set about arranging them. 'I told Luke just this morning that there's no need for him to work so hard as soon as he gets home. He should rest up a bit, spend more time with you and Beth.' She leaned forward, closing her eyes and inhaling the sweet perfume of the roses.

She acted as if Luke had been away on a business trip, to the point where at times Julie wondered if Maggie had ever really accepted the truth of what had happened. Perhaps, to her, the acknowledgment would be a terrible dishonour, and her denial was how she had managed to live with it.

'It *is* a lovely day,' Julie said. 'I think I might take Beth on a picnic, maybe up to the mountains.' She put her coffee cup on the table and, lowering Beth to the floor, stood up. 'Yes, I think that's exactly what I'll do.'

'Oh, I nearly forgot,' Maggie interjected. 'Luke called earlier. He wants you to meet him at the mill at twelve-thirty.'

'I'll see him tonight. I don't like to disturb him at work.'

She was completely unprepared when Maggie turned to her and placed a warm hand over hers. 'I know something's not right between you and Luke, my dear, and,' she spoke with some difficulty, the glistening in her eyes telling how close to the surface her feelings were, 'I pray that you'll both be able to work it out.'

Julie wanted to pull her hand away, Maggie's observations striking too close to the truth. 'Nothing's wrong, Maggie,' she said, trying to calm the rapid beating of her heart, and hoping that Maggie would let it go at that, that she would accept Julie's denial and end the conversation there.

'I'm an old woman, Julie,' Maggie replied, 'but I'm not blind. You never were a very good liar, my dear. I love my grandson and I know when he's unhappy. And he's terribly so right now.'

'No, he's all right,' Julie persisted, her face paling at the thought of all Maggie could have been observing these past few days. Did she know that she and Luke weren't sleeping together?

'And I know you, Julie.' Maggie reached out and touched the girl's cheek tenderly. 'I love you no less than I do Luke, and you can't tell me that what I see in your eyes is happiness.'

Julie closed her eyes, bitter salt tears trickling down her cheeks. She felt Maggie's arms go round her, heard her soothing voice. 'There, there, child. It will be all right, I know it will. Two years is a long time to be separated, and under such terrible circumstances.' It was the first time that she had even remotely referred to the fact that her grandson had been imprisoned. 'No matter what they say he's done, and no matter what your brother has said

to you about it . . .' Julie looked at her, startled, because
Maggie had never spoken to her about Frank. '. . . I know
that Luke is an honest man, a man of honour and dignity.'

Maggie continued, her voice gentle, 'And I know what
you've been thinking about me—you think I'm a foolish
old woman who won't face the truth of things. Well, let
me tell you, no one can say that the Marshalls don't face
up to whatever life hands them out. That's one of the
reasons we're going to the Kendalls' party tonight.'

'It isn't fair to expect Luke to be there among people
who feel the way they do about him,' Julie protested.

'Nonsense,' Maggie retorted. 'He's a proud man who's
been hurt—unjustly but not fatally. It's been difficult for
him to come back to Henderson, but this is where he
wants to be. So it's important for him to do things like go
to this party—and besides, he knows we'll be there, his
own family, and that we trust and believe in him.'

'Oh, Maggie,' Julie whispered, not knowing what to
say, so overwhelmed was she by the old woman's words,
so conscious of her own lack of support of her husband.

'I'm not finished yet. I've been watching you and Luke,
and I've seen how you're avoiding each other.'

Julie's heart thumped. Dear God, she did know. She
knew what was happening between them

Maggie continued, 'I know you planned to take Beth
and live in Calgary. You know my opinion of that and
there's no further need to discuss it. You and Luke belong
together—here, not in some city somewhere. Neither of
you would have been happy there. And I'm glad that
Luke came back when he did. I knew once he was back
you would both decide to stay.'

Julie sighed, inwardly relieved; she couldn't have borne
the humiliation of Maggie knowing to what extent their
relationship had been reduced.

'But it's not easy, no matter how much two people love
each other, to adjust to living together again after
something like this has happened. That's what I told Luke
this morning.'

'And what did he say?' Julie asked uneasily.

Maggie laughed. 'What he always says when I give

advice that isn't asked for! He told me to mind my own business and not to interfere.' She winked at Julie. 'But I never let that stop me before, so I'm not going to now.'

'What do you mean?'

'I mean that I'm going to give you both some time together. I'll take care of Beth this afternoon while you go down to the mill and tear that man away from his desk and papers. Get away from this town for the afternoon. Then, when you come back tonight, there'll be the party.' She leaned back and looked at Julie. 'Simple, isn't it?'

If only it could be, Julie said to herself as she backed away. 'I couldn't, really. I can't interrupt his work.'

'Yes, you can, and yes, you will. Besides, he wants you to meet him, remember? So off you go and make him take the afternoon off. Maybe that's what he has in mind anyway.'

'No, it's impossible.'

Maggie looked at her searchingly. 'Why? Don't you want to?' she asked pointedly.

'Of course I do,' Julie lied, determined not to give Maggie even the slightest hint of the truth. 'But it's too much to expect you to keep Beth. She's getting so active now.' The excuse sounded weak, even to her own ears.

Maggie laughed. 'I'm not dead yet, you know! And I have no intention of acting like it until it becomes a fact that I can't deny—then it won't matter one way or the other. You're going, and that's final.'

She walked over to the refrigerator and took out some wrapped sandwiches. 'I even,' she said in the exaggerated tones of a conspirator, 'fixed you two a lunch. Now go get that man of yours. I've got things to do today.'

As Julie walked reluctantly down the street towards the mill, she wondered if anyone had ever said 'no' to Maggie Marshall and made it stick. She hesitated at the gate, once more wanting to turn around and walk away, for the very thought of spending the afternoon with Luke was abhorrent to her. They no longer had any desire for each other's company. He had made it perfectly clear what he wanted from her —a bedmate when he chose, a mother for his daughter, and that was all.

Frank's car was parked next to the truck. Julie looked

at her watch and walked up the side steps, realizing she was early. It wasn't quite twelve-thirty. She opened the door to the office, which on first glance seemed empty, for the clerks and the secretary had gone for lunch; however, loud voices echoed out to her from Luke's office. She hesitated, thinking for a moment that it would be unwise to interrupt, but her hesitation was shortlived. It would be ridiculous to slink away, as if she were an intruder who had no right to be here.

Luke's angry voice sounded again from the inner office as she stopped just outside his door. She saw him lean over his desk, his face livid. She half expected him to turn and acknowledge her presence, but he didn't, evidently being too engrossed in his argument to take note of her arrival.

'I want to know why the hell Steven Jackson cancelled his account—and you haven't given me a reason I can believe yet. So try again!'

The other person spoke and Julie realised it was her brother. 'I've told you already—you can accept it or not. You're a fool if you think people will deal with you and this company the way they did before you went to prison. And you owe me more than this kind of treatment after all I've done for you over the past two years.'

A muscle twitched in Luke's jaw. 'I owe you nothing— I'm no longer sure of just what you've done for me these past two years. But I intend to find out, believe me.' He looked at his watch. 'Julie will be here any minute, so there's no need to continue this conversation. I want you back here tomorrow morning with the missing statement and some plausible explanations.' Grabbing a handful of papers from his desk, Luke threw them into his briefcase and slammed it shut.

'By God, Marshall,' Frank said angrily, 'you'll never survive in this town!'

Luke came round the desk and approached the other man, his hands tightly clenched at his sides. 'I'll survive and so will my family, Frank. And remember that,' he threatened, 'you'll be a very sorry man if she ever finds out!'

'And maybe she knows already. Maybe she knows everything,' Frank offered.

Luke stood before him, every muscle in his body taut and ready to spring. 'I'll kill you if she ever finds out,' he grated, leaving no doubt in Julie's mind that he meant exactly what he said. 'Go, before I do something I'll regret.'

With nerves screaming, Julie stepped into the room. 'I should hope you already regret all that you've done, Luke,' she challenged recklessly. Luke wheeled round to face her, startled by her sudden appearance.

'What the hell are you doing?' he lashed out at her.

'I came to——' she began, but he cut her short.

'Wait in the truck,' he ordered harshly.

Her eyes widened. 'You can't order me about like that—I don't happen to work for you!' Her anger spilled over. 'Who do you think you are, anyway? Are you so far above everyone that you think you can treat them like pawns in your shoddy games? Frank has spent the last two years tending a business that was failing because of what *you* did, not because of anything he's done. And he's been more of a father to Beth than you could ever hope to be!'

Luke's eyes blazed with unmasked fury. 'Get out of here, Julie! I told you to wait in the truck, now do as you're told.' He took a threatening step towards her.

Without stopping to consider the consequences she raised her hand and slapped him hard across the face. The sound of her palm striking his flesh, the redness painting itself on his cheek, and the sharp stinging in her hand shocked her into immobility. Even worse, Luke had seen the blow coming and had not moved to avoid it.

She heard Frank's taunting voice break the stony silence. 'Maybe we've both had enough of you, Luke Marshall. It looks as though your empire's crumbling around you and,' he slowed his words, 'there's not one thing you can do about it.'

Ignoring Frank, Luke stood facing Julie, his eyes dark and threatening. 'Go to the truck.' He spoke each word separately, and this time something in his face told her that she dared not defy him again. She whirled away from him, rushed across the office, and ran outside.

Standing by the truck, her hand on the door handle, she hesitated, filled with such a mingling of anger and hurt and humiliation that she could scarcely breathe. Luke had no right to treat her or her brother like that—damn him and his arrogance! And now what was she going to do—tamely wait for him in the truck? No way! She turned and ran across the yard and through the gates.

She was nearly three blocks from the mill when she heard the truck pull alongside of her. She kept walking, refusing to turn and look at it.

'Get in,' Luke snapped.

'Go to hell!' Julie retorted hotly.

'Don't play childish games with me now, Julie,' he threatened. 'I haven't got the taste or the patience for them today.'

She kept walking, increasing the rhythm of her furious footsteps. Without warning Luke slammed on the brakes and in an instant was standing in front of her, blocking her way. 'Damn you,' he grated, 'I told you to get in that truck. If you want me to treat you like a child, I'll accommodate you—I'll pick you up and put you in there. I'd prefer that you behave like an adult and get in on your own, but it's up to you.'

She faltered. 'Luke——' she began.

'Don't talk—just get in the truck.'

This time she did as she was told. They drove in silence out of town, towards the foothills, to the land of open space and sky. A few times Julie stole a furtive glance at Luke's profile, trying to guess what he was thinking, but unable to read anything other than anger and displeasure from his hard features.

Finally she said, 'I don't want to be with you. Can't you accept that? There's nothing left between us, nothing but dislike on both sides. Why do you insist on me living with you?'

'You know the answer to that, Julie,' he replied quietly.

'All I know is that I want to be free of you.' There was an uncomfortable silence, and she added petulantly, 'Where are we going?'

'Out to the house.'

'No!'

'Oh yes, my dear.'

'I want to go back,' she said raggedly, hating the sound of her own voice. Damn! Why was she acting like this? Why did she allow him to do this to her?

'Right now, I want to talk about what happened at the office,' Luke said coldly. 'I want to know how long you were standing there and what you overheard.'

'Well, I don't care to tell you,' she retorted.

'What did you hear, Julie?'

She threw an angry look at him. 'You know very well what I heard. Why ask?'

'Because I want to know. Now answer me.'

'I heard you insulting Frank!' She spat the words at him.

'And?'

'And all without cause. You seem intent on making other people pay for the discomfort you've suffered during the past two years.'

His face darkened. 'You use words lightly, my dear. It would be too much to expect you to believe that *I* had just cause in saying what I did to Frank. He's used me for a fool, it seems, and maybe I am just that, not to have guessed it before now.'

Julie turned her unhappy attentions to the gently rolling hills and to the snowcapped mountains ahead of them; even in June, they still had fresh snow on the higher peaks. Always the mountains were able to soothe her in times of trouble. But not this time, it seemed.

Luke slowed the truck and swung off the main highway on to the dirt road that headed straight west towards the ranch. Beyond the ranch house the road narrowed to a grassy track that led to the head of the valley. The sky was a gentle blue, but the bitter cold of winter still lay between Luke and Julie.

They came to the top of the hill that overlooked the valley, that marked the beginning of the Marshall land. Luke braked slowly and stopped. Julie felt the tension vibrating within her as she waited for him to speak. Finally she turned defiantly towards him, only to find him examining her. Strangely enough he seemed to be asking some question of himself, rather than of her, a question to which he did not give form in words.

'Don't look at me like that,' she muttered, folding her arms in front of her.

'Like what, Julie?' he asked. His voice, like his face, was unreadable. He was playing with her, she told herself, and it angered her more than ever.

'We have to go back. Beth's——'

'Not alone.' She hated how he could finish her statements. 'She's with Maggie and will be for the rest of the afternoon.'

'That's not true. I have to go back.'

'You're a poor liar, Julie,' he said as he nodded to the lunches beside her on the seat. 'We're going on a picnic, you and I.'

'No, we aren't.'

'Yes,' he insisted.

'I want to go home!' She raised her hand to strike out at him, but with a lightning-quick movement he reached out and caught her by the wrist.

'You're getting a little too free with your hands today, Julie. Don't expect to get away with it a second time.' He dropped her hand in her lap. 'Now what else did you hear, and don't bother to pass judgment—just tell me.'

'Nothing else.'

He reached over and turned her face towards him, his fingers holding her chin. She tried to shake free of him. 'Are you sure?' he pressed.

'I heard that Frank hates you as much as I do,' she taunted.

'Stop it, Julie, and answer my question.'

'That's all I heard.'

'You swear?'

She nodded.

Luke dropped his hand, unexpectantly leaning his forehead against the steering wheel and closing his eyes.

'Why is it so important for you to know what I heard?' she asked, confused by his persistence.

He opened his eyes and leaned back in the seat, staring

down the road that lay before them, but not relaxing his grip on the steering wheel.

'Well? What's your dreadful secret?'

He looked at her sharply, suddenly tense again, then ran his fingers through his thick black hair. Once again she realised how strained and tired he looked; if anything he looked worse than he had on the night of his return.

'Never mind—it's not important,' he said, dismissing her question.

Angrily she threw up her hands. 'All this for nothing? I may be naïve, but I'm no fool. You bit my head off back there and practically threw me out of the office, and now you put me through this inquisition—and tell me that it's not important. What's really going on?'

'Nothing. Just drop it.'

'Frank was really angry.'

'Poor Frank,' he said sarcastically, his eyes flashing. 'He'll be getting exactly what he deserves from me when I get the whole picture straight.'

If he was waiting for her to argue with him in his judgment of her brother, then he could wait, she decided. He wouldn't listen to her anyway. She turned and looked down over the valley. A nagging feeling in the back of her mind told her that he was omitting something crucial in his explanation, and that the omission was perhaps the reason for his increasing tension during the past few days. 'What are you going to do now?' she asked.

He turned and looked at her. 'Is that all you have to say about how I've treated your poor brother?' he asked sarcastically.

'Would anything I say change your mind about him?'

'Not a bit.'

'Then it's between the two of you. You'll work it out the way you see fit.'

'What's this—a little wifely support? Or is that too much to hope for?'

Julie ignored his sarcastic question, and it was as if he lost interest in the whole subject of Frank. 'We might as well go to the ranch,' he said.

'And if I don't want to come?'

'That's of no consequence to me and you know it. You'll

come with me wherever I choose to go.' He leaned forward and turned on the ignition. 'We'll have lunch up at the house.'

He drove until the road narrowed to a grass track over the rolling hills to the head of the valley that lay cradled between the towering stone peaks. The firm line of his mouth and the stubborn thrust of his jaw told her that he wouldn't change his mind, so she sighed and resigned herself to the long afternoon ahead of her. But, she told herself resolutely, she would never resign herself to remaining with him. Some day he would willingly give her her freedom. Some day.

The house was situated at the head of the valley, the Little Bow River flowing on one side, the foothills spreading eastwards and to the south, with mountains rising like majestic sentinels to the west.

They had often gone up into the mountains, and had spent their honeymoon there, travelling by horseback up into the high country, making their base the cabin that Luke and his grandfather had built together when Luke was a young boy, spending long summer days and nights in the total contentment of each other's presence. The memory of such days swept over her now as they gained the top of the hill which brought the house, and the pass into the mountains behind it, into view. How could such a love end in such bitterness? she wondered wearily.

Luke stopped the truck and stepped out, walking slowly forward to look down on the valley which lay below them. She came up beside him, acutely aware of the significance to him of what he was seeing. He stood, motionless and intent, looking down upon his land, and she didn't need to ask if this was the first time he'd come here since his return; it was more than obvious that it was.

'God help me,' he whispered, 'how I've longed for this place!'

It was well beyond noon and the hot mid-afternoon sun was pasted in the sky high above them. The clean, grey mountains rose before them, cutting the silken blue as they reached up to the heavens. Julie could only guess the feelings that held Luke in their grip as he gazed at last into the healing face of freedom after two years of captivity.

Eventually he turned his attention to the house, completed in his absence—not what he'd intended, she knew, for he had wanted to build it himself. Yet she was sure he would be satisfied. When Frank had brought her here, she had been stunned by its likeness to what they had envisioned together. Detracting nothing from the land that held it, it was a part of the hills and the mountains. She waited for him to speak.

'Frank tells me that you didn't go down to the house.'

Somewhere in that seemingly innocent statement she sensed a challenge. 'No,' she said bluntly. 'I saw no reason to.' She didn't tell him of the emotional cost to her of seeing it completed, of how it had brought to the surface memories of a time that could never be again.

'Since it's to be your home, perhaps you'll find that reason enough,' Luke replied icily.

She shrugged, finding nothing to say, and turned back to the truck. After a few moments he followed her and they drove the remaining distance down into the valley and up to the house.

She followed him up the steps and along the veranda, their booted footsteps echoing on the wood. Luke opened the door and stood back, allowing her to enter before him. Something in his stance indicated a kind of ritual, but she ignored it, for its only meaning would be that the house was a part of the Marshall property, as she herself was—something else that was important to him because he owned it.

Julie felt him watching closely for her reaction. To herself she had to admit the absolute loveliness of the place; to him she would admit nothing. She walked into the living room and looked around her.

It was uncanny how close it was to their ideal, to what they had planned and discussed with such joyous anticipation so many times. The interior was finished in pine, the floors covered here and there with hand-hooked rugs. At one end of the room was the fireplace, grey stone taken from the mountains that beckoned to them from just beyond the windows. The hearth was raised and stretched from wall to wall, while the fireplace itself was from floor to ceiling. The whole room was breathtakingly beautiful, and it was exactly as they had planned it. She could not take her eyes from it.

Luke's voice interrupted her thoughts. 'The main bedrooms are upstairs, as we decided.' He lifted an arm and pointed with a sweeping gesture. 'I had Frank add an extra one, so there are four rooms upstairs, including the master bedroom.' Julie saw that they all opened out on the hallway, open on one side and supported by huge, hand-hewn pine beams. One could stand there and look down on the living room below. 'Downstairs, along this side and the back, are the kitchen, the library, and two guest rooms.'

She looked around, in awe of what had been done to capture space and yet free it at the same time. She was also amazed to realise how familiar Luke was with it, even though this was his first time here. In silence she walked into the library to see the floor-to-ceiling bookshelves, built into the walls, then went on to view the kitchen and the two guest rooms. Yes, it was as they had planned, but so much more as well.

'It's huge, Luke. There's so much space,' she breathed.

'I'm afraid I've developed a very definite need for space since I've been away, Julie,' he commented drily.

She looked up at him, suddenly realising that the changes in design were part of his response to his experience in prison. The ceilings in every room downstairs were open to the beams; he had even avoided closing those in. She smiled unconsciously.

'What's that for?' he asked.

'What?'

'The smile.'

'Oh. I was just thinking that in your pursuit of openness and space, it's rather surprising that you decided to go ahead with our plans for a roof.'

Luke laughed more easily than she had heard him since his homecoming. She thought too that she saw, for a brief moment, a melting of the anger that always lay surface-deep in his eyes. Embarrassed, she turned away to look again at the library. 'A fireplace in here as well,' she remarked. 'You've spared no cost anywhere, Luke.'

He looked at her sharply, as if there were more to her

words than she had intended. 'Come,' he directed abruptly. 'Let's look at the upstairs and see what you think.'

They wandered through the rooms, looking in closets and touching the polished smoothness of the pine walls. It was truly superb. An amazing feat of secrecy as well, she thought. No one had known the house was being built, except for Frank. But who had done the labour, then? Surely if anyone from Henderson had worked on it there would have been talk?

'How did Frank manage to keep this place a secret from all the prying eyes and ears of Henderson?'

'Workers came in from Calgary and he employed an interior decorating firm from there as well.'

'It must have cost a fortune!'

'I've never been a poor man, Julie, in case you've forgotten,' Luke replied evenly.

'No, I know,' she said absently, as she moved into the master bedroom. She stopped suddenly, barely beyond the threshold. This room was carpeted in a pale ice blue. At the windows hung drapes, their texture that of filmy white clouds. Sliding glass doors opened on to a balcony that looked out on the field sloping gently down to a stand of tall white birches that lined themselves along the river, its ice-cold water fresh and clean from the mountains that rose behind it.

Against one wall was another fireplace, a smaller duplicate of the one in the living room. In the ceiling was a skylight, open to the Alberta sky, and all that it could be—soft summer blue or black velvet peppered with stars or the shimmering iridescence of the Aurora Borealis. Open to space and light and freedom. Here in their bedroom, he had indeed tried to leave off the roof.

She could feel him waiting for her response. 'I think . . .' she stopped, trying to swallow the lump that had formed in her throat, to hide the pain that had brought tears to her eyes. 'I think it's lovely, quite lovely.'

She felt Luke stir behind her, felt his arms come round her and pull her back against the solid bulk of him. 'It's for you, Julie—all of it. And for us.' There was a sadness in his voice, despite the fact that he spoke of gifts. 'We must resolve this thing between us,' he said more urgently, 'before it tears us so far apart that there's nothing that can be done to repair the damage.'

She moved out of his arms and this time he didn't try to hold her or force her to stay.

'It's already too late, can't you see that?' She swept her hand, gesturing to all that surrounded them. 'This house is beautiful, I admit, but it's like a final, tragic gesture— an empty gift, and quite meaningless to me. A statement from the past that whispers of all we'd hoped and dreamed of. But it's echoing into nothingness, Luke. We have no love to contain such dreams any more. You've seen to that. Two years ago you destroyed any hope we ever had of living the dreams we shared.' She stood facing him, her eyes pleading for release. 'Let me go, Luke. I can never be happy with you again. There can be no tomorrows for us. All our tomorrows have died, and this house would only be a prison for both of us.'

Abruptly he walked away from her, swung back the glass doors and stepped out on to the balcony. Julie saw him grip the railing with both hands, holding tightly, his knuckles white with strain. 'God help me, Julie, I can't let you go. I can't,' he groaned. 'And as God is my witness, I never will.'

'And as God is my witness,' she blurted, 'some day you'll have no choice. I *will* have my freedom from you, Luke, I will!' She turned and ran from the room, down the steps, and out into the late afternoon sunshine.

Minutes later he followed her, closing the door firmly behind him. His face, once again, showed nothing. He walked slowly towards the truck. He was a powerfully built man, whose sheer physical strength she feared now as she had never done before. She wondered how long it would be before he did, in fact, turn his wrath upon her.

She had not expected him to remain for the picnic lunch, and probably, she thought, he didn't really want to, but he was much too stubborn to given in. Lifting the basket from the truck, he seized a blanket and strode towards the river, not once looking back, but obviously expecting her to join him.

She followed grudgingly, walking past him down to the

river, where she stood with her back to him, desperately aware of him sitting there alone on the blanket. Well, he could have his picnic lunch if he wanted it so badly, she told herself, but he would eat it alone. He did just that, apparently accepting her unspoken decision, neither asking her to join him nor coming to stand with her by the river.

Afterwards they drove back the way they had come, this time, however, stopping at the ranch, where they were greeted by Jake Simms. Julie didn't get out of the truck to join the two men as they stood talking in the middle of the yard, but merely nodded and smiled at Jake when he called out a friendly hello. Then they turned, still deep in conversation, and went into one of the barns. Nearly a half hour passed before Luke finally returned, not offering any apologies for having kept her waiting.

'That was plain rudeness, Luke Marshall, going off and leaving me sitting here all this time,' she said crossly.

'You've got two good legs. If you weren't so intent on playing the martyr you'd have gotten out and joined us. Nothing we had to say was private. Don't you think that perhaps Jake might have found your behaviour a little peculiar?'

'I don't happen to care what he thought,' she retorted.

He shrugged. 'And I don't care to participate in your spoiled-brat games, Julie. You're a woman, an adult, so why don't you act like one?'

Knowing he was right didn't help matters, and this ended the conversation until they were almost in Henderson. Then Luke said quite suddenly, his voice businesslike and cold, 'If there's anything you want changed in the house, or anything added, just tell Jake and he'll take care of it.'

'Well, thank you,' she replied with mock graciousness, then some demon prompted her to add cuttingly, 'How long do you think it would take him to have it levelled to the ground?'

If she expected any reply to her comment, she got none. Luke neither spoke nor turned to look at her, but stared stonily at the road that lay ahead of him.

CHAPTER SIX

IT was dark before they reached Henderson. Luke drove directly through town, pulled into the driveway and got out, walking immediately round to her side. He opened the door, smiling at her as he did, mockery glinting in his eyes. 'At least you can't accuse me of rudeness this time.'

Julie leaped out, marched up the steps, and angrily flung open the door. As she walked into the foyer she was unable to block out the irritatingly steady rhythm of his footfall behind her. He quietly closed the door, as if to accentuate the noise she had made.

Margaret came out of the library to greet them. 'Ah, you're home,' she said, ignoring Julie's temper-flushed cheeks. 'You'd better hurry, it's about an hour's drive to Calgary, you know.'

Julie frowned. What was she talking about?

Margaret saw the look on her face and laughed. 'I knew it—you've forgotten all about Sam Kendall's dinner party, haven't you?' She looked at the stately grandfather clock which stood by the library door. 'As I said, you'd better hurry.'

'I thought you were coming with us,' said Luke.

'I was, but I'm not feeling up to par. Just a little tired, that's all,' she added quickly when Luke glanced at her in concern. 'Beth will be just fine with me, so I don't want you two worrying. We'll both have an early night.'

Damn, Julie thought, pursing her lips. She'd forgotten about the party. Well, this was one time that she wouldn't be coerced into doing something she didn't want to do. She certainly wasn't going to a party with Luke, where she'd have to face all those people and their hateful, curious stares. She just wasn't going.

'I'm not going, Maggie,' she said heatedly. 'I'm not up to exposing myself to those people you insist on calling your friends—I don't want to stand among them like some kind of freak for them to examine.'

89

She turned and ran up the stairs, not looking back to see the effect of her words on either Luke or Maggie. No sooner had she closed the door behind her than it was roughly thrust open by Luke, who slammed it forcefully, unable to hide the violent fury that blazed in his eyes.

'Is that what you think I am?' he demanded roughly, taking a single step that brought him to stand before her. Reaching out, he seized her by the arms and shook her. 'A freak in some sideshow?'

'No,' she faltered. 'I said that's how they see us. It is, and you know it, if you'd only admit it.'

'I don't happen to give a damn about what anyone thinks of me. They aren't my judges. No man is my judge!' A pulse beat furiously at the base of his throat.

'Oh, no,' Julie laughed, a little hysterically. 'You're above all that, aren't you? You're the mighty Luke Marshall, who can do whatever you want and there's no one to tell you that you're wrong. Well, think again, Luke. Two years ago twelve people did just that, in case you've forgotten. And most other people would agree with them!'

He drew his hand back so suddenly that she stepped backwards, afraid that he was about to strike her; but then, with his hand still suspended in mid-air, he drew a deep breath, and slowly curling his fingers into a tight fist he lowered his arm. 'Don't push me too far, Julie,' he rasped. 'I'll only take so much!'

She didn't heed his warning. 'Don't tell me that you truly have the nerve to face those people?' she continued, oblivious to all the danger signs. 'After what you've done, how can you have the audacity to go into that house and mingle with them?'

'Damn you!' he breathed. 'Get dressed—or I won't be responsible for my actions!'

'I will not!' she retorted, defying him further. 'I'm through with doing everything you tell me to, do you understand?'

He gave an ugly laugh. 'You, my dear wife, have a lesson to learn about pride. You're coming with me to that party if I have to dress you myself and carry you there bodily. If it's embarrassment you're afraid of, then I would strongly suggest that you not call me on this one.'

She knew as surely as she stood before him that she dared not fight him any more; he would do exactly as he'd said, she knew him well enough for that. He must have seen her decision in her face, for he nodded and turned towards the bathroom, stopping at the door to add quietly, 'One more thing, Julie. Don't you ever speak to Maggie like that again. What's between us stays between us and she's not to be drawn into it. We have no right to hurt her more than she already has been. Have you got that straight?' The tone of his voice dared an argument, but it was a challenge she was not about to pick up. She nodded mutely as he walked from the room.

Julie chose a simple dress, a long white silk with pale blue satin trim on the bodice and the hem. Deciding to wear her hair up, she stood in front of the mirror while her deft fingers quickly wove a blue ribbon to match the trim on her dress through her thick, dark tresses. Looking at the face of the girl who stood before her, she was not unpleased with her efforts. Unfortunately, she felt none of the excitement or pride she used to feel whenever she went out with Luke.

By the time she was ready, he had gone downstairs. Turning off the light, Julie tiptoed into Beth's room to whisper a goodnight to the sleeping child. How blissfully ignorant Beth was of all the pain and conflict around her! And, Julie promised herself vehemently, Beth must remain that way.

A little more subdued than usual, Maggie was waiting in the foyer. Tonight she looked suddenly older, more vulnerable. With an ache of contrition Julie realized that she was probably the cause. Walking over to Maggie, she put her arms around her and hugged her tightly. 'I'm sorry, Maggie,' she murmured, kissing the cool, wrinkled cheek. 'I'm tired, I guess. But that's really no excuse for me to have spoken to you the way I did.'

'It's all right.' Margaret smiled back at her and patted her gently on the arm. 'I know that tonight might not be easy, but I know too that it has to be done. I think Luke understands that. You're still so very young, Julie, but you'll realize in time that your husband has a great deal of pride. It's not always an easy thing to have, because it demands a lot of one and sometimes the price seems much too costly.' Her voice quivered. 'Stand with him, Julie. He needs you so much right now, and he loves you so much too—even if his pride won't let him tell you in words that you can understand.'

Julie blinked away tears, fighting back a suffocating lump in her throat. She was about to reply when the front door opened and Luke came towards them. His eyes roamed over her possessively. 'You look lovely,' he said quietly, and offered her his arm.

She hesitated a moment, and then, remembering that Maggie was standing there watching them both, she walked over to him and tucked her fingers in his sleeve. But the gesture was not solely for Maggie's benefit, she was honest enough to admit that to herself. Something deep within her wanted her to stand beside Luke, to walk forward with him into the night; it was a feeling that had surfaced so quickly, so unexpectedly, that it frightened her. Was her mind, as well as her body, going to betray her? But none of these thoughts were evident as Julie said goodnight to Maggie and walked gracefully from the house.

As they began the drive into Calgary it was raining lightly, a soft June rain that carried with it all the sweetness and promise of summer. The windshield wipers moved back and forth in a continual rhythm as Julie settled into the plush velour seat, content for the moment to think of nothing but the wet, glistening road in front of them, the steady roar of the powerful engine, and the gentle fall of the rain.

She stole a look at Luke, handsome in his dark green suede suit, his hands competently controlling the wheel of the Porsche, and remembered how much he used to like driving this car. She had forgotten how he could look equally at home and just as distinguished in his working clothes, blue jeans and a shirt, as he could dressed in a business suit or a tuxedo, and just as competent behind the wheel of his truck as in his sleek silver-grey Porsche. Now the very presence of him, the clean masculine smell of his skin, were rousing more memories than Julie could bear. Forcing herself to look away from him, she stared at the white line as it slid by in the darkness, finally leaning her head back into the soft headrest and closing her eyes.

She must have slept, she realised with a start, for when she opened her eyes, the rain had ceased and there below them lay an evening's vision of Calgary, a city of lights stretching out for miles in front of them, with its well-lit office buildings downtown to the south, and the Calgary Tower, a tall finger tipped with light, pointing skywards. She sat up and stretched.

'So you're awake. You must have been tired,' Luke observed, expertly manoeuvring the high-powered car through the heavy traffic.

Someone was always going somewhere in Calgary, she thought, suddenly liking the bright lights, the movement, the people all around her. It had been a long time since she had come into the city, and just how much she had missed her trips here with Luke was being brought forcibly home to her.

'You look like a kid with an ice cream,' he commented easily.

She'd not been aware of his scrutiny. 'Yes, I was thinking how nice it is to be here again. It's been so long, I'd almost forgotten.'

'Yes, I know what you mean,' he replied wryly.

Julie looked across at him, grateful that some kind of truce seemed to be in effect between them; the violent anger that had erupted between them back at the house appeared to have evaporated. She just might manage to enjoy the evening after all.

Sam Kendall and his wife Mildred had a home in Houghton, thirty miles from Henderson, but spent most of their time in Calgary. They owned a huge house on a beautifully manicured acre of prime land in the south-west part of the city. Sam had been a rancher, a lumberman, an oilman, and the president of three companies, as well as the best friend of Luke's grandfather for nearly four decades. He was also a friend of James Marshall's grandson, and, Julie had to admit to herself, the invitation to his home was a genuine one.

Mildred Kendall was a tall woman, as tall as the husband, whom she adored. She laughed a lot, and seemed to genuinely love the parties she gave so often. She had never had any children but had never seemed to regret that fact, for all she had wanted in life was to love and be loved by Sam Kendall.

Now Mildred greeted them at the door, speaking to them as if Luke had never been away. 'Why, here you two are at last! I'd expected you much earlier.' She smiled down at Julie. 'Well, my dear, you look lovelier each time I see you. You're a lucky man, Luke Marshall, to have caught this one.' She winked at him as she reached out and took Julie's wrap, then added more seriously, 'Welcome back, both of you. It's so good to have you here again.'

There was no doubting her sincerity, and Julie felt the warmth rise in her face. How many times had she refused one of Mildred's invitations over the past two years because she had been unable to face the other guests? Now she regretted her actions, ashamed of having cut all the ties with this hospitable woman.

'Come on, you two, you must mingle and greet old friends. If you'll excuse me, I'll search out that husband of mine—I know he wants to see you, Luke.' With that Mildred moved off into the crowd.

Luke stepped back and allowed Julie to precede him into the room. She stopped, suddenly confused by all the faces, by the sound of so many voices all talking at once. Who, she wondered, ever listened at such affairs? She felt Luke's steadying presence, mere inches away from her, and the reassuring pressure of his hand on her arm.

'You'll be fine,' he murmured.

Was it her imagination or had many of the faces turned to stare at them? As if he could read her mind, he moved forward to stand beside her. 'Head up, Julie Marshall,' he said firmly.

She stared into the room, and all the faces seemed to be the faces of strangers. Her instinct told her to leave, told her that this was not where she belonged, but the pressure of Luke's hand gave the contradictory message, that escape was impossible. She was here because Luke had wanted her here, because he had ordered her here.

Resentment at being subjected to this ordeal flamed again within her. Well, if Luke wanted a command performance, then he would get one, she decided petulantly, flashing him a brilliant smile as she freed her arm from his hand, stepped into the crowded room, and murmured with acid sweetness, 'Well, dear Luke, what are we waiting for? Act proud and pleased to be here.' He might have forced her to attend the party, but he could not make her stand sedately and obediently at his side throughout. She walked away from him.

Although her first glance into the mass of talking and laughing faces revealed no one she knew well enough to approach and speak to, a calmer, more searching look revealed familiar faces; then, to her relief, she recognised her brother Frank, standing off to the side, talking to a man she didn't know. Instantly she moved in his direction, smiling and nodding at people as she passed by them. Once, aware of Luke's watchful gaze following her, she looked back and was pleased to see Sam Kendall approaching him; the diversion would be enough for her to lose herself, albeit temporarily, in the somewhat boisterous crowd.

She reached Frank. Obviously glad to see her, he smiled and kissed her lightly on the cheek. Thankful that he was showing her no animosity after the terrible argument she had witnessed at the mill, she returned his welcome. 'Frank, it's good to see you. I was hoping you'd be here.' She squeezed his hand, as he introduced her to the man to whom he had been speaking. Julie missed the name but gathered he was from Lethbridge and was 'in oil'. Listening politely to their shop talk, she managed to add a few words here and there, but was glad when he moved off to join his wife, leaving her alone with Frank. 'I wanted to talk to you about this afternoon,' she said immediately.

His smile vanished, his face darkening as soon as she'd spoken. 'Maybe we should avoid the subject—it might be healthier for our relationship in the long run.'

'That's just it,' she replied seriously. 'I don't want it to affect us. You're too important to me. Can't we keep "us" separate from what's going on between you and Luke?'

He looked at her, his eyes questioning. 'I'm not sure that that's realistically possible, Julie. He's managed to destroy our father, caused you untold pain, and now that he's come back all the thanks I'm getting for keeping his business afloat during his absence are insults—the man's demented!' He looked into the crowd, speaking discreetly low but with intense feeling. 'Considering all that, I find it difficult to understand—and impossible to accept—that you've changed your mind about leaving him, knowing the kind of man you're married to.'

It was on the tip of her tongue to tell him why, to reveal the terrible threats Luke had resorted to; but she was afraid to, for it might well cause a confrontation between the two men that could end in her losing Beth altogether. She couldn't risk that, so she replied quietly, 'It's my decision, nevertheless, Frank. All I can do is ask you to accept and respect that, and try not to let it influence our relationship.'

'That might not be as simple a thing as you make it sound,' he replied, his eyes trained on her face. 'The lines are drawn between Luke and me now—everything's coming out in the open. It may be impossible to exist between the two of us and not choose sides. You may have to say exactly where you stand.'

Julie looked down at her hands, nervously twisting her wedding band on her finger. 'What's between you and Luke is your business—I have no intention of interfering.'

'And how will you feel if things go badly for Luke?'

'What do you mean?' She looked up quickly, not understanding the tone of his words.

'He's not welcome back in Henderson. There are a lot of hard feelings about what's happened. He may be forced to leave. He may have no choice.'

'And what's that got to do with you?'

'To be blunt, Julie, I'm one of those who'd like to see him gone. He should never have come back in the first place.' He was watching her closely, seeking to gauge the exact effect of his words. 'How does that make you feel?'

She squared her shoulders and looked at him directly. 'I believe I've already answered that question.'

His eyes narrowed. 'Why *did* you decide to stay with him, Julie?' he demanded bluntly.

She was thrown by the question and backed away from him, alarmed that he was venturing too close to the truth. 'Why?' he pursued. 'Do you love him?'

'That goes without saying,' she stammered weakly.

'Nothing in this world goes without saying,' he replied, the look of calculation still in his eyes.

Julie had to convince him to drop this line of thinking. With a sheer effort of will she pulled herself together. 'I'm his wife, Frank, and I want to be his wife—I was a fool to have considered living without him. And that's the sum total of it, so leave it at that, please.'

Staring back at him, she tried to guess the effectiveness of her words. Did he believe her or not? Relief flooded over her when he laughed aloud and patted her on the arm. 'We do look for intrigue in this life, don't we? Forget what I said, Julie, and rest assured that nothing will change between us—as long as that's what you want, of course?'

'Yes,' she murmured, 'that's what I want.'

'Good. That's settled, then.' He took possession of her arm. 'Now come with me. There are some people here you haven't seen for ages—you've been out of circulation far too long.' He bent down and whispered in her ear. 'I think perhaps our mutual friend Richard Buchanan might even be coming later.'

Julie cast a quick glance around her, searching for a glimpse of Luke, but couldn't locate him. He was probably off talking business with Sam . . . business, after all, was the most significant thing in his life. Hadn't he destroyed other people's lives in order to keep the power it gave him? But she mustn't think of that now . . . blindly she followed Frank.

Precisely how long she stayed by his side she wasn't certain, but somehow she managed to make polite, light conversation, to laugh in all the right places, even to introduce topics of her own. As the evening progressed, she gradually came to realise that her earlier apprehensions about the party had been largely groundless. No one avoided her, or made snide comments about her husband;

her old acquaintances seemed genuinely pleased to see her again.

Despite her resolution to forget about Luke, she more and more often found herself searching the crowd for his face, for a glimpse of his tall, imposing presence. The room was getting very warm, and the smoke was bothering her eyes. She put a hand to her forehead, feeling suddenly oppressed by all the noise and laughter, and taking another sip from the wine glass that Frank had kept so assiduously filled all evening. He at least was looking after her, she thought, forgetting that it was she herself who had sent Luke from her side.

Frank leaned towards her and whispered in her ear, 'Richard just came in and he's heading this way.'

Julie looked up and directly into Richard's handsome, clean-shaven face. In the same instant she heard Frank offer some half-mumbled excuse as he moved away to join someone behind her. Warmth rushed to her face; she found herself unable to meet Richard's level gaze.

'Did you come with Frank?' he asked coolly.

'No.' She gestured nervously at the people around her. 'With Luke. I haven't seen him since we arrived.' She risked a shy smile, then dropped her eyes.

The silence stretched out between them. Finally, Richard offered quietly, 'Could we perhaps find somewhere to be alone, away from all this noise? I'd like to talk to you.'

'I don't know. Maybe it wouldn't be such a good idea, Richard,' she murmured, hesitating and trying to gather her confused thoughts. As she looked around her, all the faces suddenly wavered and tilted. She closed her eyes, trying to steady herself. 'Perhaps that would be best,' she whispered, wanting only to escape from all these people, from all the noise and confusion.

'Over here,' he said, leading her across the room to the library. He opened the door, let her enter, then followed behind her, carefully closing the door and leaning back on it until it clicked shut. Julie giggled, then covered her mouth with her hand.

'What's so funny?'

'It's just that watching you now, I almost expected you

to lock the door as well. A gesture to add to our conspiracy.'

He moved towards her. 'Is that how you view this, as
our little conspiracy?' His voice was cold and hard, and
displeasure showed in his face. 'Don't be silly,' she
replied, straightening to face him. 'It amused me, that's
all.'

'And have I amused you as well, Julie?' He moved
closer and she could see in his face what she had never
seen before. Kind, gentle, considerate Richard was
angry.

'I asked you a question.' He threw the words at her.
'Do me the courtesy of answering it. Have I been in your
life merely to amuse you these past months, until your
husband returned?'

'What are you saying?' she gasped.

'Exactly that. You're an intelligent woman, Julie—I'm
sure you understand what I'm saying to you.'

She hadn't expected this from him. She started to walk
past him, but he stopped her intended flight by stepping
in front of her and blocking her way. 'Let me go!' she
ordered.

'You owe me that much, I thould think.'

'I owe you nothing.' Her eyes communicated her frustration and hurt. 'Why is it that everyone feels I owe
them something? My life isn't my own any more -it's
parcelled out to you, to Luke, to Frank. I'm tired of being
torn in so many directions and I'm tired of people telling
me what I should think and why I've done things!' Her
voice was distraught as she fought back tears, realising
that she was saying too much, was making herself far too
vulnerable.

Nevertheless, she was unprepared when Richard
reached out and put his arms around her. 'I'm sorry, I
didn't mean to upset you. But I've been so worried about
you. It's been ages since we've talked. If you must know,
Julie, I was hurt and angry when I learned of your change
of plans. I've been through hell not being able to see you
or even call you, not knowing what was happening to
you.' He held her tightly, his mouth caressing her hair.
'How I've missed you, my sweet Julie!' he breathed, his

mouth finally claiming hers.

She leaned against him, overpowered by the strength of his feeling for her, too dazed to protest. Briefly she closed her eyes and remained still in his arms, wanting only a peaceful place to rest and be protected. But then her mind told her of the unfairness of what she was doing and she gradually eased herself out of his arms. 'I've missed you as well, Richard,' she began, 'and I'm sorry about the way I've handled things —even though it seemed the best way at the time. But I know now that you deserved more than that from me.' She placed a hand on his cheek. 'Dear Richard, you've been such a good friend ... I never meant to hurt you.'

'It's all right, Julie,' he interrupted. 'Forget what I said.'

'No, let me finish, please.' She had to explain to him, to make him understand, once and for all.

'I love you dearly, Richard,' she said slowly, 'but as a friend, only as a friend. There can never be more than friendship between us—please try to understand that.' She shook her head. 'I've handled so many things badly these past months but, believe me, it was never my intention to hurt you. I do appreciate all that you've done for me and Beth and I shall always value you as a friend. But I don't love you, Richard, not in the way you want me to love you. I've already told you that.'

She felt the warm flush on her face, knowing that she had had too much to drink; she hadn't eaten lunch, of course, because that had been the ill-fated picnic with Luke. If she felt faint, it was her own fault ... she closed her eyes, resting a trembling hand on the table beside her, and tried to regain her balance, her focus.

'Are you all right?' She could hear the concern in Richard's voice, but neither of them heard the door to the library open behind them.

'Yes, of course.' She straightened her back and took her hand from the table. 'It's just so warm in here,' she whispered. But she had to know if he had understood, had accepted her words, and so she persisted. 'Can you forgive me? Can you see that I did what I thought was best?'

'Best for whom?' he asked quietly.

'For all concerned.'

He moved closer, lightly running his fingers along the soft skin of her arm. 'I guess I have to accept that our relationship has ended, but I still find it impossible to understand what you've done. I've been with you a great deal during the past year and I know what you've been through. I simply can't see how after all the plans you'd made, that you could give them up as soon as that man walked back into your life.'

'You'll have to accept that, too, Richard,' she replied as steadily as she could, trying desperately to focus on his mouth, to concentrate on his words. 'It's what I've done. Plans change, decisions get altered.' Again she touched her forehead with shaking fingers. How could it be so warm in here?

Confused, she looked up at Richard. 'Where's Luke?' she mumbled, taking a faltering step away from him. She needed Luke. A terrifying blackness was closing in on her, and the bookshelves on the wall before her were dissolving and melting into the darkness, until she was alone with the deafening roar that raged in her head. She pressed her hands to her ears, her hands that were now ice-cold. 'Luke——' she whispered.

She would have fallen had Richard not reached out and caught her, placing an arm around her waist and gently leading her to the chesterfield.

'Take your hands off my wife!'

She fought back the blackness, for it was Luke's voice, Luke, whom she had needed. . . .

'She's ill, man,' she heard Richard respond impatiently, as he lowered her to the couch. 'Get her a drink of water —something!'

Her vision focused enough to see Luke walking steadily towards them, his hands clenched into fists at his side. She saw him, with lightning speed that gave the other man no warning at all, reach out and roughly shove Richard out of the way.

Shocked and uncomprehending, she pulled herself up. 'Luke, what are you doing?'

'You can ask that?'

'Richard was just trying to help me—why did you treat him like that? What's he ever done to you?'

'Your question might be more accurately phrased, if you asked what he's done to *you*. I was most impressed with this charming little love scene. Perhaps you can duplicate it for me later.' Reaching out, he pulled her roughly to her feet. 'Get your wrap, we're leaving.' He turned to Richard. 'Don't ever come near her again,' he rasped, 'because I won't be responsible for what happens if you do!'

CHAPTER SEVEN

JULIE was never certain of how she was able to walk from the library and through the maze of faces in the living room. She saw Frank standing in the front hall, but he made no move to come to her and for this she was thankful, for she did not think she could stand any more conflict tonight. She shivered to think of what might have happened if Frank had tried to intercede between Luke and Richard.

In a switch of mood that confounded her, Luke said their goodnights to Mildred and Sam, his voice sounding genuinely warm and appreciative as he thanked them for the party. Then he manoeuvred her out the door and down the steps to the car. Neither of them spoke as they drove out into the late night traffic in the brilliantly lit streets. At first Julie felt too deathly ill to speak, then, as she gradually recovered her poise, anger at Luke's irresponsible and unreasonable actions began to churn inside her and kept her silent.

She expected him to head north-west, out of the city and back to the valley, but he didn't, at least not immediately. For nearly half an hour he drove around the city, at speeds close to, if not surpassing the limit, his hands tightly gripping the steering wheel, his face rigidly set.

Finally she said stiffly, 'Just where are we going, anyway?'

'Round in circles. Or hadn't you noticed?' he said savagely. 'We're driving around until I cool off enough to decide where we're going. What we're going to do.'

Suddenly frightened, she said, 'We've got to go home.'

A muscle twitched in his jaw. 'Look, just be quiet, will you? I don't want to talk to you.'

Julie heeded his warning and sat back in silence, trying to keep her mind blank. At least her head had cleared and she no longer felt faint or nauseated. Instead tension thrummed along her nerves, and in a futile effort to dispel it she tried to keep her anger alive and burning within her.

Finally he flicked on the signal light and drove down the exit ramp, heading back towards Henderson. The car raced through the night, swallowing up the miles. At one point she was on the verge of telling him to slow down, but then thought better of it and said nothing. She was relieved when they reached the town, although it was a shortlived relief, for Luke drove straight past the turn to Maggie's. She looked across at him quickly. 'Where are we going?'

'We aren't going back to Maggie's tonight. We're going out to the house.' He pushed his foot down on the accelerator, the roar of the engine underlining his statement.

'Maggie will worry,' she said as calmly as possible, trying to keep her tone neutral so as not to incite him further. 'And Beth——'

He cut her off. 'Don't argue, Julie—we're going, and that's final.'

A heavy sense of foreboding seized her in its frigid grip. She wanted only to throw open the door and run from him, to escape. Instead, her fear cloaked in a false calmness, she leaned back in the seat and pretended to rest, even to sleep, while all the while her head was teeming with plans to get away from him as soon as possible.

At the house Luke braked sharply. The headlights of the car stared off across the fields as he sat motionless, his hands still holding on to the steering wheel.

Stupidly, she did not hold her tongue. 'I'm surprised you subjected your precious car to the dirt roads—I thought you reserved the truck for them. But of course you're mistreating all your property lately, aren't you, Luke?' Instantly she regretted her sarcasm, for it sparked him into action.

'Get out,' he grated.

'Why should I?' she retorted childishly.

'Try me, Julie. Just try me.'

Sullenly she got out of the car and went up the steps, knowing that it was useless to fight him. Besides, she wasn't going to be so stubborn as to sit in the car all night. The door was unlocked and she walked inside, reaching out and turning on a light as she passed. The menacing click of the door closing behind her echoed in her ears and she shivered as she turned to face Luke.

'Goodnight,' she said coldly, starting for the stairs.

He laughed, although there was no humour in the grim line of his mouth. 'So you think it's going to be that easy, do you?'

She turned to face him, to fight him now, knowing that she had nothing to lose. Recklessly she cried, 'You make me sick, do you know that? Your behaviour was disgusting tonight, and I won't be seen with you in public ever again. Do you hear me, not ever again!'

He stepped towards her. 'My behaviour? You have the gall to talk about my behaviour when you sneak off like some little tramp to be with your precious Richard.' His hands were curled into fists. 'You didn't even care that I was there. What did you expect me to do? Tell me that.'

'Strangely enough, I expected you to behave like a rational human being, to find out what was really happening. But oh no, not you! Is that how you learned to behave in prison?' She no longer cared what she said, wanting only to hurt him. 'You're a fool if you think I'm going to stay with you, Luke Marshall. I hate the man you've become. Frank was right—I was crazy to have married you in the first place, and even crazier to have stayed with you now!'

She'd said too much. Darkness filled his eyes and tension screamed in every line of his body. Warily she backed towards the stairs.

'Well, my sweet and loving wife, perhaps we can add

one more regret to that long list you seem to have.' He loosened his tie and pulled it off, all the while moving slowly towards her.

'No!' she breathed, her eyes wide with fear.

'Yes. Oh yes, Julie. If you can put out for Richard, surely you can manage a semblance of willingness for your own husband.'

'Stay away from me—I don't want you to come near me! I don't want you to even touch me. How I hate it when you touch me!'

He stopped suddenly and stood staring at her, all the anger melting from his eyes, leaving only the deep, dark mark of pain. Briefly he closed his eyes. 'Dear God, Julie,' he whispered, 'go to bed.' Then he turned and walked outside on to the veranda.

Julie looked again at the clock. Three-thirty. She sighed, knowing that she was hungry for sleep, yet was too restless, too pursued by terrifying thoughts. Slipping out of bed, she walked over to the balcony, slid back the glass doors, and stepped out into the cool night air. Below, the fields and the trees by the river were bathed in the silver light of the full moon. How deceptively peaceful and quiet the whole world seemed now! It was the kind of night she loved, with the darkness lined with silver light, softened and given a texture of its own, something tangible that she could almost feel against her own body. How she longed to be a part of all she looked upon, to rid herself of the pain and anger that Luke had brought home with him.

She went inside, picked up her dress that lay crumpled on the floor by the bed, and slipped into it, not bothering with the small buttons. Nor did she bother with shoes. She would go barefoot as she had as a child. She knew exactly where she would go, where she must go.

She ran across the field, her strong slim body filled with the joy of the earth around her, the night wind caressing her hair, her face, with gentle fingers. The rhythm of her breathing matched the rhythm of her movements and she felt she could run for ever . . . all she wanted was to be free.

The field was sloped down to the stand of white birches which lined the river. It had been the river that had called to her and she came to stand in the shadow of the tall trees, listening to its eternal movement and flow. Fresh and clean and free. Free, she thought again. Who could stop its flowing?

It moved more slowly at the bend, gradually widening into a stillwater. Julie slipped off her dress, letting it fall to the grass and stepped out of it, then walked to the edge and waded slowly into the water. Its coldness was shocking and she inhaled sharply. But it was clean and free and she would be a part of it.

She moved further into the river, up to her waist, to her breasts. Finally, submerged in coldness, she struck out, swimming with the strength and purity of the river, a part of it, feeling it glide over her nakedness.

After a while, the stiffness growing in her wrists, her arms, her legs, she swam back to the shore and walked slowly up the grassy slope, at last cleansed of all the tensions that had held her in their iron grip.

Suddenly, ahead of her, a branch cracked, its sound thunderous in the night silence. She stood perfectly still, her eyes straining to penetrate the shadows, then moved cautiously towards her dress, her pulse pounding in her ears.

Luke stepped out of the darkness, his white shirt bright in the moonlight. 'Go away!' she ordered, grabbing at her dress to cover her, holding it in front of her. He had followed her, had probably watched her all the while. 'Did you think I was going to run away? Is that why you followed me?'

He stood there, his hand resting on the trunk of the tree. 'No,' he breathed. 'I came to watch you. I've always loved to watch you.'

'I want you to leave me alone.' She began to walk past him, but he reached out and stopped her, pulling her back against him.

She could feel the tension in him, the strength and power of his body. With every fibre of her being, she was swept by the longing to touch him, to feel his body against hers again.

'I forced you last time, Julie,' he said softly. 'Now I want to touch you without anger. I need to. I won't hurt you.' His voice was the gentlest of whispers, a part of the wind, a part of the river, calling to her, asking her to come with him. 'I have the strongest wish for you now, my Jul.' Slowly, as if he were performing a sacred ritual, he took the flimsy white dress out of her hands and dropped it to the grass.

She stood before him, thin and strong in her nakedness as he reached down and gently touched her face, his hands moving down across her shoulders and over her small breasts. She felt the warmth of him, of her own desire rush through her. 'Luke,' she whispered.

'Here, Julie. I want you here.' His dark eyes shone bright with his desire for her. She nodded and waited for him as he unbuttoned his shirt, never taking his eyes from her. 'You're lovely, my Jul,' he murmured, as much to himself as to her.

He drew her down beside him, holding her tightly, the warmth of his skin a sharp contrast to the coldness of hers, which was still damp from the river. His fingers brushed lightly over her, his feather-light touch revelling in the glory of his possession of her, slowly warming her and drawing her response.

Her hands roamed through the silken thickness of his black hair, then downwards to trace the finely chiselled features of his face, lines that were pure and strong and precious to her touch. He was beautiful, simply beautiful, she thought, as she closed her eyes and sighed.

'My Julie, my Jul,' he breathed again, shuddering beneath her touch as her fingers trailed down the thick mat of dark hair on his chest and fumbled with the leather belt of his trousers. She felt the tension of his stomach muscles against her nakedness, then, finally, the strong warmth of his legs entwined with hers.

They lay thus for a long time, exploring each other, discovering once again all that they had never really forgotten, all the joy of what they had shared so many times before they had been separated; they made love with a passion that grew more insatiable with each touch.

'Oh, God, Julie,' Luke whispered, his warm breath

fanning her face and his lips claiming hers, probing and tasting the sweetness of her mouth. She pressed herself closer, responding to the demands of his desire.

His heart pounded with a rhythm that was both primitive and beautiful as he finally claimed her, carrying her to the edge of ecstasy and beyond, making them one with the power and the strength of his body's passion for her, his search for the freedom realised in their union.

They lay by the river, cradled in each other's arms, blanketed by the light of the silver moon, caressed by a warm wind. Spent and fulfilled once again, both glorying in the utter and total joy of their closeness.

Julie had no idea how much time passed before they got up, dressed, and wandered up to the house. Across the living room, up the stairs, along the hall to the bedroom ... when he took her in his arms and drew her down on the bed, she knew they were going to make love again and welcomed it with all her heart, so that when he spoke it was an effort to focus on his words. 'Tell me now that you don't belong to me, dear Julie.'

The first quiver of tension touched her nerve ends. 'I—what do you mean?'

'I mean you're my wife. My wife, my lover, my woman—don't ever forget it.' Roughly his hand stroked the smooth swell of her hips and his voice thickened. 'I don't want you seeing Richard Buchanan again. Do you understand?'

Above, through the skylight, the myriad stars glimmered, cold and remote. Julie's voice was as sharp-edged as glass. 'Richard? What's he got to do with this?'

'I saw the two of you tonight in the library.'

'That was nothing——'

'The man's crazy about you. Do you think I'm so devoid of brains that I can't see that?'

Her protests died in her throat, because essentially what Luke had said was all too true. Richard did love her, had made no secret of his feelings and his desire for her. Before she could think of anything to say, Luke reared up on one elbow, his body a dark silhouette. 'If only you could see yourself—the picture of guilt! He was your lover, wasn't he? While I was in prison, Richard Buchanan was your lover——'

Julie twisted free of his hold, and the pale wash of moonlight delineated the agitated rise and fall of her breasts. 'He wasn't!'

'I don't believe you. I saw you both tonight, I heard what you were saying. Besides, you've already admitted it. How could you *do* it, Julie?'

The anguish in his question cut short her anger like a knife. She leaned forward, lightly resting her fingers on his arm. 'Luke, let's stop this,' she said urgently. 'Please— it won't get us anywhere. I was alone for two years and Richard was my friend. He's a good person and he helped me through some difficult times. And that's all.'

'But you don't deny he's in love with you.' His eyes were black pits, totally unreadable.

'No, I don't deny that.' She shrugged helplessly. 'How can I?'

Luke pounced, as swift and lethal as a mountain cat. 'So all through those months you encouraged him, and then, two weeks before I got out of prison, you served me with divorce papers and planned to move to Calgary. For God's sake, Julie, how gullible do you think I am?'

Again that underlying anguish in his voice, although this time she ignored it, too angry to care. 'You haven't listened to a word I've said, have you? Your mind's been made up from the start and nothing I can say or do will make any difference. Believe what you will, Luke Marshall, and see if I care.'

'You'll care,' he said icily. 'For one thing, you won't see your precious Richard again. You won't phone him or write to him, and you won't go near Calgary without me. And secondly . . .' his eyes raked her tumbled hair and mutinous, wide-held eyes, '. . . you'll stay with me as my wife. Do you understand?'

Her voice broke. 'Luke, you don't love me any more— don't tie me to a marriage that for both of us has become a cage, another prison. You don't need that any more than I do.'

For a moment his shoulders slumped, as if all his virility and strength had abandoned him, leaving only the shell

of a man. 'That's how you see it—a cage,' he said heavily.
'I guess it's just as well we had this little conversation—
there can be no doubt where we stand, can there? I'm
sorry, Julie—cage or no cage, you're still married to me
and Beth is still my daughter. And that's the way it's
going to stay!'

As he turned away from her, her breath caught in her
throat, for his movements were those of an old man.
Scarcely knowing what she was saying, she whispered,
'Luke . . . Luke, please don't let's do this to each other.
Where are you going?'

'I'm going to sleep downstairs. Oddly enough, the
thought of sharing a bed with a woman who despises
me doesn't appeal.' She flinched as if his words had been an
actual physical blow, and he added savagely, 'Don't look so
stricken—or you'll tempt me to stay.' His hands clenched to
fists at his sides. 'And you might not like that, Julie. . . .'

Before she could guess his intentions, he seized her, his
fingers digging into her arms like claws, his kiss a brief
and ugly violation. Then he thrust her away so that she
fell back against the pillows. 'Goodnight,' he rasped,
adding with cruel mockery, 'Pleasant dreams!'

Through a haze of tears she watched him stride across
the pale carpet and disappear through the open door,
pulling it sharply shut behind him. As if this was a signal,
the tears began to pour down her cheeks and she buried
her face in the pillow to muffle the sobs that crowded her
throat. Luke hated her . . . believed the worst of her . . .
yet would not set her free. Their lovemaking, that had
been like a brief, magical return to a lost paradise, had
been nothing but a mirage, vanishing at the sound of his
voice, erased by his ugly accusations—and leaving her
more alone than she had been for months.

Eventually she cried herself to sleep, but not until the
first faint light of dawn was reflected in a wash of rose
and gold on the far slopes of the mountains.

When Julie awoke, the house was very quiet. She had no
idea of the time, although she sensed it must be past mid-
morning by the clarity of the sunlight that poured through
the windows above the bed. Her body was tangled in the

sheets, and like the memory of a dream came recollection of the night before. Suddenly terrified that Luke might return and find her like this, she scrambled out of bed and hurriedly showered, of necessity getting dressed in the gown she had worn to the party. Her long skirts swishing, she walked downstairs, and as she did so heard the back door open and the clatter of boots on the kitchen floor. Luke . . . it had to be Luke. Head held high, she walked into the kitchen.

'Good morning,' she said coldly.

He had been filling the kettle at the sink. With a deliberation that was almost an insult, he placed the kettle on the stove and turned on the element before acknowledging her presence. Sardonically he looked her up and down. He, she noticed resentfully, was wearing dusty jeans and tooled leather boots, his cotton shirt open at the neck, his Stetson thrown casually on the counter. 'You've already been out,' she said, stating the obvious.

'Yeah. Want a coffee?'

'Why didn't you wake me earlier?' she demanded. 'We've got to go straight home—Maggie will be worried sick.'

'I already phoned her.'

'Oh . . . how's Beth?'

'Fine.' He repeated patiently, 'Coffee?'

'Yes, please.' She perched on one of the tall stools along the counter, her dark eyes wary, sensing that there was more to come.

He poured boiling water into the mugs. 'You've got it wrong, anyway, Julie—we can't go home. Because this——' he tapped the counter for emphasis, 'is home.'

'Home is where Beth is.'

He brought over her coffee, his eyes lingering deliberately on the shadowed hollow between her breasts. The heat rose to her cheeks; only a few short hours ago, his head had rested there . . . 'Home, my dear Julie, is going to be where I am. We're moving out here permanently as soon as it can be arranged. You and I and Beth.'

Her mouth was dry. 'We can't leave Maggie alone.'

'Maggie accepts that our staying with her was only temporary. She's known about this house all along.'

'I didn't know that,' Julie said stiffly.

'Why should you?'

She stirred her coffee angrily, trying to ignore the first nibblings of fear. 'I don't want to live out here—I like it in town.'

'Come off it, Julie, I know you too well for that. You've always loved this place as much as I have.'

'I'm glad you used the past tense,' she said sharply, knowing with a sinking sensation in the pit of her stomach that she was afraid to be out here with Luke, twenty miles from all that was familiar. Twenty miles from Maggie, and her comforting, unobtrusive presence. Twenty miles away from all the things that tended to keep Luke, this black-haired stranger who was her husband, at a safe distance. Last night they had made love out here . . . would he expect that every night?

'Julie, we always planned to move out here—you know that.'

'That was two years ago, Luke. Things are different now.'

'They certainly are,' he said bitterly. 'I wouldn't have believed anyone, let alone you, could change so much in so short a time.' He slammed down his mug. 'There's no point in arguing. We're going to live here at the ranch, Julie, the three of us, whether you want to or not. There's no reason why we can't be moved in by the end of the week.'

She drank the last of the coffee, too stubborn and too proud to let him see how afraid his words had made her. 'Very well,' she said coolly. 'There'll be a lot to organise— we'd better go back to Henderson.'

He looked momentarily disconcerted, as if he had expected her to keep on arguing with him, but all he said was, 'Fine.' Then, as she stood up, he suddenly grinned, an uncomplicated smile of pure amusement at the incongruity of their attire, and with a flourish offered her an arm. 'Ready, Mrs Marshall?'

It was the old Luke, fun-loving and carefree, achingly handsome, his black eyes sparked with laughter. The long months of separation vanished like smoke as Julie laughed back at him, linking her arm with his as they walked out

of the back door into the summer morning. But then the
brilliant sunlight, which would allow no secrets, fell on
the new lines in Luke's face and on the first touch of silver
in the hair over his ears. Reality returned. The old Luke
was an illusion. This was the real man, the man who had
stolen and lied and gone to prison. Who for two long
years had ignored her existence. The pain was like the
twisting of a knife in Julie's heart. The colour left her
cheeks, and she stumbled and would have fallen but for
Luke's support. 'What's wrong?' he demanded. 'Julie, are
you all right?'

She could be nothing but honest. 'I forgot,' she
muttered. 'For a minute or two it was as though we were
young again, just as we were when we first married. . . .'

He stopped dead, his lean fingers warm and sure on
her arm. 'But that's wonderful, Julie—don't you see? It
means we *can* forget. And more and more we *will* forget.'

Numbly she loosed herself from his clasp. 'No, Luke,'
she said hopelessly. 'It doesn't work that way. We can't
pretend that none of it happened—the theft, the trial, the
months in prison. We're two different people now.' She
pushed her hair back from her face, attempting a smile.
'I'm sorry- - this is all my fault. It won't happen again.' It
can't, she thought silently to herself. Because it hurts too
much.

Something in her tense white features stilled whatever
Luke might have said next. His face bleak with frustration,
he ushered her to the car and helped her in, and in silence
they drove away from the sun-bathed hills.

CHAPTER EIGHT

TRUE to Luke's word, they had moved into the new house
by the end of the week, nor had it been a very difficult
job: a matter of transporting clothes, Beth's playpen and
toys, and their personal effects. Maggie had proved perfectly phlegmatic about the change, promising to come
out and visit them at least weekly; Julie herself, once the

die was cast, found a peculiar sense of satisfaction in rearranging the furniture, hanging the pictures to suit her eye, and making brightly coloured curtains for Beth's room. Her earlier fears of being so isolated with Luke seemed groundless, for she saw less of him at the ranch than she had in Henderson. He worked all day with the hired hands, saved an hour or so after supper to play with Beth, and then immersed himself in ledgers and account books all evening.

Towards Julie he maintained a surface politeness that covered a remoteness both mental and physical, for which at first she was grateful. He never touched her; he had moved his clothes into the bedroom farthest from the master bedroom and there he slept; he made nothing that could be construed as a sexual approach. She had called him a stranger, and as such he had obviously chosen to behave—he could have been a well-mannered guest with no desire for friendship or intimacy. As the slow summer days and warm star-spangled nights drifted by, his restraint, from being a relief, began to irk her—even though she was fair enough to admit that she was the one responsible for it. *She* had said it was too late to recapture their earlier intimacy, hadn't she? That it was impossible to go backwards? It was more and more obvious that Luke had taken her words to heart, to the point where she began to wonder if he even wished to re-establish any kind of husband-and-wife relationship. She was piqued to find him so totally indifferent to her, particularly as she knew she was looking her best, her skin tanned and honey-gold from the hours she spent outdoors with Beth, or riding Jewel's Dancer. But worse than pique was loneliness. She loved Beth, loved her dearly, but the company of an eighteen-month-old child was not always enough. She wanted adult companionship—Luke's companionship, she thought uncomfortably, remembering all too well how she had always been stimulated by his enquiring mind and breadth of knowledge. Yet—and the thought seemed to slam her against a brick wall—that mind was the same one that had systematically misappropriated money that belonged to someone else, that had lied and cheated and stolen.

Because he was so withdrawn, she found herself watching him with eyes no longer blinded by anger and pain. He too was tanned now, and had gained back the weight he had lost. But there was a tension in him that there had never been before. His smile was less frequent. Unless he was with Beth, he rarely laughed. On more than one occasion when he had been indoors for some time, she had seen him stare with hunted eyes at the walls, as though they were encroaching on him, and then push back his chair, striding out to the veranda where he would stand with his head thrown back, drawing in deep breaths of the clean night air. She had shrunk from intruding on him when this had happened, sensing that he was battling demons too dreadful to be shared.

But there came one evening, well into July, when she felt she could no longer remain aloof . . . it had been a hot day, and after Beth had had her usual afternoon nap, Julie had taken her to the river's edge to play in the shallows where the crystal-clear water rippled over the stones. Then they went back to the house for Julie to prepare supper, which the three of them ate together. Beth was intent upon learning to feed herself, a process which involved inordinate amounts of food being distributed on the high-chair and her face and very little actually making its way into her mouth. In the end Luke inserted the final few spoonsful and said with mock sternness, 'You're a mess, Beth Marshall!' wiping chocolate pudding from the child's ear.

Beth chuckled in delight, letting loose one of the strings of unintelligible syllables which were her present means of communication, and waiting expectantly for Luke's next move. He blew noisily into her neck and she buried her little fists into his hair, tugging at his curls. Luke yelped in protest, raising his head, and with disarming suddenness Beth rested her cheek on his chest and closed her eyes.

The man looked down at the child and something in his unguarded face brought a sheen of tears to Julie's eyes. They looked so right together, Beth and her father, a rightness which was only superficially related to the silky black hair and dark eyes they had in common. They loved each other, Julie thought. The big black-haired man who had appeared from nowhere had become an integral part of Beth's world in the past few weeks, just as the child had stolen her way through all Luke's defences to find his heart. As Julie stood by the sink, letting the water run over a plate long ago rinsed clean, it struck her for the first time that she was trapped into this marriage by more than Luke's threats. She had known all along that she could not bear to be separated from her daughter; but now she recognised how cruel it would be to separate father and daughter, to rip apart the bond that had been developing between them under her very eyes. To deprive Luke of his daughter, Beth of her father—how could she do it?

'You'll flood the sink.'

Dazedly she pushed back her hair. 'What?'

'Turn off the tap before the sink overflows.' As Julie numbly did as she was told, Luke added, his eyes fixed on her taut face, 'You look as though you've just lost your best friend.'

'No—no, I'm all right.'

He had lifted Beth from the high-chair and the child was now curled trustingly against his chest. 'She's beginning to love me, certainly,' he said, with the uncanny ability he had always had to discern Julie's thoughts. 'But that doesn't mean she'll have any the less love for you, Julie.'

'It's not that,' Julie disclaimed incautiously. 'But how will I ever be able to free myself from our marriage now? Now that Beth loves you as well as me. . . .'

His arms must have tightened involuntarily, for Beth wriggled in protest. Luke set her down on the floor and straightened to his full height. Although he spoke in a low voice, for the sake of the child, there was no mistaking the corrosive bitterness underlying his words. 'So you still think of leaving,' he grated. 'I thought you knew from the day I came back that that was impossible—but oh no, you still imagine you're going to be able to run away from reality, don't you? What are you planning to do— hide in Richard's arms?' He leaned forward, and the very restraint in his voice was more of a threat than any shouting could have been. 'I'll never let you go, Julie—get that into your head once and for all!' Grabbing his Stetson from the table, he shoved it on, and said shortly, 'I'm going out. I could say don't wait up for me, but then I know you won't anyway, will you, Julie? You'll be glad to see the last of me for a few hours, won't you? Well, allow me to tell you there are other women who don't feel that way.'

'Luke, where are you going?'

'Why do you care? After all, think how convenient it would be if I end up in the ditch somewhere. You'd get the ranch and the house and Beth without having to put up with me. Plus you'll get my money.'

'Luke, I never. . . .'

Their voices had risen and from the floor Beth gave a little whimper of distress. With a muttered expletive that held utter frustration, Luke slammed out of the back door, and a minute later Julie heard the roar of the truck. Running to the window, she watched it turn around, the tyres throwing up a shower of dust and gravel as with reckless speed the vehicle headed down the road to Henderson. For once ignoring Beth's fretful cries, Julie leaned her forehead against the cool glass. Luke was like a volcano, she thought, with a surface calm that lasted for days, yet could erupt in moments into a torrent of hot and angry words. One careless phrase from her had triggered him off, and now he was gone—and gone where? To another woman? Someone who would welcome his embraces and give him the love and laughter he no longer had at home? Sick with an emotion she knew could only be jealousy, Julie automatically began the usual round of evening chores: clearing away the meal, bathing Beth and putting her to bed. Afterwards she knitted for a while, watched a little television, tried to read a book, but nothing could hold her attention. The quietness of the house pressed on her ears. Her aloneness seemed absolute, as though it would never end. Finally she went to bed and for a long time lay awake in the darkness, watching the breeze waft the curtains in a slow ghostly dance.

She must have fallen asleep, for there was the illusive sense of time having passed before she found herself sitting upright in bed, her ears straining for the noise that must have wakened her, her heart hammering. Sliding out of bed and throwing her housecoat around her, she tiptoed down the hall to Beth's room, but the child was sleeping peacefully, spreadeagled on the bed in total abandon. So it had not been that . . . taking her courage in her hands, she went to the end of the hallway, to the room Luke had been using. The door was ajar. Horribly conscious of the banging of her own heart, she peered around it.

The room was empty, the bedcovers undisturbed. Julie clung to the door-frame, feeling physically ill, her knuckles white with strain. So Luke had not been joking when he had made reference to another woman—he had meant every word of it. Perhaps right at this moment he was in another woman's arms, another woman's bed. She fought back the nightmare images this evoked, for what did it matter, after all? She didn't want him, did she? She did not love him any more . . . so why should she care where he spent his nights, or with whom?

Slowly she straightened, loosening her hold on the door. At one and the same time she felt bone weary and yet wide awake, so wide awake she knew there was no point in going back to bed. Her bare feet soundless on the carpet, she padded downstairs, with the vague idea of getting a book to read. A light had been left on in the study, the bar of gold falling across the polished pine flooring. Julie hesitated, her brow furrowed. She hadn't been in the study last night, had she? Without giving herself time to think, she walked boldly forward, pushing open the door.

The man at the desk looked up with a start. 'Julie! What the hell are you doing up at this hour?'

She felt such an irrational surge of relief that her knees went weak. 'I thought you were still out,' she stammered foolishly.

Pointedly Luke looked at his watch. 'At three a.m.? Hardly.'

Her unruly tongue blurted, 'You said you were going to see someone else—another woman.'

His hands, which had been adjusting a pile of receipts, grew still, and in one keen glance he encompassed his wife's slim figure, her chin lifted proudly, but her eyes full of unconscious pleading. 'I was angry when I said that, Julie,' he answered slowly. 'I didn't mean it. You, of all people, should know that—you know you're the only woman I've ever wanted or will ever want.'

Inexplicably she felt like crying. 'Oh, Luke,' she said helplessly, 'I wish——'

'——that the past two years hadn't happened? So do I, Julie. But they did happen, didn't they? We can't erase them—we can only try and live with the results.'

He had been staring down at his hands as he spoke, the overhead light casting his deep-set eyes into shadow and highlighting the strong jut of his cheekbones. He looked tired and careworn and somehow defeated, and Julie was overwhelmingly aware of the desire to step nearer, to gather him into her arms and to hold his head to her breast. And if she were to do that, she knew exactly what would happen: they would make love again, she and Luke, and she would feel all the heat of passion and the surging fulfilment that he could bring her. But afterwards—and her mind flew back to their lovemaking on the banks of the river—there would be only bitter loneliness, and an isolation all the worse for their transitory closeness. She could not bear that again . . . her tentative move forward froze and she said at random, gazing down at the papers and ledgers, her voice sounding disembodied in her own ears, 'What are you doing?'

'Still trying to make sense of the accounts for the mill for the past two years. There are several discrepancies I can't figure out. And the DeWitt contract—it just seems to have disappeared from the books.' As though suddenly recalling himself, he said sharply, 'I shouldn't be telling you that, Julie, it's strictly confidential. Right now no one else knows about that contract except me.'

She said as calmly as she could, 'I'm not likely to discuss it with anyone,' even as she spoke trying to ignore the cold fingers of fear that brushed her nerve ends. Wasn't this how all their trouble had started? So what was Luke up to now, talking about missing contracts and discrepancies in the books? Was it going to start all over again?

She was unaware how clearly her thoughts were written

on her face until Luke gave a muffled exclamation. 'Don't look at me like that!' he said harshly. 'What do you think I'm doing—stealing from the company again? At least give me credit for a little intelligence, Julie. I'd hardly be likely to try the same game twice.'

'Oh, please, I didn't mean——'

'Like hell,' he interrupted rudely. 'You know perfectly well that's what you meant.' His eyes went around the civilised, orderly room with its rows of books on the shelves and its collection of Inuit sculpture, as if it were a cage and he the animal trapped within. Shoving back his chair, he got to his feet, and she saw that his whole frame was shaking slightly. His fists were clenched at his sides, his jawline tense with an effort at self-control that flooded her with compassion. But his eyes passed over her, blind with an inner battle, and then he was blundering towards the door, narrowly missing her.

'Luke!'

He did not even hear her. He thrust his way through the door and she heard the rap of his boots on the living room floor and the click of the latch on the front screen. It mobilised her into action. She fled after him, across the room and out on to the veranda. He was standing there, half bent forward, drawing in great gulps of air, hands gripping the railing as if he were a drowning man and it the lifeline.

Aware only of his suffering and of a deep, instinctive need to help, Julie grabbed him by the sleeve, the folds of her housecoat swirling about his feet. 'Oh, Luke, was it that bad?'

He glanced down at her, eyes like black pits, and she was not sure that he even knew who she was. 'I couldn't get out,' he said hoarsely. 'I couldn't take Whistler and ride for miles across the plains. I couldn't see the sweep of the sky or the expanse of stars at night. The world had shrunk, and I was forced to shrink to fit it.'

One last reminiscent shudder and he grew still. She rested her cheek on his shoulder and whispered, 'Luke, I'm so sorry.'

This time when he looked down at her, there was recognition in his gaze—recognition and then withdrawal. 'You,

along with the rest of Henderson, thought I deserved it—
if you steal, you should be punished. So spare me the
sympathy, Julie.'

She said, each word falling clearly on the cool night
air, 'I'm not sure anyone would deserve it. To take a man
who all his life has roamed free, and shut him up behind
bars—no, I don't think you deserved that, Luke.'

'Guilty or not guilty, eh?'

She hesitated. 'That's right. Guilty or not guilty.'

Very softly he said, 'But you still think I'm guilty, don't
you, Jul?'

Unconsciously she moved back a pace. Her eyes
dropped. 'I don't know how else to explain what
happened, Luke. If you didn't take the money, who did?'

'Julie, I'm no millionaire, but I've never wanted for
anything as far as money is concerned—so why would I
risk my freedom, my marriage, my good name, just to
steal money from the mill?'

She stared at him in perplexity. 'I don't know,' she
fumbled. 'I've never really known how much money you
had—it didn't seem important.'

'I certainly never have been so desperate that I would
have had to steal.'

'But this house—you were planning to build it back
then. It must have cost an awful lot.'

Luke banged his fist against the rail. 'You just can't
bring yourself to trust me, can you?'

She wanted to—God, how she wanted to! 'Then who
took it?' she cried. 'Tell me that!'

'I can't,' he said flatly.

Losing all caution, she demanded, 'Can't or won't?
Which is it, Luke?' He hesitated fractionally, and it was
the final straw. 'You don't care, do you?' she said wildly.
'You don't give a damn about your marriage—about me.
Strong and silent Luke, hiding behind a cloak of secrecy—
I hate you, do you hear me? I hate you!'

Sobs bursting from her throat, she whirled and ran for
the door, her last image that of Luke standing by the
railing, making no move to stop her, his face a frozen
mask.

*

The next day Julie took Beth into town with her, ostensibly to do some shopping and have a visit with Maggie, but in actuality simply to get away from the ranch—and from Luke. She bought Beth a couple of sunsuits and a bright pink plastic boat to float in the river, then left the store, walking slowly to accommodate the child's short legs. Momentarily dazzled by the bright sun, she did not see the light-haired young man coming towards her, his eyes hidden behind polaroid glasses, his whipcord slacks and cream-coloured shirt immaculately pressed.

'Hi there, Jul. Hello, Beth, how's my favourite girl?'

'Frank!' Julie exclaimed in delight. 'What a lovely surprise. I've missed you since we moved out to the ranch.'

'You've got your husband out there—you don't need my company.'

Puzzled by the edge in his voice, she said, 'I'm always glad to see you, Frank, you know that.'

'What's Luke up to, anyway? We sure aren't seeing much of him around the mill.'

Beth tugged at her hand and Julie bent to pick the child up. 'Hush now, we're going to Grandma's in a minute. Luke? Well, he's spending most of his time at the ranch. He's out all day—I think he almost has to be, Frank, after all the months in prison. It's as though he can't stand to be indoors for too long.'

'So he didn't enjoy his stay in prison, eh? Too bad.'

Again there was something in his voice she could not define—a blandness, almost a note of gloating. But that was impossible . . . she said sharply, 'Of course he didn't—how could he?'

'Pity he hadn't thought of that earlier, isn't it?'

The fact that she had had somewhat similar thoughts herself did not make her any the less uncomfortable now. It was not often she was out of sympathy with Frank; but today, with the memory raw and fresh on her brain of Luke's body shuddering in the cool night air, she could not tolerate her brother's mocking.

'He's paid for whatever he did, Frank—so let's leave it

at that, shall we?' Impossible to tell Frank's reaction to her words behind his dark glasses, and she added peevishly, 'I do wish you'd take those things off—I hate them.'

'Beth likes them, don't you, love?' He slid them down his nose, peering at the little girl over the rims, then sliding them back up again, and the child gurgled with delight. Repeating the performance, Frank said casually, 'Someone's got all the books from the mill—is it Luke?'

'Well—yes, I guess so.'

'What does he want them for?'

'I don't know, Frank. He mentioned some discrepancies in the accounts, I believe.'

'I see.' A pause before Frank added with rather overdone casualness, 'He didn't say anything about any contracts, I suppose? The DeWitt one, for instance?'

A cold hand clutched Julie's heart. What had Luke said? . . . no one knows about that contract except me . . . 'How did you know about that?' she demanded.

Even behind the concealing glasses she could tell Frank was taken aback. 'What do you mean?' he countered. 'Why shouldn't I know about it? I work at the mill, remember?'

'Luke said no one knew about that contract.'

Imperceptibly Frank relaxed. 'He meant the general public, silly—not me. I'm the accountant, after all.'

'That's not what he told me, Frank. He said *no* one knows about it; it was strictly confidential.'

Beth reached out for Frank's glasses and he pushed her hand away irritably. 'So that's the line he's going to take, is it?' he asked softly.

'What do you mean?' Julie asked, wishing the subject of the contract had never come up.

'Oh—nothing. Sorry, Jul, I shouldn't have said that. The trouble is—oh, hell, I hate to say this, because I know he's still your husband and you're still living with him—but I just don't trust him. That contract—well, you don't need to know all the details, but it was a very important contract, and it was because of Luke, I'm afraid, that we didn't get it. So I would suspect he's trying to do a whitewash job now. Trouble is, who's going to take the rap?'

People were jostling them on the sidewalk, and the heat bounced up from the pavement. But Julie felt very cold—cold and afraid, for if the nightmare were to begin again she could not bear it. In her arms Beth wriggled crossly, trying to grab Frank's glasses again, and Julie said with unaccustomed sharpness, 'Stop it, Beth!'

'I'm holding you up,' Frank said lightly. 'Can I give you a lift anywhere?'

'No—no, thanks. The car's parked just up the road. But, Frank——'

'Forget everything I said, hon—it was indiscreet of me.' He chucked Beth under the chin. 'See you later, sweetie. By the way, Julie, an old friend was enquiring after you——'

Her attention was more on the ache in her arms from Beth's weight, and on the unease Frank's remarks had generated. 'Oh?'

'I was in Calgary the other day and had lunch with Richard. He wanted to know how you were, what you were up to. I had to tell him, of course, that you and Luke had left Henderson and were living out at the ranch.'

Julie flinched, ashamed to realise how little thought she had given to Richard lately. 'How is he?'

'Missing you, Julie. You know, you'd only have to say the word and he'd come and get you and Beth and take you both back to Calgary with him, I know he would. The guy's eating his heart out for you.'

'I can't help that! I'm a married woman, Frank, not a young girl who can pick up and go as she chooses.'

Frank's breath hissed through his teeth. 'Luke's got some kind of a hold over you, hasn't he? I thought he must have——'

'Don't be ridiculous!' she snapped, knowing he was getting too close to the truth for comfort.

'Why else would you stay with him? Not because you love him, I know—spare me that routine.'

It was Luke himself who had killed her love, she thought in a wave of black despair that blotted out the busy street, the heat, the child in her arms—leaving only the ugly image of Luke's frozen face, as clear in her mind's eye as if he stood in front of her. Then, from a long way away, she heard Frank's voice again, and forced herself to listen.

'You don't have to stay with him, Julie. You don't even have to go back today. I'll drive you in to Calgary, and you can go to Richard's—he'll look after you.'

Go to the city. Get herself an apartment and a job. Find a play-school for Beth. It was all manageable. She could even do it in such a way that it would be virtually impossible for Luke to trace her. In a city of thousands of people, a young woman and a small child could vanish from sight. It would be a new life, a new beginning. 'No, Frank,' she said steadily, 'I can't do that.'

'Why not?'

'I don't know—I just know it's impossible.' She glanced down at her watch. 'I've got to go, I want to catch Maggie before lunch. Nice talking to you, Frank. 'Bye!'

Before he could say anything else, she had quickly turned away and was threading her way along the sidewalk towards the car. It had not been 'nice' talking to him at all, she thought wryly, as she strapped Beth into the car seat. But oddly enough the deep unease that he had evoked had been pushed aside. In its place was the recognition that flight was no longer possible—she could not run away from the ranch, or from Luke. In some strange way her place was there with him . . . and although beyond that she could not go, she was also aware of a kind of peace. Something—she scarcely knew what— had been resolved, and for that she was grateful.

Resolutely turning her mind ahead to the visit with Maggie, she checked her rear-view mirror and pulled out on to the street. Maggie was delighted to see them; they had lunch in the back garden and then, while Beth had her nap, the two women sat in the shade of the birch trees chatting about this and that, easy conversation with no disturbing undertones. When Beth woke up, Julie stayed a little longer so the child could play for a while before being confined to the car seat, then the two of them set off for the ranch. The town of Henderson was soon left behind and ahead of them lay the highway, leading arrow-straight to the rolling foothills and the snow-capped peaks; as she drove, Julie found she was humming under her breath. She did not want to analyse her feelings too deeply; she only knew that her instinctive rejection of the idea of moving to Calgary had settled something in her mind. In the few short weeks that she had lived at the ranch, it had become home. She was going home. . . .

Luke's truck was gone when she drove into the yard, but she had not really expected him to be there. She settled Beth on the kitchen floor with a pile of pots and pans to play with, put a prime rib roast in the oven and made some pastry, still humming to herself under the cover of the racket Beth was making. An hour or so later she was just taking an apple pie out of the oven when she heard the clatter of Luke's steps on the back porch. Straightening with the pie in her hands, she smiled at him with all the pleasure of her discovery in her face.

She had tied her hair back with a ribbon; she was wearing faded jeans and a flowered shirt, the sleeves rolled up; her face was innocent of make-up. A less seductive outfit could hardly be imagined. But her cheeks were flushed from the heat of the oven, and her eyes liquid with a new-found warmth, and there was a lilt in her voice as she said prosaically, 'Hello. You look dusty and tired, Luke—had a hard day?'

'Yeah, you could say that—mending fences. Hot as Hades out there, not a breath of wind. I think I'll have a shower right away . . . you seem very pleased to see me.'

Julie put the pie on the rack and closed the oven door. Facing him squarely, she said, 'Yes, I guess I am.'

'But only last night you told me you hated me.'

So she had . . . she had forgotten that. She blushed, her eyes dropping in confusion. 'I did, didn't I? I'm sorry, Luke—I was upset.'

Another pause. He was unbuttoning the front of his shirt and pulling it out of the waistband of his Levis, his forearms and hands grimed with dust. 'Perhaps you had reason to be. I know I'm not the easiest person in the world to live with, Julie. The trouble is. . . .'

'Yes?' she said, wanting only to encourage him, for she sensed that their few brief words had been, however inadequately, at least an attempt at genuine communication.

Sitting down on one of the chairs, he pulled off his boots, then stood up, shrugging out of his shirt. 'Look,' he said abruptly, 'let's take the day off tomorrow—I've done nothing but work since we moved out here. Why don't I give Maggie a call and see if she'll look after Beth, and the two of us will disappear for the day. We can take the horses, pack a lunch, head up into the hills—how does that sound?'

He was draping his shirt over the back of the chair, almost as though purposely avoiding looking at her. Dirt was ingrained in the lines of his face, and his eyes were shadowed with weariness. He *did* need a day off, Julie knew, for he had been driving himself unmercifully since he had come back to the ranch; and he was asking her to share that day with him. It would be like the old days, she thought with a catch in her throat—the two of them going off together on horseback. 'I'd like that,' she said in a small voice, even as she spoke wondering if she was crazy to risk any closer involvement with him.

For a split second something flashed in his eyes and then was gone. 'Good,' he said impersonally. 'I'll give Maggie a ring and then I'll have my shower. I won't be long—that pie smells too good!'

Maggie had arrived by eight-thirty the next day, the morning sun glinting in her white hair and bright blue eyes. 'Morning, Julie, Luke,' she called, as they came out on the veranda to greet her. 'Where's Beth?'

'You don't even come to see me any more,' Luke grumbled with mock ferocity.

Maggie hugged him. 'That's right,' she said cheerfully. 'Is she up yet?'

'Indeed she is,' Julie said ruefully. 'She's seeing how much of herself and the kitchen she can cover with cereal. Come on in.'

An hour later Julie and Luke were ready to leave, box lunches and water canteen thrown in the truck. Waving goodbye to Maggie and Beth, they drove off to the corral and saddled up the horses. Somewhat sheepishly Luke said, 'Do you mind if we go north? I could check on the haying and we could ride along the fence line. Then we could follow the creek up into the hills.'

'Some day off!' she teased, adjusting her stirrups to a more comfortable level as Jewel's Dancer whickered impatiently. Julie shoved her hair under her Stetson, her movements pulling the thin cotton of her shirt taut over her breasts and momentarily Luke's eyes rested there before he swung himself up on the prancing stallion. Making a great play of gathering up the reins, Julie found herself suddenly hoping with all her heart that up there in the hills under the empty blue sky she and Luke might make love again, and she would be allowed to recapture, however briefly, the intimacy they had shared at the river's edge so many long nights ago. It was as though this wish freed something tight-held in her psyche, and as she gripped her knees to Dancer's sides and rode with Luke out of the corral she was aware of a deep, primitive joy that she was to spend the whole day at her husband's side. She was tired of being treated as a stranger, tired of all the anxiety, suspicion, and pain of the past few months; just for one day she was going to forget it all, to forget the past and pretend she and Luke were the close and loving companions they had been three years ago . . . she dug in her knees so that Jewel's Dancer surged ahead of Whistler, and yelled in challenge, 'I'll beat you to the first fence!', her smile as bright as sun on water.

It seemed as though her gaiety infected Luke. They raced along the rutted trail side by side until Luke finally drew ahead and Whistler's hoofs threw up clouds of dust in Julie's face. She slowed her mount to a lope. Luke glanced back over his shoulder and pivoted Whistler to ride back and meet her. 'Going kind of slow, weren't you?' he drawled, his teeth very white in his tanned face.

Her breast heaving, she pulled a face. 'You know darn well I was going as fast as I could, Luke Marshall!'

'Winner of the race ought at least to get a kiss.'

He edged closer until their legs were bumping against each other and bent to kiss her, contriving a very thorough kiss considering the circumstances. When he drew back there was a reckless triumph in his dark eyes. 'Glad you're here, Julie,' was all he said, but for the girl it was enough.

'So am I.'

They rode on, in half an hour arriving at the field that was being mowed and baled; more than a third of it was already done, spotted with triangular stacks of bales. The four-man crew stopped the machinery at Luke's approach and they talked briefly together, Jake Simms explaining a difficulty they had had with the baler twine; as she sat quietly by, Julie could sense the innate respect the crew had for Luke, knowing it was nothing to do with the fact that Luke owned the ground they were all standing on; it was something Luke had earned over the years working side by side with them, and to her it indicated more clearly than words that these fields were where Luke belonged, where he needed to be.

In the most northerly part of Luke's land, they rode through the herds of white-faced cattle, the calves skittering away from the horses. Luke gave a cursory glance at the waterhole and more carefully studied the fence line. 'It's in good shape,' he pronounced finally. 'Better than I thought it'd be. Once the hay's in, I'll get Jake to send out a crew with new barbed wire. In the meantime, why don't we find a place to eat?'

'Thought you'd never get around to it,' Julie said pertly, and was rewarded by one of Luke's lazy grins.

They meandered up the hillside, picking up a creek that had originated high above them in the mountains, and following it until they came to a dense stand of poplars, leaves rustling in the breeze. The shade was welcome, for the sun was directly overhead, blazing in the clear blue sky. Sliding to the ground, Julie removed Dancer's saddle and tethered the horse to a tree, rubbing the sweat-stained flanks with a handful of dry grass. Then she walked over to the bank of the creek, splashing water on her face and taking a long, cooling drink. Luke dropped to his knees beside her, muttering something rude under his breath as he inadvertently got water down his neck. Julie giggled, on impulse dipping her hand in the stream and flicking the icy droplets in his direction.

She saw the laughter leap into his eyes. He reached out and grabbed her by the waist, insinuating his cold hands under her shirt. She shrieked in protest, trying to wriggle free, but his hold only tightened and his eyes were suddenly very serious; her protest stilled and her lips met his half way in a kiss of such mingled tenderness and passion that she was lost. From a long way off she felt herself being lifted and carried; then she was lying on her back in the sweet-scented grass, her face and hair surrounded by wildflowers, the sunlight dancing in her gold-flecked eyes, and he was kissing her again, slowly, deliberately, as if he had all the time in the world.

Her whole body rose up to meet him. Their clothes were shed, although afterwards she had no recollection how or when. Naked to each other under the restless shadows of the poplar leaves, they answered need for need, desire with desire, as together they climbed the sun-drenched slopes of a mutual passion, and together at the summit cried out in passion's earth-shaking release.

CHAPTER NINE

CRADLED in Luke's arms, his silky head resting on her breast, Julie gazed up at the ceiling of translucent leaves, clear green against a distant dazzling blue. She and Luke had never, not even in the first joyful months of their marriage, made love quite as they had just then; it was as though, in the fragment of an afternoon, each had slaked a two-year thirst, fed a long and desperate hunger—yet had done so with tenderness and love. Love . . . she closed her eyes, her fingers gently caressing his nape, as the inevitable conclusion flowered within her. She loved Luke . . . she had never stopped loving him. None of her anger and rejection had destroyed that love, for it was too deeply a part of her to be destroyed. Buried, yes—certainly she had buried it—and mistakenly she had concluded it was dead. . . .

'What are you thinking?'

She opened her eyes, her face shadowed by his head. 'That was beautiful, Luke,' she said shyly, reaching up and stroking his cheek with her fingers. 'Thank you.'

'It was just as beautiful for me,' he answered, his voice rough with an emotion Julie could only guess at. But one thing she saw, and it caused the first faint brushing of fear, as delicate as the wings of the brightly coloured butterflies that flitted through these meadows—he did not look happy. Instead he looked haunted, his black eyes inward-turned to visions she could not imagine. . . .

'What's wrong?' she blurted. After such a sharing of their bodies' needs, he surely could not keep from her the secrets of his mind?

'I—Julie, I don't know. I wish——'

She held her breath. 'Yes?'

'If there were only you and I—and Beth too, of course—we'd be all right. It's the others that get in the way. . . .' He fell silent, rearing up on one elbow, shredding at the grass with restless fingers.

'We're alone now,' she coaxed. 'Can't you tell me what's bothering you?'

'I can't! Not now. Because if I do, it will ruin it,' he said with such violence that she jumped. 'But I'll have to tell you sooner or later, I suppose . . . oh, Julie!' He fell across her and his kiss was such a blend of desperation and hunger that his words were pushed aside. He took her in silence, his hands and body rough in their demands, as if his very intensity could subdue the devils within him. Afterwards he held her for a long time, and she knew with a sinking heart that he had failed, for there was tension in the arms that were around her, and a grimness in the line of his mouth.

Eventually they got up and dressed, saddling up the horses and leaving the little copse without a backward glance. By an unspoken consent they rode straight home. For Julie the day that had started with such high hopes, hopes that their lovemaking had more than fulfilled, had been spoiled. She was afraid again. And because she had finally realised that she still loved Luke, she felt achingly vulnerable to that fear, and of all that it might signify.

It was late evening before she and Luke were alone again. Maggie had stayed for dinner, regaling them with all Beth's exploits during the day; if she noticed the strain between Luke and Julie, she was wise enough not to interfere. All she said as she left was, 'Call me any time you need time to yourselves. Beth is a darling, but she does need a lot of attention and it's always good to get away for a while.'

Julie recognised the understanding and compassion under Maggie's briskly spoken words and said warmly, 'Thanks, Maggie. Take care of yourself. Goodnight.'

The door closed behind her. 'Why don't you make us both some more coffee and we'll drink it in the living room,' Luke said with an effort at normality which did not deceive the girl at all. As she poured cream into the jug, and re-heated the coffee, she could only wonder what Luke wanted to discuss with her. It would be the height of irony were he to offer her her freedom, she thought wildly. Now, when she did not want it.

But when they sat down in the living room in chairs that faced each other, yet were a careful distance apart, and Luke started to talk, Julie realised she never would have guessed what was on his mind. His first words were: 'I've decided to sell the mill.'

She stared at him blankly, wondering if she had heard rightly. 'Sell the *mill*? What on earth for?'

Moodily he gazed down at the carpet. 'I don't want it any more. It's a reminder of things I'd prefer to forget, for one thing. And for another, my place is out here. You remember that originally I only took on the mill because my grandfather had died—not because I wanted it. I'm a cattleman, Julie—not a business man or an administrator spending his time behind a desk in a nice white shirt.'

True enough, as far as it went. Feeling her way carefully, Julie said, 'But the mill's been in the Marshall family for generations—how will Maggie feel about you selling it?'

'I haven't told her—or anyone else—yet. But I think she'll understand. I hope so, anyway.'

'But Luke, rather than selling it—which seems a bit drastic—why don't you keep the ownership and put someone else in as manager? Then you wouldn't have to bother with it.'

'I don't want to do that, I want to get clear of the whole thing. Besides, who would I get?'

She said excitedly, 'Well, there's a very logical choice—

Frank, of course. I'm sure he'd really like that, Luke. It would give him more of a challenge, more of a sense of importance—I think he needs that.'

'No, Julie,' said Luke with icy calm. 'Frank is the very last person I'd have.'

She shifted in her chair. 'The last person? I don't understand.'

'You don't have to. Just take my word for it.'

'Frank's the obvious person to get,' she persisted. 'He virtually ran the place single-handed for two years, so he already knows the job inside out. And if you got him as manager you could leave the mill in the Marshall name, which I'm sure Maggie would prefer, and yet be freed of any of the day-to-day responsibilities. It would be ideal.'

Luke drained his coffee, putting the mug down on the coffee table with a sharp crack. 'Julie, I've already said no. So just drop it, okay?'

She could hear her voice rising in frustration. 'Will you kindly tell me what you've got against him?'

'That's just what I won't do.' He leaned forward persuasively, the lamplight gleaming in his raven hair. 'Look, I'm sorry now I even told you. I didn't think you'd care if the mill was sold, I thought like me you'd just see it as—as an albatross off our necks. Because that's all it's been for the past two and a half years, believe me.'

With deadly precision Julie asked, 'And whose fault is that?'

Luke made a visible effort at control. 'I don't want to get into a discussion of what happened two years ago. The past is past, Julie, trite as it may sound. I'm talking about the future, trying to improve it for both of us, and one way of doing that as far as I'm concerned is to sell the mill. Then I can concentrate on building up the ranch, try some new feeding techniques, experiment with some of the new types of grain—without having to run in and out of town two or three times a week because of the mill.'

Despite herself, she could see the force of his arguments, and she too made an effort to keep calm. 'I do understand what you're saying about the ranch, Luke. I've always known it was your first love and that you only ran the mill for your grandfather's sake. What I don't understand is your attitude towards Frank—what has he ever done to you to deserve that?'

Abruptly Luke got to his feet. 'I'm not going to discuss Frank with you, Julie. Not now, anyway.'

She too stood up, her fists clenched at her sides, her eyes molten with anger. 'No, you'll run away from that, won't you, just as you ran away from everything in the courtroom—don't talk about it, and that way maybe you can pretend it doesn't exist.' Her voice broke. 'Luke, why can't you learn that's not the way to handle things? The mill—there must be something badly wrong at the mill for you to talk about selling it . . . can't you tell me what it is? Share it with me? That's what wives are for, isn't it?' She faltered to a stop, her cheeks paling. 'Unless, of course, it's something you can't tell me. Something you've done wrong—oh, God, Luke, not again! I couldn't bear to go through it again. . . .'

She was quite unaware of the tears streaming down her cheeks as she stretched out a hand in unconscious pleading. Viciously Luke struck it down and the ugly sound of flesh on flesh was very loud in the room. 'The slightest little thing and you immediately suspect me of the worst, don't you?' he grated. 'Trust isn't a word you even begin to understand. Well, this time you'd better try and trust me, Julie, because if you don't we're going to be right back where we started. So instead of jumping to one of the worst possible conclusions about me, why don't you try looking at Frank for once? Maybe he's not quite the blue-eyed boy you think he is.'

'You're crazy, Luke,' she whispered. 'Frank's always done his best for you. And you're not even grateful!'

He gave a bark of laughter, so totally devoid of humour that Julie winced. 'If you only knew the irony of that, my dear,' he said grimly. 'And now, if you'll excuse me, I think I've had enough of this—I want to do a bit more work on the books before I go to bed. But you might as well know that my decision's already made—I'm going to sell the mill.'

Full circle, she thought dazedly, watching him stride across the room to the study, closing the door behind him with a decisive snap that seemed symbolic, for he was shutting himself away from her by more than the physical barrier of a door. It was as though time had kaleidoscoped and she was smothering under the weight of suspicion and fear that had overwhelmed her two years ago. Was his sole reason for selling the mill his need to devote all his time on the ranch? Or were there other, less savoury, motives? And why was he so bitter against Frank—Frank, who could not have helped him more if Luke had been his own brother?

There was no answer to the questions. Suddenly worn out, she carried the coffee mugs back into the kitchen and rinsed them out, then trailed upstairs to bed. The day had begun so brightly, culminating in the exquisite joy of their lovemaking, and of her realisation that at some elemental level she had never stopped loving Luke ... but now it lay around her in ruins, destroyed by words, by suspicions and anger. Earlier in the day she had hoped that Luke might spend the night with her, but now she knew better than to expect that. Lying alone in the big bed, she fell asleep eventually, and woke the next morning to the sound of Luke driving away in the truck. Her plan fully formed in her mind, she got out of bed, dressed Beth, and cooked breakfast, then went to the phone, dialling the number of the mill.

'May I speak to Frank Taggart, please?'

'One moment, ma'am.'

Then Frank's voice on the line. 'Hello. Taggart here.'

'Frank, it's Julie.' She hesitated, as for the first time it occurred to her that Luke might not approve of her action.

'What's up, Julie? I'm kind of busy, so if it's just a social call——'

'No, no, it's not that. Frank, I have something to tell you—or maybe you already know.' She plunged on. 'Luke's planning to sell the mill. Had you heard about that?' Dead silence on the line. 'Frank, are you still there?'

'Yeah ... did you say what I thought you said? Luke's going to sell the mill?'

'That's right. He told me last night.'

An expletive echoed down the line. 'Did he tell you why?'

'Well, partly. He wants to spend more time at the ranch.'

'He knows damn well he can spend all the time he likes at the ranch right now — I do most of the work that keeps this place running. So that won't wash. Where is he now?'

'I don't really know. Somewhere on the ranch.'

'What time does he get home?'

'Around six, usually.'

'Okay. Listen, Julie, don't tell anyone else, have you got that?'

'Maybe I shouldn't have told you. . . .'

'You did the right thing. Hopefully this way I can stop him from making a bigger mistake than last time.' Before she could ask what he meant, he said, 'I've got to go, Jul. And listen — thanks.'

The connection was cut. Slowly Julie replaced the receiver, wishing irrationally that she had never phoned Frank. Luke was in the wrong over this, she was sure of it—yet even so, she felt as though she had gone behind his back, violating an unspoken loyalty. Oh, damn. . . .

The day dragged by. As if she was attuned to Julie's mood, Beth was unusually fractious, demanding to be picked up, refusing to be amused by all her usual toys and games. Luke did not come home for lunch and was late enough for supper that the steak was overdone, and the potatoes boiled dry, neither of which contretemps improved Julie's temper. Immediately after the meal Julie went upstairs to get Beth ready for bed, leaving Luke alone at the kitchen table with his coffee; she had, she realised bleakly, absolutely nothing to say to him.

She had just finished putting Beth in her cot when she heard through the open window the sound of a car approaching, then the slam of its door, and looking out, she saw Frank striding towards the house, tailored jacket slung across his shoulder, tie loosened. With a sudden premonition of disaster she ran lightly down the stairs, intending to forestall Frank should he be wanting to discuss the mill. But she was too late. From her stance in the hallway she could see into the kitchen. Frank was already there, leaning over the table, and she could hear him speak as clearly as if she was in the room with him. 'What's this I hear about you planning to sell the mill?'

Luke sat up a little straighter. 'Now who told you that?'

'Julie. At least *she's* loyal to me.'

'More loyal to you than to me, obviously.' Julie flinched, not deceived by the softness of Luke's tone of voice—he was angry, she knew, and found herself wishing again she had stopped to think before phoning Frank. Then maybe she wouldn't have done it. . . .

'She has more reason to be, I would have thought,' Frank said with a calculated spite that Julie found disturbing.

Luke took a deep breath. 'You didn't come out here just to trade insults, surely, Frank? So why did you come?'

'You can ask a damn fool question like that! I came out to find out if it was true, of course—if you are planning to sell the mill.'

'Oh yes, that's true enough.' Lazily Luke leaned back in his chair, lacing his fingers behind his neck. 'I even have a prospective buyer in mind—Sam Kendall, from Calgary. You already know him.'

Frank leaned forward, his pale eyes intent on the man across the table, and with crystal clarity Julie saw them as opposites: Frank, her brother, fair-haired, well-dressed, essentially a man of the city; and Luke, her husband, raven-dark, tanned and muscular in his work clothes, a man of the land. Opposites, yes—but more than that. Opponents. Men who were about to clash. And there was nothing she could do to stop them.

'The mill's been in Marshall hands for four generations——'

'——which is no reason why it should continue to be. Or are you forgetting that I disgraced the Marshall name, Frank?' his voice deadly quiet.

'That's over and done with—you paid the price and now it's finished.'

'That's where you're wrong.'

'Luke, you've got to get on with living.' Frank leaned

forward, a lock of hair falling boyishly across his forehead. 'I can understand why you might not want anything to do with the mill now—so let me take it over. I'm the logical choice.'

Julie drew in her breath. Inadvertently Frank had used her very words. How would Luke respond this time?

'You and Julie must be in cahoots,' Luke said silkily. 'How charming to see a brother and sister so attached to each other, both working away for my own good. And how unfortunate that the answer's no.'

'Come off it, Luke——'

Moving as quickly as a striking snake, Luke stood up. '*You* come off it, Frank. Let's quit playing these little games and try telling the truth for a change. You know as well as I do why I won't allow you full control of the mill. And you know why I'm selling it. What about the DeWitt contract, Frank?'

Julie heard Frank's indrawn breath, saw his hands clench on the back of the chair. 'What about it?' he blustered.

'I want to know what happened to it. Just as I want to know about a few other things you did—or didn't do—while I was so conveniently in prison.'

Some of the colour had returned to Frank's cheeks. 'I was trying my best to clean up the mess you'd left behind,' he said roundly. 'If I did a less than perfect job, you have only yourself to blame.'

Almost conversationally Luke remarked, 'You really are an incredible liar. Which is another reason why I'm firing you.'

There was a charged silence. 'You can't fire me, Luke Marshall.'

'I can and I will.'

'What are you trying to do—make me the scapegoat for what happened two years ago?'

'How can I possibly do that when a court of law found me guilty? You were there, remember? Testifying against me.' Luke rested his knuckles on the table and leaned forward. Unconsciously Julie had been creeping closer and now she trembled to see the implacable hatred in Luke's eyes, eyes that were trained on her own brother.

'I'm getting rid of you because I can't stand the sight of you. I want you out of the mill and out of Henderson. I'll give you a week, Frank, and if you haven't resigned by then, so help me God, I'll fire you!'

'You do that and I'll smear your name from one end of the town to the other!'

'That's already been done.'

Two men, both of whom she loved, and they were turning into strangers in front of her eyes. Strangers who looked capable of murdering each other . . . suddenly Julie could stand no more. 'Stop it, you two!' she exploded. 'How can you be so hateful to each other——'

Luke's head snapped around. 'So there you are. Do you always eavesdrop on other people's conversations—besides relaying confidential information to your brother as soon as my back's turned? You've developed some charming habits while I was away.'

Her half-formed plan of apologising for phoning Frank died stillborn on her lips. 'You didn't tell me it was a state secret,' she seethed.

'I didn't think I had to.'

Refusing to be sidetracked, she went on, 'You're not serious about firing Frank?'

'Never more serious in my life.'

'Luke, you can't! He kept the mill running all the time you were gone.'

'He mismanaged it so badly that the only choice I have left is to cut my losses and sell it,' was Luke's grim reply.

'I'm sure he did the best he could.'

Frank intervened roughly, 'Julie, lay off. The guy's crazy if he thinks he's going to get away with firing me.'

'It's not a question of getting away with it,' said Luke with exaggerated patience. 'I own the mill. I can hire and fire whom I please. It would save you both a lot of trouble if you could get that straight.'

Perhaps it was the edge of contempt in his voice that he did not bother to disguise that triggered Julie's temper. 'So you'll get rid of Frank just as you got rid of my father! That seems to be your way of thanking the people who try and help you out, doesn't it, Luke?' Recklessly she added, 'When are you planning to get rid of me? Am I next on the list?'

'No, Julie,' he answered, every word clipped. 'You stay with me.'

Completely ignoring Luke, Frank said to his sister, 'You're a fool if you do. He's got it in for the Taggarts. First Dad, he eased him out and let him die—just another useless old man, after all. Now me. So why don't you beat him to it, Jul? Get Beth and come back with me tonight.'

'She'll do that over my dead body,' Luke rapped. 'Beth stays here. If Julie wants to leave without her, that's up to her.'

Only yesterday Julie had been swept with happiness in her rediscovery that she loved Luke. But now it seemed impossible that the man who stood quite still by the table, his eyes coal-black and impenetrable, his face set and hard, was the same man who had made such impassioned love to her under the poplars. In an anguish deeper than any she had ever experienced, she whispered, 'Let us both go, Luke—Beth and me. You don't need us. You don't need anyone.'

'Beth is my daughter—she stays.'

'You know I can't go without her!'

'That's your problem, isn't it?'

'How can you be so cruel, Luke?' she cried, her pride in tatters. 'Please let me go.'

'*You* can go—I already told you that. But not Beth.'

'You hate me, don't you?' she whispered. 'You only put up with me because I'm Beth's mother.' She drew a long, shuddering breath. 'If that's the way you want it, Luke, that's the way you can have it—but I don't want you to lay a finger on me again, do you hear?'

So acute had been her pain that she had almost forgotten Frank's presence. Now he threatened, 'You touch her, Luke Marshall, and I'll have the police out here so fast you——'

Wearily Julie interrupted, 'Don't be so melodramatic, Frank. You can hardly get the police if a man chooses to sleep with his wife. I think you'd better go—I've had enough of all this.'

Was it her imagination that for a split second as her

brother's eyes rested on her they were as cold and inimical as Luke's had been? Then he walked over to her, and the nightmare sense of distortion was gone, for he was once again the Frank she had always known and looked up to, the big brother who was her protector and friend. 'Okay, I'll go,' he said gently, resting his hands on her shoulders, and talking as if they were the only two people in the room. 'But I hate leaving you here, and I want you to know if you need anything, anything at all, you can call me—day or night. Have you got that?'

'Yes.' She reached up and kissed his cheek. 'Thanks, Frank.'

'You've got my home phone number and for the next week at least you can reach me at the mill during the day.' His pale eyes flickered momentarily in Luke's direction, as blank of expression as a mountain cat's, and Julie shivered. 'After that, we'll have to see, won't we?' Frank finished softly.

She could take no more. Moving back abruptly, she repeated, 'You'd better go. I'll keep in touch.'

'Okay. 'Bye.' He brushed past Luke and ran lightly down the back steps. In a moment his car door slammed and the sound of its motor gradually diminished in the distance.

Julie sank down in the nearest chair, resting her head on her hands and feeling utterly drained. But worse than the physical exhaustion was the terrifying realisation that history was repeating itself, for once again she was enmeshed in conflict between the people she loved, in events she could not understand. Cut off from reality, adrift in a desolate landscape where nothing was as it appeared to be. . . .

Something heavy came to rest on her shoulder. She looked around and saw that it was Luke's hand, and realised he was standing very close to her. She shrank away from him, pushing his hand off. 'Don't!'

'Julie, we've got to talk——'

Frantically she got to her feet, facing him like an animal at bay. 'No, we don't! We have nothing to say to each other, Luke—it's all been said.'

'Frank's poisoning your mind against me.'

'That's got nothing to do with it,' she cried wildly. 'I

just want to be left alone!' Whirling, she ran from the room and up the stairs, going to her own room and slamming the door shut behind her. With some confused idea that he might try and follow her, she shoved a chair under the handle before throwing herself face down on the bed, the tears already running down her cheeks. In a very elemental way she had been telling the truth when she had said that Frank had nothing to do with her present state of emotion; she was not crying because Luke and Frank had quarrelled, not even because suspicion against her husband was once again rearing its ugly head. No, it was not that simple. She was crying because she loved Luke, loved him with all her heart—and he did not love her. All along he had been putting up with her because of Beth, tolerating her presence because it gave him access to the daughter he loved. For there was no doubt that he loved Beth . . . as there was equally no doubt he despised Beth's mother. And there was nothing she could do to break free, for she could not possibly leave without Beth. She was trapped. Every day she would have to see Luke, to eat with him and talk to him, to share the same roof, to sleep within fifty feet of him. Loving him, and knowing herself unloved . . . it would be unbearable.

Smothering her sobs in the pillow, she must eventually have fallen asleep, for her next conscious impression was of light, soft pearly light diffusing through the tall window. Her eyes were aching from the tears she had shed; her body felt lethargic, as though every limb was weighted down. Moving very slowly, she pulled on a housecoat, splashed cold water on her tear-swollen face, and went to check on Beth. The child was still sleeping, her tiny hands loosely curled on the pillow. So it was not Beth who had woken her . . . then her body tensed, for she heard the sounds of movement from downstairs. Luke must just have pulled on his boots, for where before there had been only silence, now there was the tattoo of his heels on the pine flooring. Poised to run should she hear him coming upstairs, Julie waited, her face set with misery. It would have been better, she thought numbly, if she had never realised she still loved Luke, far better. Then the knowledge that he was using her as a means to keep his daughter would not have been such a devastating blow. . . .

To her ears came the echo of footsteps on the back stairs, followed by the closing of the back door. Suddenly brought to life, she ran swiftly down the hall to Luke's room. Edging the curtains open a fraction, she gazed down into the yard. Luke was striding across the grass to the parked truck, a looped rope across one shoulder, a saddlebag in his other hand. Even from this distance he looked confident and alert, the very image of a man about to spend his working day in the place he loved. He flung the gear into the back of the truck, then swung himself up into the seat, driving away without a backward glance. No cares on his mind, she thought bitterly; for him nothing had changed. But for herself the whole world had turned upside down and she had no idea how she would be able to cope; even as she stood there watching the dust cloud from the truck waft across the fields, she felt fresh tears well up into her eyes.

Silence settled on the house once more. Silence and a sense of isolation so total that Julie recoiled from the window with its view of fields and hills and hovering, encroaching mountains. She was dwarfed to insignificance by the landscape. It did not need her. It would go on without her as it had always gone on, vast and uncaring. She could leave it and it would never notice. She could leave. . . .

The car, silver-grey in the morning light, was parked by the side of the house. A set of keys was in her hand-bag—at least they had been yesterday. Hurrying back to her room, Julie searched through the contents of her handbag, the keys, of course, being the very last thing she found. So she still had them . . . it had obviously not occurred to Luke to remove them.

Without making any kind of a conscious decision, Julie went to her room and began folding clothes into a suit-case—dresses and skirts, suitable for the working world, rather than the jeans and cords she wore around the ranch. Blouses, sweaters, jewellery, shoes . . . her fingers moved nimbly even as her ears were straining for any sounds that might indicate Luke's return. It was foolish to think he would, yet today would be just the day he might have forgotten something. . . .

By the time she had finished her own packing, Beth was awake. Because Julie was in a hurry, Beth chose to upset her cereal bowl and spill her milk, and it seemed to take forever to clean up the kitchen, dress the child in fresh clothes, and gather up all the paraphernalia Beth would need. Finally Julie was ready: everything loaded in the car, Beth strapped in her car seat, the house left locked and empty. Purposely Julie had left no note, for she did not want Luke to follow her. Now as she stood by the car the windows of the house seemed like eyes, sad and forlorn, abandoned. All morning she had acted without thought, automatically doing all the things that needed doing. Now, for the first time, the enormity of what she was about to do hit home. She was leaving Luke. Taking their daughter and running away, heading for the anonymity of the city. Running for her life . . . yet as she looked around her, she knew that in a very real way, she was tearing herself up by the roots. She, as much as Luke, belonged here. It was home.

A fine drizzle was falling, blurring the foothills, blotting out the mountain peaks. On the plains all the shades of green and gold were softened, blending into one another, making of the landscape an abstract painting, an impression of space and colour that was gentle and serene. And she was leaving this to go to the noise and confusion and dirt of the city . . . blinking back more tears, Julie got into the car, forcing herself to turn the key in the ignition.

No more backward thoughts, she decided with a kind of desperate resolution. A clean break from Luke and all he represented in terms of lost love and pain and disillusion was the only possible answer. She would be destroyed if she remained with a man who despised her. Ahead of her lay a very different life, certainly, but to the best of her ability she must make it rewarding, fashion a new life for herself and for Beth. She would have to ask Richard for help to get started, that seemed unavoidable, but it would not be for long. She would make herself independent, free of emotional entanglements. She turned the car around and headed east.

The worst parts of the journey were driving past the corral and stables, every nerve on edge in case Luke should see her, and then driving through Henderson, knowing she was purposely avoiding any contact with Maggie. Once the town was behind her, Julie relaxed slightly, soothed by the swish of the wipers on the windshield, able to chat to Beth and even sing her little songs. The next hurdle was coping with the increasing flow of traffic as she approached the environs of the city; she had a fairly clear idea of where she was going and finally found a parking spot within walking distance of Richard's office. But by now it was lunchtime, and it would be useless to try and phone him for at least an hour.

Conscious of the fact that her money was in limited supply, Julie bought a light lunch for herself and Beth in a downtown café, deliberately dawdling over the meal to give Richard time to get back to the office. Then, Beth perched on her hip, she dialled his number in a phone booth. 'May I speak to Richard Buchanan, please?'

'One moment, please.'

Richard's voice, clipped and impatient. 'Buchanan here.'

'Richard, it's Julie.'

A blank silence. 'Who?'

She took a steadying breath. 'Julie Marshall. From Henderson.'

'Julie! Sorry, I wasn't thinking straight. How are you?'

'Well, that's why I'm calling,' she said nervously. 'I'm here in Calgary with Beth. I've left Luke.'

'I see.' Another silence. 'Are you planning to stay in Calgary?'

'I hope so.' She laboured on, aware that the conversation was not going quite the way she had thought it would. 'I'm hoping you still have a job to offer me.'

'Lord, Julie, I'm sorry. That position was filled two weeks ago. I thought you'd given up the idea of coming here, you see.'

'I had—but then I changed my mind.' Beth was becoming a dead weight, and awkwardly Julie tried to shift position.

'Look, I've got to go. I've got a meeting sharp at two. Can you entertain yourself this afternoon? Then why don't you come to my apartment around six or six-thirty? I should be home by then, and we can talk this whole thing over. If I'd only known you were coming, I could have left the key with the doorman.'

'You're sure that's all right?' she faltered, disconcerted by what she could only construe as an unflattering lack of welcome in his attitude.

'Of course. See you around six-thirty.'

'Thank you.' But his receiver had already been replaced.

Julie hoisted Beth up into her arms and hurried along the crowded, rain-wet sidewalk to the car. The afternoon stretched ahead of her needing somehow to be filled, although she had no idea how. Now that she was off the phone it occurred to her that she did not want to be in Richard's apartment this evening, for it was the logical place for Luke to start looking for her—if, indeed, he did look for her, and always provided he could find out the address. She felt a faint spark of hope. Luke had only met Richard once, and it was not likely Frank would reveal the address. So perhaps she was worrying for nothing—which still did not resolve the problem of this afternoon. If she had been on her own, she would have gone searching for an employment agency and a rental agency. But the rain had settled into a steady downpour, and the thought of trudging along the streets with Beth was mind-boggling. For similar reasons the zoo was out; and the planetarium did not seem quite the place for a one-year-old. Beth settled the problem herself by falling asleep in the car seat, so of necessity Julie had to stay where she was, staring through the windshield at the never-ending flow of traffic and trying not to fret over her enforced inactivity.

When Beth awoke she was irritable and hard to please, obviously wondering why she was cooped up in the car, and in desperation Julie drove to one of the indoor shopping malls and wheeled the child around in a cart, when that palled letting her explore one of the children's play areas. The time dragged by. After only a few hours in Calgary, Julie would have given almost anything to be back at the ranch and in her own house—almost anything but the thought of living with Luke, she thought painfully.

Finally it was time to leave for Richard's. He lived in a luxurious, ultra-modern apartment building, on the tenth floor. To her amusement the uniformed doorman eyed Julie somewhat askance, and she could only assume Richard was not often visited by young women complete with a baby, a dilapidated teddy bear, and a nappy bag. The elevator whisked them upstairs and then Richard was opening the door and ushering them in. 'Hi, Julie. Hello, Beth.' He hesitated, then quickly kissed Julie on the cheek. 'Sorry about this afternoon. It was a high-powered meeting, no way I could get out of it. Would you like something to eat? Or——' He quizzically eyed Julie's strained face and shadowed eyes '—how about a drink?'

She plunked Beth on the floor and straightened, pushing her hair back from her face. With a confused idea of job interviews she had dressed this morning in a mauve linen skirt with a flowered blouse, and now she felt crumpled and grubby, and very tired. 'A drink sounds marvellous,' she said, horrified to hear her voice quiver.

When Richard came back into the living room with the drinks, he flicked on the television for Beth's benefit, and under cover of the cartoon soundtrack said to Julie, 'Now, what's up?'

Her voice still with a tendency to wobble, Julie briefly recounted the events of the past couple of days, omitting only that she and Luke had made love high in the hills. 'The trouble is,' she concluded, 'I've discovered I still love him, Richard. I guess that never changed. I was fooling myself when I said I hated him. I almost wish I did hate him, it would make it easier. . . .' Her words trailed off.

'Which is a nice way of telling me that even though you've left Luke—because you have, haven't you?— there's no particular hope for me,' Richard said drily.

'I'm sorry, Richard.' She reached out and touched his sleeve. 'Truly sorry. I came to you today because I didn't know where else to go. Frank—well, I could have gone to Frank, I suppose, but he's been behaving so strangely lately. I don't really understand him. . . .'

'Surely you're not just now realising Frank hates Luke's guts?'

'Don't be silly, Richard—of course he doesn't,' she retorted.

'Julie dear, he does. And has done for as long as I can remember.'

'He has no reason to hate Luke——'

'He has every reason in the world. For all that I'm no psychologist, even I can see that Luke has everything Frank wants—money, social position, power. And a beautiful wife, who happens to be Frank's sister. I'm quite sure he saw your marriage as the last straw—a going over to the enemy.'

'Not Frank!' Julie protested, with the frightening sense they were discussing different people.

'Frank's one of the best poker players in the county— keep that in mind,' Richard said cryptically.

With the feeling she was fighting a rearguard action, she said, 'It's Luke who hates Frank, not the other way round.'

'Believe what you like, Julie,' Richard replied with faint impatience. 'What I've said to you is only my opinion, of course. Anyway, it's neither here nor there. What we should be discussing is your future. What are your plans?'

'Get a job. Find a playschool for Beth, and a small furnished apartment,' she said steadily.

He grinned reluctantly. 'Can't deny your spunk, at least! Another drink?'

With faint surprise she saw her glass was empty. 'I shouldn't really——'

'Come on. You're not going anywhere tonight. You can stay here until you find an apartment.'

'I'm scared Luke will follow me.'

'He doesn't know where I live—and Frank will be the last person to tell him. Just as well, too. I've no desire for a second encounter with your husband.' Richard came back with a second drink. 'A friend gave me a casserole, so I've put it in the oven. Have you got something for Beth?'

She took a sip of her drink and leaned back in the

chair. Richard's living room was furnished in rather more modern style than she cared for, but there was no denying its comfort, and for the first time that day she began to relax. Slipping off her shoes, she tucked her feet under her. 'Yes, I've got babyfood with me. Oh, Richard, it's good to be here—I'm starting to feel half human again.'

'Good.' He eyed her reflectively. 'You can say what you like about loving Luke—but you've only been away from him for a matter of hours and already you're looking better. The guy's no good for you, Julie. If you can make this break and get established on your own—and I'll help you any way I can—it'd be so much better for you, I'm convinced of it.'

Although there was no doubting Richard's sincerity, she wished she was half as convinced. 'Thank you, Richard . . . perhaps you're right.' She sighed. 'All I know is that when I got up this morning I had to get away from him.'

'That's a start.' He stood up. 'I'm going to make a salad. Today's paper's over there—why don't you start looking through the "help wanted" ads and see what you can find that might be suitable?'

Grateful for his pragmatic attitude, for she had been a little afraid he might make emotional demands on her for which she was not ready, she got down on the thick mushroom-coloured carpet with the newspaper, somewhat hindered by Beth who wanted to crumple the paper into balls. There were a number of hopeful leads, which she and Richard discussed over the meal. Then he got her suitcase out of the car, and she settled Beth down for the night.

Richard had put a James Last record on the stereo, had loosened his tie, and was sitting beside her on the chesterfield going over the list of vacant apartments when the door buzzer sounded. He went to answer it and she could hear the distorted voice speaking over the intercom, then the buzzer as Richard pressed the lock release. 'It's Frank,' he said. 'Odd, he hasn't dropped by for quite a while. I wonder if he knows you're here.'

In a minute or two there came a tap at the door, and Richard went to answer it. From her vantage point on the chesterfield Julie saw the door suddenly swing inwards as though pushed, and heard a voice that was not Frank's demand, 'Julie's here, isn't she? Where is she?'

She was not surprised. She had somehow known that Luke would come after her. Slowly she got to her feet as Luke brushed past Richard and came into the hallway; she stood still, a slim straight figure in her full skirt and flowered blouse, her face watchful and guarded. Without any particular emphasis, she said, 'How did you know where to find me?'

Across the twenty feet or so of carpet that separated them Luke gave one swift glance around and stared at her. 'It didn't take much brain work to figure out you'd run to Richard. After that it was only a question of getting his address from Frank.'

'Frank told you?'

He grinned unpleasantly. 'After a little coaxing, yes.'

With a polite attempt to make of Luke's visit a social occasion, Richard said, 'Can I offer you a drink?'

'No. I'm not staying.' With deliberate challenge Luke added, 'I've come to get my wife and my daughter and take them home where they belong.'

Still very much the urbane host, Richard said, 'I'm not sure I agree with you—that they belong with you, that is. Julie—and you know this as well as I do—is not the type of woman to leave her husband unless she feels she has good reason.'

'Oh?' said Luke nastily. 'Aren't you reason enough?'

Richard flushed. 'Julie didn't come here with any idea of marrying me——'

'She couldn't very well. She does still happen to be married to me.'

Bravely Richard ploughed on. 'She came because she'd become so unhappy living with you that she couldn't stand it any longer.'

Ferociously Luke snapped, 'Basically none of this is any of your business, Buchanan. Julie, get your stuff together. Where's Beth?'

'It happens to be my business because I care for Julie,' Richard persisted. 'I don't like to see her unhappy. I think you both should——'

'Shut up!' Luke barked. He took one step towards Richard, who held his ground with a steadfastness Julie could only admire. 'I don't give a damn what you think. Julie's my wife and she's going to live with me. And both of you might as well get that straight.'

He was still standing in the hall, obviously with no intention of going any further. Dressed in his work clothes, Levis and a faded denim jacket, he towered over Richard. He looked tough and dangerous, as though he was holding himself back from physical violence by only a thin thread of control; he also looked aggressively masculine, the male come in search of his mate, as powerful and unpredictable as a cougar in mating season.

Knowing she was the only one who could lessen the tension, Julie said very quietly, 'Do you only want me back because of Beth, Luke?'

Luke's head swung around to her. His eyes were burning like coal, and instinctively she knew he would tell her the truth. 'No,' he said equally quietly. 'That's not why I want you back. I want you back because you belong to me. You're my woman.'

It was enough. He was still a stranger to her, still the man who had lied and stolen, the man who could make love to her with passionate tenderness yet speak of her as a belonging—but at least he wanted her for herself. Turning to Richard, she said, 'I'm sorry I've embroiled you in all this, Richard. I have to go back with him—I don't really understand why, I just know I have to.'

Ignoring the fact that Luke was watching every move, she reached up and kissed Richard's cheek. 'You've been a good friend to me—a better friend than I've been to you. Thank you. I hope—well, I think it's best you forget about me.' She looked over at Luke, her face pale and unsmiling. 'We'd better wake Beth up. My suitcase is in her room.'

She led the way into the spare bedroom. Beth was curled in a ball in the very middle of the double bed, her curls ink-black against the pillow. Very gently Luke reached over and picked her up while Julie tucked a blanket around her. Drowsily the child looked up, recognised Luke, and allowed her head to flop forward against his chest, as the thick, dark eyelashes, so like her father's, flickered shut again. She looked so tiny and defenceless in Luke's arms that Julie felt tears prick at her eyes. If there was one thing she could never fault in Luke, it was his gentleness with Beth. . . .

'Where's the car?' he asked softly, so as not to disturb the sleeping child.

'In the basement parking area.'

'Okay. Can you manage the suitcase?'

They left the bedroom together. Richard was waiting in the hall. 'Goodbye, Richard,' Julie said. 'And thanks again—for everything.'

Beside her she heard Luke speak. 'Sorry if I was abrupt with you earlier, Buchanan, I wasn't thinking very straight. You've been a friend to Julie at a time when she needed one—I realise that now. Thanks.'

Knowing she would never understand the male psyche, Julie watched Richard and Luke shake hands, rather awkwardly because of Beth. Perhaps Luke would always have the ability to take her completely by surprise at times—certainly the generosity of his last speech had done so.

It was only when they arrived at the car that she thought to ask, 'How did you get here?'

'Jake drove me in the truck. So now he can drive it back—he's parked outside.'

'You were that sure you'd find me?'

'Yes. If you hadn't been at Richard's, I'd have turned the city upside down until I found you.'

He had unlocked the car and now lowered Beth into Julie's arms. Then he threw the case into the trunk, and came around to the driver's side. Only then did she ask, 'Why?'

He glanced over at her. 'I don't know that I can explain why, Julie. Nothing very rational about it, I guess.'

Skilfully he backed around the concrete columns, and then drove up the ramp and pulled in by the curb. 'There's the truck—I won't be a minute.'

She watched him dash across the road, the pavement slick and shiny with rain, the puddles reflecting the over-head street lights and the red and yellow lights of passing cars. When he came back and was seated beside her again, he said as if there had been no break in the conversation, 'Will you leave me again? Tomorrow or next week or two months from now?'

'I don't think so, Luke. I think we're caught in this marriage, you and I—for today and tomorrow and all the tomorrows to come. We can't escape.'

He was weaving in and out of the traffic and each approaching car threw his profile into brilliant relief. He said very carefully, 'Do you see it as a prison, Julie?'

'I don't know—I honestly don't know,' she answered unhappily. 'It isn't as it used to be, I know that.'

'But we can't go backwards, can we? Life's not like that. We can only go forwards, and do the best we can with what's left.' He looked over at her and her heart went out to him. He looked tired and older than usual, and the deep sadness in his eyes made her want to weep. 'Let's make a pledge,' he said quietly. 'Let's both try and do the best with what we have. For better or for worse we *are* married to each other—let's try not to tear each other apart as we have been doing. Would you agree to that?'

She was filled with a terrible sense of hopelessness. She and Luke, who had had such a bright and beautiful beginning, were now reduced to the lowest level, of promising not to hurt each other. They had fallen that far in three short years. And what did they have left? The love that had burned so brightly between them—that was gone; that she still loved him was of little use, for in a marriage the love could not be one-sided. The trust was gone. She had thought she knew him through and through, and that knowledge had been a mirage, a false image—his true colours were those that had been painted in the courtroom, the ugly colours of untruth and theft. Yet she could have sworn that the man sitting beside her now was being painfully honest with himself and with her as it was possible for a man to be . . . oh, God, where would it end, this endless circle of doubt and confusion and pain?

'You don't want to make that promise? Is that why you're so quiet?'

He would not beg, not Luke. But there was such deadness in his voice, such utter desolation, that she said quickly, 'No, that's not it—I was just thinking, that's all.' Moving Beth's weight to one arm, she rested her other hand on Luke's knee. 'I would like to promise to do the very best I can.' Loving you as I do, she added in the silence of her heart.

Briefly he rested his own hand on top of hers. 'I make that promise, too.' Then he smiled at her in an apparent effort to relieve the solemnity. 'And now I have a proposal. Why don't we take a couple of days and go up to the mountain cabin? Maybe it would be good for us to spend a bit of time alone together.'

'At the cabin? Oh, Luke. . . .' They had spent their honeymoon at the cabin. How could she bear to go back there now, under these so very different circumstances? 'You were the one who said we can't go back,' she said in a low voice.

'It will be a new beginning, Julie.'

No, she cried silently. No, it isn't that easy! Revisiting a place where they had been happy would not bring back the happiness. On the contrary: it would only counterpoint how woefully they had strayed.

'Please, Julie? Let's at least try it.'

She could not refuse him when he asked like that. Helplessly she said, 'All right.' In an effort to be practical she added, 'What about Beth?'

'You could run her in to Maggie's in the morning. Then we'd leave after lunch—mid-afternoon or so.'

He had it all worked out. She gazed down at her hands, loosely linked around Beth's sleeping body; her wedding band gleamed gold in the semi-dark. 'I guess that would be all right,' she said, trying to put a little enthusiasm in her words, but succeeding only in sounding very tired.

'Why don't you try and sleep a little? We won't be home for an hour or so.'

Obediently she let her head fall back and closed her eyes, her ears absorbing the rhythmic swish-swish of the wiper blades and the hiss of tyres on the wet road. Soothing, repetitive sounds that lulled her into a doze. . . .

CHAPTER TEN

THE next morning Julie gathered up all Beth's things and drove her into town. The first stop was the drugstore to pick up baby powder and shampoo. On her way back to the car, Julie heard a gruff male voice call her name. 'Miss Julie!'

She turned, already guessing who it was: old Tom Mossman, who had worked for several years before his retirement as one of the foremen in the mill. He had left Henderson, she realised with a sinking heart, before the trouble had begun, to settle on a small acreage outside of Cochrane; she had not seen or heard of him since then.

'Hello, Tom,' she said warmly, holding out her hand which he clasped in his own calloused palms. 'You don't look a year older.'

His sharp blue eyes twinkled under bushy white eyebrows. 'You always had the knack of making a fellow feel good.' With the license of his years he went on bluntly, 'You look older, Julie, and not very happy. I only heard last year about Luke being in prison—couldn't believe my ears. Whoever framed him must have done one hell of a good job to have made it stick, because anyone with half a brain would know Luke would never have done what he was accused of. Luke Marshall steal from the folks who depended on him? I never heard such nonsense in my life!'

Julie stared at him. 'You knew Luke for a long time, didn't you?'

'Since he was a little guy, sneaking out of school to go fishing in the creek. Don't get me wrong—there was always lots of mischief in him, plenty of high spirits. But he'd never do anything that would hurt anyone else—not Luke.'

In a strange way she felt as though a weight had been lifted off her shoulders. 'A lot of the townspeople seem to think he did it,' she ventured.

'That's because they got touched where it hurts—in their wallets. Find the real thief and they'd forget Luke quick enough.'

Could he be right? But he was still speaking ... 'As long as *you* believed in him, and his grandma, and the ones closest to him, I don't reckon the opinion of the town would bother Luke overmuch.'

A summer breeze lifted a strand of her hair, blowing it across her face. 'But I didn't, Tom,' she said flatly, and somehow it was a relief to spill it all out. 'At the trial he wouldn't even defend himself, and then he wouldn't let me visit him and he didn't write ... and if he didn't do it, who did?'

Tom looked at her quizzically. 'Well now, I don't know about that. Would have to be someone in the right position, wouldn't it? Your dad and your brother were both right there, weren't they? Never did quite go along with that brother of yours. He had eyes that reminded me of an old coyote I once knew who'd steal the food right from under your nose and sneak off into the woods before you could say "boo".'

'It couldn't have been Frank!' she protested vehemently.

'Well now, I didn't say it was. All I know is it wasn't Luke, and that if he took the rap and wouldn't tell you why, there was a reason, and a damned good one, you can be sure of that.' He grunted. 'Too bad you let him down, though.'

Tom had always been one to call a spade a spade. 'I did, didn't I?' Julie said faintly, suddenly overwhelmed by the enormity of what she had done. Somehow, despite all the evidence, she should have stood by her husband. ...

'You were pretty young, mind you,' Tom said. 'And all by yourself, and with a baby on the way, I hear.'

She brightened. 'Yes—would you like to see her? She's in the car.'

As Julie lifted Beth out of the car seat, Tom said with great satisfaction, 'Spitting image of her dad, and a beauty like her mum besides. Another few years and you'll have your troubles keeping the boys away.'

Julie giggled. 'You're a hopeless flatterer! Tom, you must come for a visit. We're going up into the mountains for a couple of days, but once we're back, I'd love you to come and stay with us—will you do that?'

'How about Friday?' he said promptly. 'Don't have to be back at my place until Monday or Tuesday. It'd do my heart good to see Luke again.'

They made the necessary arrangements and then waved goodbye. Her brow puckered thoughtfully, Julie drove on to Maggie's. She had the feeling she was standing on the brink of a discovery that would change her life, yet she was frightened to commit herself, to take that final step that might radically alter her relationship with those who had been closest to her—her father, her brother, her husband.

While Beth was busily engaged pulling Maggie's saucepans out of the cupboard, Julie said under cover of the noise, 'Maggie, you never believed Luke stole the money, did you?'

If the older woman was startled by Julie's introduction of a subject they had always assiduously avoided, she did not show it. 'I'm sure he didn't,' she said quietly.

'Then who did?' Julie blurted. 'It would have had to have been my father or Frank, wouldn't it? There was no one else in a position to do it.'

Maggie sat down at the table, her blue eyes compassionate as she saw the conflict in Julie's face. 'Your father isn't here to defend himself, Julie.'

The girl sank down in the opposite chair, burying her head in her hands. 'Not Dad—it couldn't have been Dad!' She raised her ravaged face. 'But if it wasn't Dad, then it has to be Frank!' Now that she had started, she couldn't seem to stop, and all the confusion that had been bottled up for too long came tumbling out. 'I believed that Luke did it—I didn't see how else it could be explained. But now I'm beginning to think I've done him a terrible wrong, and he'll never forgive me for it.' Her words were increasingly incoherent. 'That's why he doesn't love me any more, because I called him a thief and a liar! How can I blame him for not loving me? I'm no better than the townspeople. Oh, Maggie, I've ruined our marriage. . . .'

Maggie got up, grasping Julie firmly by the shoulders. 'Hold it, now,' she ordered. 'First of all, have you told Luke any of this?'

'No,' Julie quavered. 'I'm only just discovering it myself.'

'Okay. Well, before you talk of ruining your marriage, try explaining it all to Luke. And secondly, Luke has some explaining to do himself. It's all very well to be the strong and silent type, but it's not always easiest on those around you. He owes you some kind of an explanation of why he behaved as he did.'

Slowly Julie raised her head, Maggie's common-sense attitude bracing her as no amount of sympathy would have done. 'I guess you're right,' she said slowly.

'Of course I am. Luke's not the easiest person in the world to live with. But one thing I'm sure of—he's honest.' She added briskly, 'Now, I'm going to make you a quick lunch before you head back.'

It was after two when Julie got back to the house. Luke's truck was parked outside, the saddlebags in a heap on the ground nearby. Suddenly shy of facing him in the light of so much new self-knowledge, she walked slowly up to the veranda.

She need not have worried. As she climbed the steps, Luke came out of the house with an armload of tack. 'There you are,' he said casually. 'Want to get changed? And pack a couple of changes of clothes, won't you? I think once that's done, everything's just about ready to go.'

'Fine,' she said with a quick, meaningless smile. 'I won't be long.' Conscious only of a profound sense of anticlimax, she ran upstairs.

Within the hour they had saddled up the horses and were on their way. Although at first they followed the northerly route they had taken before, they soon branched off to the west, climbing steadily all the time, giving the horses their heads and allowing them to set their own pace. After three hours they were high in the hills and Luke called a halt for supper. As he lit a small fire, Julie went to the stream with a billycan for water, looking

around her appreciatively. They were completely out of
sight of any other human habitation, the two of them
alone in a wilderness world of hills and mountains, trees
and rocks and tumbling water. The boughs of the pine
trees sighed in the wind, while high overhead an eagle
soared with widespread wings on air currents invisible to
the eye. But it was the mountains that dominated the
scene. For thousands of years they had thrust up to the
sky, and for thousands more they would remain, massive
and awe-inspiring, the high peaks tipped with snow.

'How about bringing the water, Jul?'

Hurriedly she filled the billycan with the ice-cold water
and carried it back to Luke. 'I was daydreaming,' she
said lightly. 'How very insignificant this——' her arms
indicated the sweep of forest and the majestic mountains
'—makes you feel.'

Luke hung the billycan from three forked sticks; a frying
pan with two sizzling steaks was already on a rack over
the fire. 'Mmm, you're right,' he said absently, turning
the steaks. 'Hungry?'

'Starving! Is the coffee in the haversack?'

They ate in a companionable silence, amused to see a
grey-plumaged spruce grouse stalk out of the woods and
with great dignity beat a stately retreat when it sighted
them. After the meal they cleaned up quickly, because
Luke was anxious to reach the cabin before dark. As they
followed the trail up the banks of the creek they saw a
cow moose and her calf cross the water ahead of them
and plunge into the woods, and twice the horses flushed
more grouse, the whirr of wings incredibly loud in the
cool evening air. The mountains were closer now, the
lower slopes crowding almost to the opposite banks of the
creek; on their right was the dark impenetrable forest of
alpine fir and white pine, home of bear and deer and elk.
The creek was widening, and Julie knew they were approaching the lake. Finally the forest opened in front of
them into an alpine meadow that edged the mirror-
smooth waters of the lake. The sun had set behind the
mountains, giving the lake the patina of gold, making of
the trees on the far shore stark black silhouettes. The cabin
itself was set on the slope of the meadow. Built of logs and

roofed with weathered planks, it had faded into its environment so naturally that it took a minute for Julie to discern it in the twilight.

'Two or three weeks ago I had Jake bring a couple of the men up here to clean it up,' Luke remarked. 'The squirrels had found their way in, so it was a bit of a mess.' He dismounted. 'I wouldn't have wanted to get here much later. By the time we look after the horses and get a fire started and unpack everything, it'll be time to settle for the night.'

They had not discussed sleeping arrangements, although Julie knew the cabin had two double bunks. Would she be sharing a bed with Luke? Was that part of the promise she had made? One thing was sure—she lacked the courage to ask.

Luke hobbled Whistler and Dancer while Julie carried in the gear. It was nearly dark now, and it was a relief to light the oil lamp, and start the woodstove; the crackle and snap of the kindling made a cheerful sound of welcome. As she stood by one of the bunks shaking out her bedroll, Julie looked around her, and for a moment it was as if it were three years ago when she and Luke had first come here, late on the day of their wedding. The same rough flooring, the same pine beams and crudely hewn furniture; the same bearskin rugs on the floor. That night so long ago she had felt shy and uncertain and afraid, for she and Luke had never made love before. Tonight she seemed to have many of the same feelings; as Luke walked in the door, shutting it carefully behind him to keep out the insects attracted by the light, she was aware of her nerves tightening uncomfortably. He picked up his saddlebags and went over to the other bunk, matter-of-factly unstrapping his bedroll and spreading it out.

Julie turned away, for she had her answer. The pattern that had been set ever since Luke had come home was to continue—they would sleep apart, like two chance-met strangers.

He apparently noticed nothing amiss, busying himself by putting some water on to heat and hanging up their gear. 'It's been a long day—I'm just about ready to turn in. Are you, Jul?'

'Yes, I am tired,' she said. It was partially true, for the

emotional strain of the past few days had taken its toll. But she knew that one touch of his hand, one kiss, would dissipate that tiredness as though it had never been.

'There's hot water here if you want to wash. I'll just go out and check the horses.'

He was treating her as if she were his sister, or a distant acquaintance, she thought resentfully, as she splashed some water on her face and soaped her hands and arms, rinsing them off quickly, and slipping into a softly pleated nightgown of thin, pale yellow cotton. She had braided her hair for comfort on the journey up; when Luke came back in, she was brushing it loose with vigorous strokes until it fell about her shoulders with the dark sheen of satin.

She was perched on the edge of the bunk in one of her favourite postures, one foot tucked underneath her, not looking at him as she kept mental count of the number of strokes. Momentarily he stood still, but the catch in his breath was lost in the hum of the woodstove and Julie was oblivious of the tightening of his jawline. Then, as if nothing had happened, he walked over to the oil lamp and said levelly, 'Is it okay if I turn this off?'

She put down the brush and, very conscious of him watching her, slid under the blankets. He turned down the wick until there was only the faintest glow of light left. His black hair and black eyes became part of the blackness around him and as he moved across the room to his own bed she could see only the pale gleam of his face and arms. Then she heard the faint sounds of his clothing as he undressed, the rustle of the bedding as he climbed into the bunk. 'Goodnight, Julie. Sleep well.'

Her throat was tight with unshed tears. 'Goodnight,' she responded, turning her back to him, her eyes staring through the darkness at the pine board wall in a frustration that was more than just physical. She had wanted to tell him of her new-found conviction that he was innocent—but how do you tell a man who has treating you as a stranger that after two years you have suddenly decided he is not a criminal? She felt lonely and unsure of herself, for to have him in the same room, yet totally unreachable, filled her with an acute misery that she could only keep to herself. She could not, it was certain, share it with him. . . .

She fell asleep eventually, insensibly soothed by the gentle murmur of the fire and the vast surrounding silence of the night. And she awoke to terror, to a body thrashing in the other bed, to a harsh voice repeating endlessly, senselessly, 'No, no, no. . . .'

She lay still, eyes wide open, heart pounding, briefly suspended in the no-man's-land between sleep and wakefulness. Then memory rushed back: the long journey to the cabin, the sense of an ineradicable distance between her and Luke, her unhappiness as she fell asleep . . . Luke too must have fallen asleep, for now he was dreaming, caught in the toils of a nightmare. . . .

She scrambled out of bed and ran over to the other bed, tripping over a rug as she went. 'Luke! Wake up.'

But her voice did not reach him. She grabbed his arms. 'Luke! Please, wake up!'

He shook her off as if she had been an insect and she stumbled backwards, suddenly terrified. She had never heard sounds from a man such as were coming from his throat—harsh sounds, no longer recognisable as words, but filled with a horror, a despair, that made her want to weep. She could not stand it any longer. She *had* to wake him up. With all her strength she grabbed him by the shoulders. He heaved himself away from her and again she heard that dreadful litany, 'No, no, no. . . .'

'Luke, I beg you—wake up!' she screamed, shaking him as hard as she could, then feeling herself being flung against the wall as he broke free. Her sharp cry of pain as her elbow struck a beam was quite involuntary, but it accomplished what her words had been unable to do. Luke's body suddenly stilled. Her eyes more accustomed to the darkness, she sensed him sit up. He was breathing in harsh gasps. 'Who's there?' he demanded.

'Luke? It's Julie,' she whispered, and suddenly she was sobbing with pure relief that he was released from whatever ghastly visions had been torturing him.

'Julie? Where are you? Hush, dear, don't cry.'

He was holding her close, and beneath her cheek she could feel the frantic racing of his heart. 'Oh, Luke, what was it? I couldn't wake you up——'

'I must have been dreaming. What did wake me? Did you cry out?'

'I was trying to shake you and you threw me against the wall,' she confessed, her voice wobbling in spite of herself.

'God, I'm sorry—I didn't hurt you, did I?'

'I'm all right.' She clutched at him convulsively. 'I'm so glad you're awake. Please—tell me what you were dreaming about.'

He fell back on the pillows, bringing her down beside him, and said harshly, 'I can't, Julie——'

'Was it about the prison?'

'Julie, it's not fair to even try and share it with you.'

She was struck by a new thought. 'You have this dream quite often, don't you?' she said, more as a statement than as a question. 'But because we've not been sleeping together, I haven't known about it until now. Am I right?'

'Yeah . . . a couple of times a week, usually.'

'Then you'd better tell me about it so I'll know what to do another time.'

'Wake me up any way you can,' he said with such heartfelt fervour that she almost laughed.

'I see. Well, next time just refrain from throwing me across the room, okay?'

He buried his face in her neck, inhaling the scented warmth of her skin. 'You're so sweet, Julie. So sane and kind and gentle. I needed you those two years—you don't know how much I needed you. But I couldn't bear to have you visit me there—it was no place for you.'

She didn't want to argue that now. Instead she repeated patiently, 'So tell me about the dream.'

His body shuddered reminiscently, and in a primitive flood of protectiveness she tightened her hold on him. 'It's hard to describe,' he said slowly. 'It's not so much the concrete images as the feelings that go along with them. I'm in a series of rooms. I leave one through the door, thinking I'm going to get out, but it leads into another one the same—painted grey all over with a window with bars on it and a door ahead of me. And when I go through that door it goes into another room and I know I'll keep going forever from room to room and I'll never get out and feel the sun and the wind on my face. . . .'

He was trembling. Tears were trickling down her cheeks and falling on his skin, and all Julie could do was hold him, for there was nothing she could say.

'Don't cry,' he said again. 'It's all over now.'

'I wish you could have shared it with me before,' she whispered painfully. 'But I can understand so well why you couldn't. You probably thought I'd say you deserved it——'

'Never that, Julie.'

She ignored him. 'Because all along I thought you'd done it, Luke. But not any more.' She felt the absolute stillness of his body and laboured on. 'I don't know who did it, I'm not sure I even want to know, but one thing I know and that is that you didn't.' She was crying again, the tears pouring from her eyes. 'I'm so sorry, Luke. I should have known you couldn't have done it. I should have trusted you. You must hate me for the way I behaved. . . .'

'No,' he said in a strange voice, 'I don't hate you. But I don't understand why you're changed.'

A sob hiccupped in her throat. 'I don't really, either. It's a combination of a whole lot of things—seeing you with Beth, the changes in Frank, seeing how the ranch hands respect you.' She stumbled to a halt, wishing she could say, 'Realising I still love you', yet somehow not able to bring herself to say the words.

'I see,' he said, although she was not sure that he did.

'I wanted to tell you before we went to bed, but you seemed . . . so far away. I just couldn't.'

'I can understand that—and it's largely my fault. One of the reasons I haven't been sleeping with you, Jul, is because of the nightmares.' He shifted restlessly. 'I guess I didn't want you to know about them. I was afraid you'd think I was playing for sympathy.'

'But I know about them now, don't I? So you don't have to worry about that any more. . . .' Greatly daring, she ran her fingers up his chest, pulling gently at the dark tangled hair. 'We could sleep together now, couldn't we?'

'You wouldn't be propositioning me, would you, Mrs Marshall?' he drawled, a note in his voice that made her nerves shiver with excitement.

'And if I were?'

'I might be tempted to do this. . . .' He kissed her slowly, lingeringly. 'And this. . . .' drawing his hands along the whole length of her body and pulling her close to his own.

It was she who was trembling now, and she who pulled his head down so they could kiss again. Something had been freed within her by her confession and heartfelt apology to Luke; she felt as she had when she had married him, full of love and longing, with an overwhelming need for the closeness that desire can bring. Boldly she took the initiative, guiding his hands to her breast and holding his palm so he could feel her quickened heartbeat, nibbling at his lips with her teeth, sliding her limbs to lie along the heavy warmth of his thighs. As if sensing her need, Luke allowed her to lead them deeper and deeper into the maze that was physical passion, until they were lost to everything but their frantic urge to become one, to break down all the barriers and for that brief, transitory moment that was out of time, be as one flesh.

And then it was over, and Julie was left with the exhaustion that was satiation, with a peace as calm as the dawning of the sun over the rim of the prairie. Her eyes drooped shut and her breathing slowed as she drifted into a deep and dreamless sleep.

Luke did not fall asleep immediately. His arm curved around Julie's shoulders, he held her close, his troubled black eyes gazing upwards at visions only he could see.

CHAPTER ELEVEN

THE next day would long remain in Julie's memory. The weather was perfect, a bright sun in a cloudless sky, with the slight touch of coolness in the air that the altitude brought. In daylight she could now see that the meadow was adrift with wild flowers, red and orange and yellow, white and pink, waving gently in the breeze; the surface of the lake sparkled in the sun. They swam and lay on the shore to dry; they hiked farther up the trail to see the waterfalls cascade over the rocks; they canoed on the lake and Luke caught a three-pound rainbow trout which they cooked for their supper over an open fire by the lakeshore, watching the sun die in a dazzle of orange and gold behind the jagged peaks of the mountains. Then they made love in the grass under the glimmer of the first distant stars. . . .

It was a day spent in the present. By an unspoken consent they did not talk of the past or the future: the day in its perfect beauty was enough, and it was as though each of them wanted to drink of its pleasures to the full, undisturbed by the realities that would inexorably claim them when they went back to the ranch. The day ended with them falling asleep again in each other's arms.

There was cloud cover the next morning and the air was cooler, the wind whipping the wild flowers into a frenzied dance and making white-capped waves that splashed against the lakeshore. 'Let's take the horses and go farther up the pass,' Luke suggested. 'If we go in a northerly direction, we should be able to get a glimpse of the icefield. It's a good day for riding, not too hot.'

Julie packed a picnic lunch and they set off, the horses pirouetting with excess energy after a day spent cropping the lush meadow grass. They climbed steadily for almost two hours through a terrain that became increasingly harsh: heaps of sharp-edged rocks on either side of the trail, the creek roiling between steep ravines, the trees growing more and more sparsely. Finally Luke said, 'Let's stop for a breather. How about over on that ledge?'

'I brought a thermos of coffee.'

'You're a wonder!' He edged Whistler closer to her and gave her a rough hug.

Her smile was dazzling, and her surroundings, which had begun to oppress her, grew less threatening. Nevertheless, as they tethered the horses loosely, and she followed Luke up the slope on foot, she was glad of his presence: this was not a place in which she would have cared to be alone. Perhaps the day itself had something to do with it; the sky was massed with ragged grey clouds, torn and driven by the wind, and there was a bite in the air that spoke of seasons other than summer. But it was, she acknowledged, more than the weather. It was the landscape itself, bleak and barren, ungiving and unforgiving. A mistake here would be paid for by death, she thought with a shiver, and the rocks and pinnacles and ledges would not even notice your passing.

She had fallen behind and now she called, the faintest trace of panic in her voice, 'Luke, wait for me!'

He turned and offered her a hand, pulling her up beside him on a flat ledge. 'Sorry—was I going too fast?'

'No—it's just something about this place. It gives me the creeps.'

He glanced at her keenly. 'Do you want to head back?'

'No, that'd be silly. We should at least see the icefield now that we've come this far.' She gave herself a shake. 'It's nothing. I'm letting my imagination run away with me.'

Luke unscrewed the lid of the thermos and poured steaming coffee into the two plastic cups. 'Here, this'll make you feel better.'

Julie sipped the coffee, warming her hands on the cup and already feeling less chilled. 'This is how I imagine the surface of the moon must look,' she said reflectively. 'Empty of life—even alien to life.'

'That's not a bad analogy,' he concurred, taking another gulp of coffee. Then suddenly he tensed, his head turning to the left, his attention strained. 'What was that?'

'I didn't hear anything,' she responded, puzzled.

'I thought I heard something up in those rocks behind us.' He remained silent a while longer, but the only sounds were the keening of the wind and the raucous cry of a raven in the valley below. Imperceptibly he relaxed, saying ruefully, 'Now *my* imagination's working overtime—you're a bad influence on me, Julie.'

'Am I really?' she teased.

'Definitely. Here I am on a working day drinking coffee with my wife in the middle of nowhere and not feeling the slightest bit guilty.' His voice roughened. 'Worse than that—not feeling the slightest urge to go back to work.

I'd rather stay with you at the cabin. . . .' Setting down his cup, he pulled her close, his lips seeking hers with a hunger that was as raw and elemental as their surroundings. She went into his arms willingly, everything blotted out but the joy of surrender, of being claimed as his own. So the shock was that much the greater when he suddenly thrust her away so violently that she was flung against the opposite ledge. Dazed and uncomprehending, she heard the rumble and roar of rocks tumbling down the cliff towards them, saw a huge boulder bounce off the ledge above them and strike the exact spot where they had been sitting, felt something strike her arm, followed by a numbing blow on her shoulder. She cowered against the overhang, deafened by the noise, blinded by the shower of rock dust, separated from Luke by a landslide of boulders that catapulted off one another as they fell to the valley below.

It seemed to last for ever. Even as, instinctively, Julie shielded herself as best she could, she was aware of a deep, engulfing fear, a horror of what she might find when the avalanche ended. Her mind screamed out for Luke—Luke, who had thrust her out of the path of the rockslide, and who maybe had not had the time then to save himself. . . .

Gradually the cacophony diminished to a rattle of small stones, the near-silence almost as deafening as the thunder of rock against rock had been. With painful slowness she raised her head, her whole body shaking with the aftermath of shock. Across the width of the ledge, half buried by debris, she could see the chequered fabric of Luke's shirt, the darker blue of his jeans. He was lying absolutely still.

She tried to call his name, but only a croak came from her throat. Trying desperately to control the trembling of her body, she moved her limbs one by one—nothing broken. She was bruised, and the hand that she raised to her cheek came away streaked with blood, but she was not seriously injured. Luke had saved her from that.

She got to her knees and cautiously began to crawl across the ledge, taking infinite care not to disturb the heaped-up rocks. But despite herself she dislodged a boulder and it fell from the ledge, crashing from rock to rock with sounds like gunshots, the noise echoing across the valley.

Knowing she had no choice, she began moving forward again, each movement as precise and careful as she could make it, and this time she reached the far side of the ledge without further mishap. Luke was half buried under rocks and stones. His eyes were shut. His face was ashen pale. Across his forehead was an ugly laceration, and over one ear his hair was matted with dirt and blood. But the most obvious injury Julie saw was where a rock fragment, sharp as a knife, had sliced through his shirt and the flesh of his arm, and the blood had soaked into his clothing.

From her shirt-tail she fashioned a tourniquet that she bound above the wound, then made a rough bandage out of his shirt. Only then did she begin to scoop away the stones that covered him, terrified of what other injuries she might find, yet knowing she had to look. Apart from cuts and scrapes where the knees of his jeans had been ripped, his legs seemed to be all right. But when she moved his upper arm very gently, she heard the scrape of bone on bone, and traced it to his collarbone.

Scarcely realising what she was doing, she had been whispering his name over and over again, and now she was rewarded—his eyelids flickered and then his eyes opened, staring straight ahead at the rock face.

The relief was so intense that Julie nearly fainted. Fighting for control, she breathed, 'Luke—oh, Luke, are you all right?'

He turned his head slightly, bringing her into his field of vision and she could actually see memory rushing back. 'Julie,' he said hoarsely. He tried to move and pain contorted his features.

'Lie still—I think your collarbone is broken.'

He was struggling to regain reality, breathing shallowly. 'We've got to get out of here.'

'It's all right now,' she said soothingly. 'The rockslide's over.'

'Someone—up there,' he gasped. 'It wasn't an accident——'

Her head swivelled and she raked the cliff above her with her eyes: nothing but grey rock. 'That's crazy, Luke—there's no one there.'

'Heard someone,' he persisted stubbornly. 'We must get to the horses. Help me up, Jul.'

She couldn't believe what he said was true, yet there was something horribly convincing in those brief, painfully uttered phrases. Bracing herself with her knees, she grasped Luke under the arms, and somehow their concerted efforts got him upright, although inevitably she caused him pain. Avoiding looking at his face, where sweat had sprung out across his brow, she loosened the tourniquet and with a valiant effort to keep her voice from wobbling said, 'What now?'

'We'll go down to the right there—that way we're sheltered by the overhang.' He gripped her arm with surprising strength. 'Julie, just in case anything happens, you're to leave me and go for help—do you hear?'

She was ripping another strip from her shirt to make a sling and said, without looking at him, 'Yes.'

He was not deceived. 'I mean it—there's no point in both of us being killed. You do as I say, Julie.'

She would have obeyed him in almost anything he asked, but not in this. She said shortly, 'We're not going to be killed.'

His fists clenched at his sides, but all he said was, 'We'd better go. Remember to use every scrap of shelter there is. And when you get to the bottom, make a dash for the horses.'

Julie would long remember the climb down the slope. She helped Luke as much as she was able, but no one could have prevented the inevitable jarring of his shoulder. His arm, she noticed sickly, had started bleeding again. Both of them would have to ride Whistler, for it would be out of the question for Luke to manage the horse on his own. But when they finally reached the trail again and had struggled over the heaped-up boulders that the slide had left in their path, there was no sign of the horses.

Julie looked around her frantically, her shoulders aching from Luke's weight. The horses would have been terrified by the landslide, no doubt of that. But had they tethered them so loosely that both had broken free? It did not seem possible.

She eased Luke to the ground, noticing with sheer terror that his head fell between his knees, then went to investigate. A snapped-off branch showed where Whistler had jerked clear. But Dancer—how had she got free? Julie could remember tying the reins around the trunk herself. And never before had Dancer run away. . . . She found her eyes darting nervously around her, searching for any illusive movements that would indicate the presence of another human. Had Luke been right after all? Was there someone, an unknown enemy, trying to destroy them? Up on the ledge she had not believed him, for she had known that many factors could start a rockslide—even the nimble-footed mountain goats had been known to do so. But now, faced with the mysterious disappearance of the horses, she was paralysed by doubt.

'Julie. . . .'

She ran back to Luke, dropping to her knees beside him. 'The horses are gone,' she said baldly.

He muttered a profanity under his breath. 'Leave me here and go for help,' he said, putting all the force of his personality behind the words.

Her eyes never wavered. 'No. I won't do that. We'll make it together, Luke.'

'Then we may not make it at all,' he said angrily.

She tried to ignore the frisson of fear that raced along her spine. 'Can you get up? We'd better get moving.'

The next half hour was like a nightmare. Every step was agony to Luke, and they had not gone far before Julie realised his injuries were more serious than she had supposed; he was lightheaded from the blow on his scalp, and limped from a badly bruised ankle. Although she said nothing to him, she could not prevent her brain from assessing their situation and realising it could hardly have been worse. They were a morning's ride from the cabin; they were without food, for all their packs were with the horses; and they were possibly under the surveillance of someone who could only be a homicidal maniac, for he had already tried to kill them once. Rationally she still had difficulty accepting that anything other than an accident of nature could have been responsible for the rockslide; despite this, she more than once found herself glancing nervously back over her shoulder, as though she could catch their possible pursuer by surprise.

The only bright spot was that it was a long time until dark. Nevertheless she did not see how they could possibly make it back to the cabin before nightfall, which meant spending the night in the open. When she looked anxiously at the sky, she was experienced enough to know that by then it would almost certainly be raining.

She struggled on, every muscle in her body crying out for rest. Eventually the trail opened out into a small clearing, where grass grew down to the bank of the creek, and she heard Luke mutter, 'I need a drink. We'll stop for a minute.'

She led him to the water's edge, where he collapsed on the grass. Removing the bandana from around her neck, she dipped it into the icy water and wrung it out, gently wiping his face and dirt-grimed hands. This seemed to revive him, so that he was able to kneel and drink from the creek, and then splash more water on his face and neck. He straightened slowly, something of the normal Luke in the hard, assessing look he gave the girl at his side. She had just finished washing her own face and was wiping it dry on her sleeve, but no amount of water could remove the blue shadows of exhaustion under her eyes or the strained line of her lips, nor could she quite control the tremor in her hands and arms that came from muscles pushed beyond their limit. 'Julie, listen to me,' Luke began imperatively. 'You must——'

He got no further. Three feet to the left splinters flew into the air from a shattered rock as the valley echoed and re-echoed with the whipcrack report of a high-powered rifle. Luke flung Julie face down to the ground, throwing himself on top of her; she could feel the pounding of his heart against her spine. He was so heavy that she was crushed into the ground, rocks digging into her cheek so hard that she whimpered in protest. He shifted slightly, his breath fanning her other cheek. 'When I move, you're to wade through the creek and hide in the rocks on the other side.'

Even though she was nearly suffocating, she managed to gasp, 'What about you? I won't go without you.'

'Don't worry—I'll be right on your heels. Okay—now!'

He rolled off her and she scrambled to her feet, making

a dash for the creek. The water was thigh-deep and bitterly cold, fed as it was by springs high in the mountains where ice and snow still lingered. Fighting against the current, Julie forged across, glancing over her shoulder to make sure Luke was following. As she clambered up the opposite bank, her feet squelching inside her boots, she reached back a hand and helped him up behind her. Together they ran for the shelter of the rocks clustered untidily at the foot of the slope, and Luke dragged her behind the nearest one. He leaned back against it, his chest heaving, new lines of pain scoring his cheeks. 'The bastard's playing with us,' he said bitterly. 'Cat and mouse. He knows darn well he's got us where he wants us and now he can take his time picking us off.'

Momentarily she closed her eyes, swamped by incredulity that this could actually be happening: that she and Luke were being pursued by a murderer. From a long way away she was dimly aware of Luke pushing her to her knees and forcing her head down; the blood rushed back to her brain and the faintness passed. 'Sorry,' she muttered. 'I'm okay now.'

'Good,' he said grimly. 'Because that brings me back to what I was saying a minute ago—before that lunatic took a shot at us. You've got to go for help, Julie, and you've got to go alone. I'm nothing but a hindrance to you at the moment. Unless you go, we'll both be killed.'

'I can't believe that, Luke.'

'He's got a rifle, Jul,' he said impatiently. 'And all we've got is the clothes we're standing up in. You've got to go!'

'And leave you behind? To be killed on your own?'

'I can hide from him until dark. And while I'm doing that, you could get back to the cabin—I'm sure the horses will be there. Then you can ride for help.'

He made it sound very plausible. But, Julie wondered, how could he hide for six or seven hours from an unknown pursuer, who no doubt had a horse, and certainly was armed? He couldn't ... she looked him squarely in the face, her small body held very straight. 'No, Luke, I won't leave you.'

'You must, Julie.' Forgetting his injuries, he reached out to seize her, and she saw agony twist his features and heard his sharp intake of breath. 'Have you forgotten Beth? One of us must get back for her sake—and it can't be me.'

Beth, their child . . . with her silky hair and her infectious laugh, her need for both mother and father . . . how could Julie bear it if she never saw Beth again? But on the other hand there was Luke, her husband, whom she loved with all her heart . . . it was the cruellest dilemma in the world.

'How can I leave you?' she cried in desperation. 'You're saying if I don't leave I'll be killed. That means you will be, too. I *can't* leave, Luke!'

Hazel eyes clashed with black and neither fell. 'I beg you to go, Julie.'

He had never begged her for anything in his life before, her proud reticent Luke. How ironic that the one time he did, she might have to refuse him. Her voice suddenly trembling, she said, 'Luke, don't you see what you're asking me? Now, when we should be together, you're asking me to leave. Once before when you needed me, I left you alone. I believed you were guilty and I wouldn't have anything to do with you. Please don't ask me to leave you again—let me stay!'

There was a long silence. She was scarcely aware that she had been crying until he stretched out his good arm and gently wiped her cheeks. 'I understand,' he said softly. 'But all the same, for Beth's sake I think you should go.'

She was crying in earnest now, and awkwardly he gathered her close, her face pressed against his sling. 'Don't cry,' he said gruffly. 'We'll stay together for a while at least, and maybe we can get out of this.' She tried to smother her sobs, aware that he was still talking. 'We'll head downstream, keeping to the shelter of the rocks and being as quiet as we can. Keep your ears open—he must be on horseback.'

She nodded, heartened by the realisation that at least temporarily they were still in this together. With him leaning on her shoulder, they set off. For about an hour all went according to plan. The rocks offered ample cover and they were following the downward slope of the ground, which made travelling easier. But then, around a bend in the creek, the terrain began to change, opening out and affording less shelter, only the dubious coverage of a few stunted pines. Julie stopped to get her breath. 'What'll we do now, Luke?' Would he insist on them separating now?

Her question was answered from another source. A second gunshot cracked through the air, the bullet ricocheting off the surface of the creek and ploughing into the grove of trees on the opposite shore. Silence fell, an eerie, threatening silence. Then, from behind them, they heard the rhythmic clatter of hoofbeats.

'He could have got rid of us ten times over if he'd wanted to,' Luke said rapidly. 'We're sitting ducks and he knows it. So there's something else up—I wish I knew what. We'll just have to take our chances and hope we can get out of this. For God's sake, Julie, if anything happens to me, run—do you hear me?'

Because she sensed he needed some kind of reassurance, she nodded. 'I will.' But, she thought, looking around her hopelessly, he knew as well as she did that there was nowhere to run.

The hoofbeats were coming closer, their pursuer obviously making no attempt at hiding his approach. For Julie it was a horrifying experience, the waiting and the sense of helplessness; unconsciously she cowered against Luke, feeling his arm come around her, and grateful for its warmth. She glanced up at him, and her heart skipped a beat. As they had stood there waiting, something had transformed him; it was as though some primitive flow of energy had raced through his veins. His eyes were still sunk in their sockets and his mouth still grooved with pain, but none of that mattered. He looked dangerous, strung up for action, as predatory as a mountain cat and just as dangerous. He would, she knew instinctively, protect her with the last ounce of his strength, with all his intelligence and formidable will. She drew a deep breath, feeling an influx of hope. Luke said softly, 'We'll have to take any chance we've got—I only wish I had a gun.'

Their gun, along with the food, had been strapped to Whistler's saddle. 'At least there are two of us, and only one of him,' she said. But then her voice died away, for horse and rider had rounded the bend in the creek and were in full view, approaching them at a slow canter. The rifle was held in the crook of the man's right arm. His face burned into her brain and her whole body froze in shock, the blood draining from her cheeks. Appalled, she whispered, 'Luke, it's Frank!'

'I know.'

Although her neck felt stiff and awkward, she turned her head to look up at him. 'You knew all along?'

'I was pretty sure. But I didn't want to say anything, just in case I was wrong.'

She murmured helplessly. 'I don't understand. . . .'

Frank pulled up his horse, a powerfully built chestnut gelding, within twenty feet of them. Like Luke, he was wearing jeans and an open-necked shirt, his hat pushed back on his head; unlike Luke, he looked in top physical condition, fit and ready for anything. As Julie watched him she saw with horror that he was simmering with excitement, his light eyes blazing triumphantly as he regarded the man and girl standing on the bank of the creek. Insolently he looked them up and down, missing not one detail of their bedraggled appearance. 'The rockslide didn't do as much damage as I thought it would,' he drawled. 'Too bad. . . .'

To Julie the whole scene had taken on an air of total unreality. She swallowed, trying to find her voice. 'Frank, what are you doing this for?'

'Ask Luke, why don't you? He knows.'

Again her gaze swivelled up to her husband's face. 'Luke. . . .'

'I would imagine it's because I threatened to sell the mill—am I right, Taggart?'

Frank must have made some movement, because the chestnut shifted uneasily, the leather saddle creaking. 'That's right,' Frank spat. 'Because you knew as well as I did what that meant—all the books would have to be audited, wouldn't they? And I hadn't had time to cover my tracks, had I? That's all I needed—time. And that's what I'm going to get!'

Feeling as though she was fighting her way through a morass, Julie said, 'What is there to hide, Frank?'

Frank gave a contemptuous crack of laughter. 'My

sweet, innocent little sister—hard to believe you can be so naïve!' He leaned forward, and the rifle slanted carelessly towards the ground. Unable to disguise the venom in his voice, he rasped, 'Why, the fact that I've been stealing Luke blind, every chance I got!'

She swayed on her feet, and Luke's arm tightened around her. 'So it was you who stole the money two years ago,' she said.

'Of course.'

'Oh, Luke,' she cried, 'why didn't you tell me?'

'Because at that point I didn't know,' Luke said evenly. 'Come on, Frank—I know you're dying to show how clever you were. Tell Julie the whole story.'

Frank laughed and again the chestnut pawed restlessly at the ground. 'Why not?' he said gloatingly. 'I've got nothing to lose. I rigged the books, Julie, so it looked as though Dad was the one who'd been responsible. I knew how you felt about Dad, and I gambled on the fact that Luke would protect Dad's reputation at any cost—and I was right.'

'So you went to prison, Luke, to protect my father,' the girl muttered brokenly.

'Yes . . . it didn't seem possible he was a thief, but all the evidence pointed to him. So I covered up for him because I thought it would kill you to find out the truth.'

'That was why you made him retire early.'

'That's right—I did the only thing I could under the circumstances, and it backfired. Being innocent, of course, he couldn't understand why I didn't need him any more. He felt useless, an old man no good for anything—so he died. I'll never forgive myself for that, Julie.'

She turned her back on Frank, almost forgetting him in her overriding need to say what had to be said. Her face vivid with conviction, she declared, 'You've got it all wrong, Luke. It's not yourself who was to blame—it was Frank.' She whirled, her eyes molten with emotion. 'You killed Dad, Frank—as surely as if you'd taken that rifle and pulled the trigger. Just tell me one thing—why did you do it?'

As they faced each other, brother and sister could have been alone in the world; for all intents and purposes, Luke no longer existed. Frank brought his mount closer. His pale eyes were like stones, his voice as cold as the waters of the creek. 'Because I hated him,' he said. 'You never knew that, did you? All those years I kept it hidden from everyone.'

'I don't understand.' How could anyone have hated her father, so gentle and loving and kind?

'I loved my mother—I loved her more than I'll ever love another woman. Everything was perfect until the summer I was thirteen and you came along. We didn't need you, we were fine as we were. And then my mother died giving birth to you. I've never forgiven you for that.'

She blurted, 'So you've always hated me as well.'

'That's right. But not as much as I hated Dad. Because he doted on you—he thought the sun rose and set on you. And the older you got, the more you looked like Mother. That was why I left Henderson as soon as I could and went to Calgary—to get away from both of you.'

Luke broke in. 'But in Calgary you were just a little fish in a big puddle, weren't you, Frank? You were ambitious—you wanted money and power, and Calgary was too big for you. So you came back to Henderson and went to work in the mill.'

'And discovered that my darling little sister was going to marry Luke Marshall,' Frank interrupted roughly, 'who had everything already—more money than he knew what to do with, the mill and the ranch, and the name of the county's most respected family. So I decided I'd kill two birds with one stone—drag that name in the mud, and my father along with it.'

'That's sick, Frank,' Julie protested in horror. 'Sick and twisted and horrible!'

He shrugged carelessly. 'Maybe ... but it worked, didn't it? Mind you, I didn't succeed with everything. I'd hoped to break up your marriage as well—I made sure none of the letters you wrote to each other were delivered, and that the messages you so trustingly passed back and forth were suitably altered. I figured that'd be enough—but if not, there was always Richard.'

The girl lost all caution. Stepping forward, she seized the reins and stared up into her brother's face. 'So it was your fault that I never heard from Luke! How could you *do* such a terrible thing?' Her breath caught in a sob. 'It was because of you that I thought he was guilty.'

He slashed down at her with the rifle. 'Let go!'

Numbly she stared down at her hands, only realising then that she had hold of the bridle. She did not even see Luke's sudden lunge forward, although she heard him groan in agonised effort as he attempted to haul Frank out of the saddle. What she did see was the rifle waving wildly in the air as Frank fought to keep his balance. Dropping the reins, she grabbed it by the stock with both hands, praying the safety catch was on, and twisted and tugged with all her strength.

The chestnut gave an outraged neigh. Tossing its head in fury as the two men struggled, it plunged towards Julie, its neck muscles a taut curve under the satiny skin. It was all Julie needed. She wrenched the rifle free, grabbed the bridle and pulled, and saw Frank topple from the saddle and fall to the ground. She heard the sound of blows and Luke's gasp of agony before he shouted. 'Run, Julie! Run!' Another sickening thud of flesh on flesh.

There was only one thing to do. She looped the reins around her left wrist, saying raggedly, 'Whoa, boy—easy, now,' as she pulled him round so she could see the two men locked together on the ground. Releasing the safety catch on the rifle, she screamed, 'Luke, get back!'

Somehow he heard her and understood. Bringing up his knees, he kicked out viciously, throwing himself backwards as he did so. Before Frank could react, Julie cried, 'Don't move, Frank—or I'll shoot!'

The silence was so abrupt as to be shocking in itself. Frank stared at her, his face a rictus of rage as he slowly sat up. 'Julie, put that down.'

Swallowing hard, Julie said, 'Don't move, Frank. I know how to use this. Dad taught me, remember? And I will use it if I have to.' Although inwardly she was trembling, there must have been something in her face that convinced him of the truth of her words. From the corner of her eye she saw Luke mounting the chestnut and felt the tug on the reins as the horse swivelled skittishly under the burden of a strange rider. She began backing away from Frank, her eyes trained on him, the rifle absolutely steady.

Luke said softly, 'Good girl, Jul. Let go of the reins.'

She let them fall to the ground. There was no more than twenty feet between her and Frank, and she kept backing away, her whole being concentrated on the rifle. Then Luke said, 'Okay—toss me the gun, Jul. Then get up behind me.'

With the barrel never wavering from the man on the ground, they managed the exchange. Julie turned her back on Frank and scrambled up behind Luke, putting her arms around his waist. Unhurriedly he said, 'You can make it back to the cabin on foot, Taggart—we'll leave some food there. After that you're on your own. If you're smart you'll never show your face in Henderson—or Calgary—again. Because the first place I'm going when I get back is to the police, and tell them the whole story. We've got your horse and your rifle as evidence and I have the account books locked up in the safe. So if you know what's good for you, you'd better make a fresh start somewhere else.' There was open contempt in his voice. 'And try going straight this time.'

Still crouched on the ground, Frank said nothing. Luke wheeled the horse and they set off down the trail at a canter, Luke apparently anxious to put as much distance as possible between them and Frank as quickly as he could—a concern Julie shared with all her heart. Once they were out of sight of Frank, Luke slowed the horse to a steady, mile-devouring jog, a gait which would, she realised, jolt his shoulder to a lesser degree. Her cheek resting against his back, she said foolishly, 'Are you all right?'

'I'll feel better once we've left the cabin,' he replied shortly. 'You did well back there, Julie—I couldn't have handled him on my own.'

'Thanks,' she whispered, feeling ridiculously like crying. Since it was plain Luke was in no mood for conversation, she remained silent, her mind reeling as all the implications of what Frank had revealed began to sink in: the foremost being that Luke *was* innocent. He had gone to prison to protect her father, who had nevertheless needlessly died; he had been abandoned by his wife and forced to wait nearly two years to see his own daughter; his name had been vilified across the county. And none of it need

have happened. Equally, all the loneliness and pain and
rejection that she had suffered had been just as senseless.
Like two puppets they had been manipulated by a man
without conscience, a man whose personality was so
warped by envy and hatred that he had become nothing
but an instrument of destruction—without pity or love.
And that man was her own brother.

It didn't bear thinking about, the damage he had
done. She closed her eyes and the rest of the journey to
the cabin passed in a daze. She surfaced to hear Luke
say, 'Here we are. And the horses are here, too. I
thought they might be.' He pulled up by the cabin
door, while Whistler and Dancer whickered in welcome.
Julie slid to the ground and Luke said, with the faintest
touch of humour in his voice, 'Sorry, Jul, you'll have to give
me a hand down. I'll never make it otherwise.'

He swung his leg over and she managed to break his
descent from the saddle. Breathing heavily, he stood still
a moment, his forehead resting on the leather, his good
hand clinging to the stirrup. Then, as he turned, she saw
that his sleeve was soaked with blood and knew his wound
must have reopened.

'I must bandage your arm again,' she said, trying to
sound matter-of-fact.

'Okay, but let's hurry. Can you bring Frank's packs?
We'll leave them here and he can take what he wants out
of them.'

She hauled the heavy saddlebags into the cabin and
dumped them on the floor. 'Luke, about Frank——' she
began.

He interrupted harshly, 'Look, let's not get into that
right now—we've got problems enough. See what you can
do with my arm, will you?'

She turned away, feeling tears prick at her eyes.
Finding a clean piece of cloth, she rebound Luke's arm,
trying not to wince at the pain she was undoubtedly caus-
ing him. He looked ghastly, not a speck of colour in his
face, his hair damp with sweat, his eyes bruised with exhaustion, and she felt fear pluck at her nerves. 'We'll both
ride Whistler,' she announced. 'That way I can help hold
you up.'

'I look that bad, do I?' he said drily. 'Finished? Let's get out of here.'

Again they mounted, this time with the other two horses on long leading reins, and turned due east. The light was already starting to fade and Julie knew that long before they reached the ranch it would be dark, and they would have to trust to Whistler's surefootedness. She could see no point in sharing her concern with Luke, who obviously had worries of his own. Since Frank's revelations he seemed to have retreated within himself to a place where she could not follow, and she had no idea what he was thinking. Their physical closeness as they rode along the trail only served to emphasise this barrier, and more than once she let tears of sheer misery trickle down her cheeks.

The journey back to the ranch was an ordeal Julie would never forget. Luke soon lapsed into a kind of semi-consciousness, his chin drooped to his chest, his shoulders slumped. Had it not been for her support, he would have fallen, she was sure, for occasionally his whole body would sway sideways and she would grab at him and cry his name and he would straighten, muttering an apology under his breath. Each time her arms felt as if they were being pulled out of their sockets, so that she was soon in a daze of weariness, her body aching for relief. At least while it was still daylight she could look around her and gain some sense of progress from their surroundings; once darkness fell, she had almost no idea where they were.

But finally, blessedly, there was the flat, grassy prairie underfoot, and Whistler, without any encouragement, picked up speed, his ears pricked forward as though he knew they were nearing home. Along the fence line, past the house, and then the square yellow lights of the ranch house came into view.

The next couple of hours were a blur to Julie. She roused Jake, and while one of the other ranch hands looked after the three horses, Jake drove her and Luke into town, not asking a single question after his first, stunned look at the two of them. In the hospital, Luke was whisked away from her; her cuts and bruises were examined and after a brief consultation between the doctor and the nurse, she was put to bed in a small room usually reserved for the parents of sick children. Sleep washed over her, submerging her in its depths.

When she surfaced it was broad daylight and Luke was standing at the end of the bed. She blinked in confusion, wondering where on earth she was. Then she noticed his arm in the sling and the piece of tape on his forehead and memory came rushing back. She closed her eyes, not even wanting to face the man at the foot of the bed. Her family, herself included, had brought him nothing but un-happiness; at the moment she didn't even see how they were going to begin picking up the strands of their lives again. Maybe if she lay very still he would go away. . . .

'Julie? It's nearly eleven——'

In spite of herself, her eyes flew open. 'It can't be!'

'It was the small hours of the morning when we got here. It's not surprising that you slept late. Do you feel like getting up now so we could get out of here?'

A simple enough question, yet it brought her fully awake, for there was a note of something like desperation in his voice. She looked around the narrow little room with its single high window and its iron cot, its washbasin and utilitarian atmosphere, and knew he needed to escape, to get outside where he could breathe.

'Of course,' she said quickly. 'Give me five minutes.' She sat up unwarily and gave an exclamation of pain, for every muscle in her body revolted against the movement.

'Sore?'

'You said it,' she agreed ruefully.

'I'll wait in the corridor. You won't be long, will you?'

Again that undertone of unease. 'No, Luke, I won't be long.' As he left the room, she hurriedly got dressed, noticing abstractedly that someone had laundered her jeans and shirt. She brushed her hair back in a ponytail, splashed cold water on her face, and was ready. He was outside in the hall, pacing up and down like a caged animal. She smiled with determined brightness. 'Ready?'

'Yeah . . . let's go.'

They went down the hallway and out of the front door, where Luke stopped for a moment, drawing a deep breath of the crisp morning air. 'That's better,' was all he said, but it was enough to remind her all over again of the

damage that had been done to him because of her father
and her brother . . . no wonder he no longer loved her.
Now that she knew the truth of what had happened, she
wondered how he could bear to live with her, for surely
she must serve as a constant reminder of betrayal and
lack of trust?

Blindly she followed him across the parking lot to the
truck. 'Are we going to get Beth?' she asked at random.

'Do you mind if we don't right now? Maggie isn't expecting us, and we could always come back into town
and get her this evening.' He looked around him restlessly.
'I just have the urge to get home as quickly as we can.'

Loving him as she did, it seemed a small sacrifice to
make; besides, she knew Beth and Maggie thoroughly
enjoyed each other's company. 'Fine,' she said equably.
'Why don't I drive?'

They drove in silence, a silence which for the girl
intensified the sense of distance between them.
Unconscious of the fact that her knuckles were white with
strain where she was gripping the steering wheel, she
stared straight ahead of her, while sheer panic stirred deep
within her. Perhaps he was going to tell her that he no
longer wanted to live with her—was that why he hadn't
wanted to pick up Beth? Because he wanted to discuss
their future—or rather, their lack of it?

By the time they reached the house, she was in a pitiable
state of nerves. She parked the truck in the shade and
they both got out. 'Let's walk down to the river for a
minute,' Luke said quietly.

Julie's heart quailed. One night, what seemed like a
very long time ago, they had made love on the river-
bank—how could she bear it if that was the place he had
chosen to tell her their marriage was finished? She
stumbled after him as they went past the house and across
the grass. So panic-stricken that she was incapable of
rational thought, she had completely forgotten the tenderness of his lovemaking up at the cabin, let alone the
fact that the trip had been an attempt to save their marriage; she could think of nothing but the pain she had
caused him, and all for nothing.

He had stopped and she almost bumped into him.

Apparently oblivious of her mood, he put his good arm around her shoulders and said softly, 'Look around you, Jul. Have you ever seen anything more beautiful in your life?'

They were standing on a slight rise overlooking the river, its crystal-clear waters sparkling in the sun. The trees on its banks murmured to each other in the breeze, the dark mass of the evergreens a perfect foil for the tremulous, pale green poplars. On their left the hills rose to meet the grandeur of the mountains, that were tipped with gold; straight ahead, as far as the eye could see, stretched the open fields of the ranch, awash with sunshine, the breeze rippling across the long grass like waves on the sea. A hawk hovered overhead, the only mark in a sky that was an endless, fathomless blue.

Julie glanced up at Luke. His face was rapt, his eyes far-seeing, and she sensed he was scarcely aware of her presence. His profile was clean cut against the granite mountain range, while a vagrant wind lifted a dark silky lock of his hair. He was at home here, she thought intuitively, as much a part of his surroundings as the hawk, soaring so wild and free. He needed this space and freedom. More, she thought with painful honesty, then he would ever need her, or indeed any other human being.

As if he had read her thoughts, he said, 'I belong here, Julie. I want to live here for the rest of my life.' He turned to face her, his black eyes very serious. 'The nightmare's over now. We're free to take up our lives again.'

'Are we, Luke?' she replied soberly. 'Can we ever be? I don't see how we can forget the past, as though it never happened.'

'We won't forget it, no.' He traced the line of her cheek with one finger and she felt her nerves shiver in response. 'I'm sorry you had to find out about Frank—I know you loved him.'

'I loved the Frank I thought I knew.' Her voice quivered. 'But that was a totally false picture, wasn't it? I really didn't know him at all. I don't see how I could have been so stupid, so deluded.'

'My dear girl, he deceived more people than you. I was taken in by him, your father was. He was totally unscrupulous—but he was also very clever, don't forget that.'

Her eyes left Luke's face to search the northward sweep of hills. 'I keep worrying that he'll reappear, with his gun and his threats and his hatred,' she confessed in a low voice.

'You don't have to worry about that,' said Luke with absolute conviction. 'I said he was clever. He knows I'm going to the police—he won't show his face around here ever again. The only thing I'm sorry for is that the word will get out—sooner or later the whole town will know what he did. It'll be hard on you, Julie.'

'Not nearly as hard as having the whole town think that it was you. Oh, Luke, will you ever forgive us for what we've done to you?'

'Julie——'

But now that she had started, she could not stem the tempestuous flow of words. 'You went to prison for my father's sake. Frank robbed and cheated and deceived you. I didn't believe in you when you needed me—how you must hate us all!' Her eyes were shining with unshed tears, but she refused to give in to them. She grasped his arm with both hands, her small face passionate with conviction. 'Just promise me one thing,' she begged. 'Please, if you ever loved me at all, don't keep me with you now if all you feel towards me is hatred or bitterness—or even worse, indifference. I couldn't bear that. . . .' She fought back the sobs that crowded her throat, despite her misery aware of a strong sense of relief that she had been as honest with him as she knew how to be.

There was a strange look on his face. 'I told you once before that I've never hated you, Julie. Oh, I've been angry with you and felt desperately uncertain of you— but that can all be laid at Frank's doorstep. It wasn't your fault that you came to believe I was guilty—my God, how could you have believed otherwise? Everything pointed to it—he'd made sure of that.'

'You mean—you forgive me?'

He gently wiped away a tear that sparkled on her cheek. 'My dear, there's nothing to forgive.'

Somehow she was in his arms, her face buried in his shirtfront, the strong steady beat of his heart of infinite comfort to her. Then she raised her head quickly, sur-

prising on his face a look of such unguarded tenderness
that she was momentarily speechless. She faltered, 'Your
arm . . .? You'll hurt it!'

Luke had worked free of the sling, she now saw. He
grinned, laughter lines fanning around his eyes. 'It'll be
all right—I wanted to hold on to you properly. You're
not objecting, are you?'

Her laugh was quite spontaneous. 'Never!' she said incautiously.

The smile faded from his face. 'Do you mean that,
Julie?'

She could feel his hands firm at her waist; her palms
were resting on his chest, the warmth of his skin seeping
through his shirt. The moment of truth had come, she
knew. The time for prevarication between her and Luke
was over—they had had too much of that, and had each
suffered from it. Knowing full well that her whole future,
all her happiness, depended on the next few minutes, she
raised her chin and said evenly, 'Yes, I mean it, Luke.
You see, I've never stopped loving you. I thought I had
for a while, I thought I hated you. But I was wrong. I
love you, Luke, and I believe I always will.' He would
have spoken but she halted him by putting a finger to his
lips. 'You say you don't hate me. But that doesn't mean
you necessarily love me any more, and I can understand
that. I'd like you to be honest, that's all. I don't want you
to feel you have to——'

Ruthlessly he interrupted, taking her fingers and pressing them to his mouth and then lowering his head to kiss
her, a long, deep kiss of naked longing and desire. 'I never
stopped loving you, either,' he said, hoarse with emotion.
'How could I? Ever since I first met you, you've been the
breath of life to me, the very heart of my being. Oh,
Julie, Julie, I love you!'

He was raining kisses on her hair, her cheeks, her
mouth. She cupped his face in her palms, her eyes shining
with joy, her mouth a soft, tremulous curve of pure happiness. 'I love you, too, Luke.'

He was kissing her again and there could be only one
inevitable conclusion to their new-found closeness. The
grass was sweetly scented, the sun warm on their skin,

and the hawk their only witness as they made love. And to Julie it seemed as though they were making love in the true sense of the words, and the pleasure that Luke was bringing her was the truest joy she had experienced for many long months, for now with voice and hands and eyes he was pledging his love to her and she was finally free to respond as she had so often wanted to—with all the generosity and love of which she was capable. Under the dazzling light of the sun with the music of the river in their ears they came together in that miraculous fusion that is outside of space and time, and it seemed as if their very intensity could erase all the pain and separation they had endured.

Afterwards Julie lay contentedly in the curve of Luke's arm. She did not think she had ever felt such perfect happiness and, knowing he would understand, she tried to put her feelings into words. 'Maybe in the long run the past two years won't have been wasted. Perhaps we'll value each other, and all the beauty that surrounds us, so much more because we nearly lost them.'

'And now we know we have each other, and Beth, and we're free to live together and love each other.'

'Tomorrow and tomorrow and tomorrow,' she said dreamily.

'For all our tomorrows. . . .'

ROMANCE